A TIME FOR PEACE

by

Sylvia Broady

Magna Large Print Books
Long Preston, North Yorkshire,
BD23 4ND, England.

First published in Great Britain in 2013 by Robert Hale Limited

Cover illustration by arrangement with Robert Hale Ltd.

The right of Sylvia Broady to be identified as the author of this work has been asserted by her in accordance with the Copyright, Designs and Patents Act, 1988

Published in Large Print 2014 by arrangement with
Robert Hale Limited

Magna Large Print is an imprint of Library Magna Books Ltd.

Printed and bound in Great Britain by
T.J. (International) Ltd., Cornwall, PL28 8RW

Mrs Vi Rabie, Mrs Hannelore Caley
and Mrs Olive Caley.
Thank you, ladies, for sharing
your memories with me.

For Julie and Mike, with love

ONE

*Kingston upon Hull, East Yorkshire,
February 1945*

Snow was falling softly. Her footsteps made
no sound as the young woman, Rose Ellerby,
hurried along the dark, empty, war-damaged
street, lit only by the silvery, shadowy moon.
Ahead of her, the door of a public house was
wrenched open and an airman stumbled out.

'Heed the blackout, you fool,' someone
shouted, and the door banged shut.

The airman fell to his knees, skidding on
the snow-covered pavement, mumbling incoherent words as he tried to struggle to his
feet.

Rose shrank back into the gloom of a shop
doorway, waiting for him to pass by, but he
tumbled backwards on the pavement. She
decided to run for it and stepped from the
shadows, her head bent against the now
driving snow. She was too late. The airman
was there, standing in front of her, staring at
her, blocking her way. She froze in horror.

He was broad and towered above her. The
strong smell of beer on his breath filled her
nostrils. Her heart thumped as he continued

to stare at her, his dark, bleary eyes looking into hers, as if he was looking into her very soul. Filled with unease, she held her breath, a sharp pain creasing across her chest. Was he going to attack her? She prepared to defend herself, but wasn't sure whether her trembling legs would respond, when he spoke.

'Ellie, is that you?' His voice was unsteady and big tears rolled down his rough cheeks as he sobbed, 'I thought you were dead.' He held out his arms to her; huge, bear-like arms.

She pressed her body against the cold pub wall as far away from him as possible.

'I'm not Ellie. I'm Rose,' she managed to stutter.

The airman peered closer into her face, his expression one of disbelief and sadness. 'Not Ellie.' He swayed against her and she felt the crush of his body against hers. She wanted to scream, but no sound would come.

'Now then, what's this?' said a stern voice. 'Is he bothering you, miss?'

The airman shifted away from her, his face grief-stricken, as the dark outline of a policeman came into view.

With relief, Rose replied, her voice a quiver, 'No, just mistaken identity.'

The policeman eyed the airman thoughtfully, then turned to her. 'You get off home, miss. I'll attend to matters.'

As she moved away, as fast as her shaky

legs would go on the snow-clad pavements, she glanced back over her shoulder. A shaft of moonlight caught the two men and she saw the policeman take hold of the airman's arm, talking to him as if he knew him.

Out of breath, exhausted, she reached Hill Street without meeting anyone else, and slowed her pace. Passing the ghostly half of the street, her eyes were drawn to where once houses had stood so proudly. Now they were reduced to rubble by the heavy raids of the German bombers on the city, targeting the docks, factories and railways. In her mind she could hear her father's voice as he read the newspaper: 'Bloody cheek, why can't they say it's our city instead of *Raids on a north-east coastal town?* That'll never hoodwink Jerries. They say when it's London and Coventry, and the likes.'

Rose went down the back passage, which ran between the terraced houses, and into the yard of number nine, Church Terrace. Their house had three bedrooms because at some stage, the second one had been made into two, and downstairs was a front room, a kitchen and a tiny scullery. Here she lived with her parents and her brother Freddie, a soldier, who was fighting in Europe. Stamping the snow from her shoes, she leaned against the brick wall to catch her breath and steady her thoughts before going indoors. She didn't want to worry her mother about the incident with the drunken airman. Dad wouldn't be home, as he was on fire watch duty in the city centre. During the day he worked in the shipyard so they didn't get chance to see much of each other.

'It's only me, Mam,' Rose called. She hung her coat on the hook on the back of the scullery door, and kicked off her wet shoes and socks, wriggling her cold toes, giving them a quick rub with a rough towel before she slipped her feet into soft slippers, her only luxury. She glanced in the tiny mirror on the window ledge, which Dad used for shaving. Her blue-grey eyes had dark circles, too many late nights, extra shifts at the factory. Pulling off her headscarf, which was tied up in a turban, she shook her shoulder-length blonde hair loose and went into the kitchen. A warm, comfortable room, with two easy chairs either side of the fireplace, polished oak sideboard, chairs and wooden stools arranged round an oak table covered with a clean, checked cloth over a green chenille cloth. The walls were distempered cream, plain with no adornments.

Mary Ellerby looked up from where she was sitting by the fireside, knitting socks for the troops. Once a pretty woman, the austerity of war and coping with make do and mend had etched worry lines on her kindly face, and her once fair hair was flecked with grey.

'Hello, love.' She put down her busy needles and got to her feet. She reached for the pan, warming on top of the side oven plate. The oven was the old traditional type, which was fuelled by the open fire and great for keeping meals warm, especially as members of the family would arrive home at different times. She lifted the lid and gave the mixture a stir, filling the room with its tasty aroma. 'Nice bit of broth, just a few carrots, onions, potatoes and Oxo cube,' Mary said.

But Rose was distracted as she looked on the sideboard. 'No letter from Harry?' She couldn't keep the disappointment from her voice. Harry was her sweetheart, a soldier, fighting somewhere in Europe. They had met at a dance and fallen in love all within the space of a few weeks before he was posted abroad. So letters were their only contact.

'Afraid not, love. If things are bad, Harry won't get much time for letter writing. I saw his mother in the butcher's queue and she hasn't had one either.'

Rose knew her mother was trying to make light of the situation and give her comfort. Hearing Harry's mother hadn't received a letter didn't quell the longing and ache of the loneliness in her heart. What man would write love letters or pour out his heart to his mother? Yes, she sighed inwardly, Harry was a dutiful son and did write to his mother, but never about the secrets that she and Harry shared. They wrote to each other, sharing their innermost feelings of love and desire, and she had no wish to reveal them. They were engaged, although not officially, because Harry was saving up to buy her a special ring. Often they wrote about their wedding plans, dreaming of the day when they would be together in their own home. She sighed again; the war seemed to be going on for ever. Then a terrible thought struck her.

'Mam, you don't think anything has happened to Harry?'

Hearing her daughter's troubled voice, Mary glanced towards her, saying, 'Of course not, love. You'd have heard. It's probably as I said, his regiment is caught up in operations or something and there's no time for letter writing, so stop worrying.'

'We had a letter from our Freddie last week and he's in Europe,' Rose pouted. Then she immediately regretted her outburst, for she dearly loved her brother. On seeing her mother's despondent face, she went to hug her. 'Sorry, Mam,' she said.

Mary sighed, heavily. 'I understand your concern, lass, but I never could understand the cruelty of war.'

As they sat down to supper, anxious to change the subject, Mary asked, 'Anything happened at work today?'

Rose worked at Clarke and Sons' factory

on a production line, filling soldiers' first-aid packs of surgical dressings into small tinned containers. The cuts on her fingers were a constant reminder of her work because the tin was so sharp. She endured what she did because it was war work and, like everyone else, she did it without complaint.

Rose told her mother snippets of gossip of a light-hearted nature, but she didn't mention anything about the sad, drunken airman who had frightened her earlier. After a while they were both quiet and Rose caught Mary's thoughtful expression.

'What's on your mind?'

Mary pushed away her empty plate, smiled and responded, 'Perhaps it would be nice for you to go to a dance once in a while.'

'But I've promised Harry–'

Mary cut in. 'It isn't natural for a girl of eighteen to shut herself away from a social life.'

Rose stared at her mother; what had brought this on?

'I go to the pictures with Sally every week, and I go to Mrs Carter's once a fortnight. I work extra to save up for when Harry's home for good. I want everything to be nice, so we can enjoy our life together.'

Mary stood up. 'I know, love, but a dance once in a while won't hurt.'

Later in bed, Rose always turned her last thoughts before going to sleep to Harry and her brother, Freddie. But tonight, another face appeared: that of the distressed, drunk airman, and she wondered what had caused his sadness.

A few mornings later, on the early work shift, over the din of the factory noise, Sally Wray, Rose's best friend, yelled, 'Rose, are you coming to the dance at the barracks tonight?'

Rose shook her head, calling back, 'It's my night for going to Mrs Carter's.'

'Lucky you,' Sally grinned, rolling her large brown eyes upwards.

Rose wished Sally would stop asking her to go dancing; it unsettled her. She didn't want to break her promise to Harry. He wanted her to be true to him and not to think of her dancing in another man's arms. For the rest of the day, she was content to indulge in daydreams about hers and Harry's future together.

Leaving work, she didn't catch the bus to Mrs Carter's, but walked to save the fare for her and Harry's nest egg. She trudged along the street, still daydreaming. The snow had turned to slush and she wished she had worn her old wellington boots.

Mrs Carter lived in a two-bedroom terraced house down Burleigh Street, off Holderness Road. Hungry, cold, and shivering, Rose knocked on the door, which was always locked even though Mrs Carter knew she was coming. Rose heard the shuffle of feet, the bolt drawn back and the door inched open.

'Take them wet shoes off; I've just cleaned the floor,' was Mrs Carter's greeting.

Rose fixed a smile on her face and said, 'How are you, Mrs Carter?'

'My lumbago's playing up,' she sniffed.

Rose moved into the kitchen to get near to the meagre fire in the grate, holding out her frozen hands to catch some warmth. The main reason why she was saving hard was because there was no way she was going to live with Mrs Carter once she and Harry were married.

She moved away from the fire and sat at the kitchen table, placed centre and dominating the cramped, furnished room. What was for tea? There was no tantalizing smell of cooking. Her stomach rumbled and she longed wistfully for her mother's cooking.

She kept her pledge to Harry to visit his mother regularly, to see that she was all right, but it wasn't always easy being pleasant to Mrs Carter. Rose sighed inwardly and said, 'I haven't heard from Harry for a few weeks, have you?'

'No I haven't. What does he care if I'm all right or not?' Mrs Carter sniffed.

Ignoring the whining tone, Rose asked, 'Do you think his regiment is on a mission?' Rose's heart contracted, hoping her beloved

Harry wasn't in danger.

'How do I know? They don't tell me anything. I'm just his mother, left all on my own with no man to care for me.' She went to the pantry, bringing back two cold meat pasties, bread and margarine, and a cake.

'Eggless sponge,' Mrs Carter said, placing the food on the table. 'If I had money I could get eggs on the black market, but I haven't so this will have to do.'

Rose glanced at the cold food, wishing for something hot, especially on such a wintry day. Instead she said, 'It looks nice, Mrs Carter.' She thought of Harry in some dark, dismal place. Was he thinking of her?

The next couple of weeks passed slowly. The sirens had sounded on several occasions and Rose and Mary went down to one of the rows of air-raid shelters at the bottom of Hill Street, thankful each time that their lives were saved, though Ted Ellerby suffered a knee injury. Ted was a robust man, having fought in the Great War, so there wasn't much which would keep him from his duties of fire-watching. He rarely missed a night and Mary often feared for his safety. Frequently, as she sat on an evening, sewing or knitting, with only the radio for company, she dreamed of happier times before the war. The nights when Rose and Freddie were young and tucked up asleep in their beds, she and Ted would talk together or have friends round for supper and a game of cards or dominos.

Mary glanced at the clock. Rose would soon be home and with any luck so would Ted. It was a rare treat for all three to sit down for a meal together. She'd made a cottage pie with a tin of stewing meat she had been so lucky to buy from her grocer. It made tasty gravy, which Ted loved, and Mary had also managed to buy a crusty cob. She glanced up as the back door opened and Rose entered the kitchen.

'You look tired,' she said, sympathizing.

Rose slumped on her father's armchair and replied, 'I'm shattered and I feel itchy and grubby. I'd love a bath in hot, bubbly water, just like I saw in the American film last week. But it will have to be a strip wash in the cold scullery,' she added miserably.

Her mother's cheery voice said, 'You have the next best thing.'

Rose looked up to see her mother with the biggest smile on her face.

'There's a letter.'

In an instant, Rose's whole being changed from one of gloom to one of delight as she jumped up, eagerly snatching the letter from the sideboard, recognizing Harry's familiar writing on the envelope.

'I'll take it up to my room,' she announced.

'Tea in ten minutes,' called Mary, as Rose disappeared up the narrow staircase.

In her bedroom, Rose drew the blackout curtains and switched on the light. The thin beam of light disguised the faded wallpaper and the worn patchwork quilt, but the highly polished chest of drawers shone brightly. She sat down on the edge of the bed.

'Harry, my sweetheart,' she said, kissing the envelope. It was then she noticed how thin the envelope was. Perhaps he had been in the thick of the fighting and only had time to pen a few lines. At least it showed he cared and knew she would be worrying about him. She tore open the envelope.

Dear Rose...

She sat on the edge of the bed in the cold room, her body bathed in sweat, her head spinning, her heart in turmoil. The letter, the words, they didn't make sense. Was it a cruel joke? Then in slow motion, she looked down at the single sheet of paper crushed in the palm of her hand. Releasing it, she held it between trembling fingers and forced herself to look at the letter again. But the words seemed to jig about the page, and she couldn't focus, her mind was too numb.

From a great distance, Rose heard her mother calling her name. But she seemed incapable of replying because all her strength had gone from her body. She felt only a vast sense of emptiness and of unbelievable despair as she curled up on the bed and buried her face in the pillow and wept.

TWO

Rose didn't hear mother's footsteps coming up the stairs, nor the knock on the door as Mary entered the room. It wasn't until she felt the gentle touch on her shoulder and heard the soft voice saying, 'Rose, what is the matter?' that she was aware of her mother's presence.

Slowly lifting her head, Rose stared unseeingly into her mother's face. Mary dropped to her knees, taking hold of Rose's cold clammy hands in hers. 'Sweetheart, what is it?' she coaxed.

Rose tried to speak, but her throat was so dry and tight. If she could speak she didn't know what to say. Her head spun and her body sank and she felt as though she was seasick, like as a child when crossing the Humber on the ferry.

'I feel sick,' she groaned.

'Put your head between your knees,' instructed Mary. Rose sat on the edge of the bed and did her mother's bidding. After a while, she felt a little better until she remembered the letter. Tears flooded again and huge sobs racked her body. Mary drew her close into the comforting circle of her arms.

'There, there, love,' Mary soothed. She stroked Rose's tangled hair, as if she were a child again, whispering words of comfort. But Rose knew the heartache she was experiencing would not go away as easily as when she was a child.

When the sobs subsided, Mary said firmly, 'Rose, you must tell me what it is.'

'The letter,' Rose whispered.

'Oh my God! Oh, Rose!' Mary's hands flew to her lips. Then she clasped her daughter closer. 'Oh, sweetheart.' She took a large gulp and not wanting to utter the words, but knowing she must, said in a shaky voice, 'Has something happened to Harry?'

Rose couldn't reply, not wanting to speak the words out loud. How could she bear the pain? Weeping, she buried her face in her mother's soft bosom. Mary rocked Rose gently, like a baby. Outside a dog barked and someone shouted for it to be quiet.

The minutes dragged slowly until a voice called into the sadness.

'Is anyone home?' It was Ted Ellerby, home from work, wanting to eat and snatch a couple of hours' sleep before he went on fire-watch duties.

'Come up here, Ted,' Mary called.

The house rang with the sound of him taking off his boots, clanging as they hit the lino floor, and his weary footfalls climbing the stairs. 'What's up?' His bulk filled the tiny room.

'Rose's got a letter.'

Ted moved from the doorway and scooped up the letter lying on the clipped rug, and read it. Then he exploded. 'The bloody...!' A stream of expletives, which neither Mary nor Rose had heard Ted utter before, filled the room. Both women stared at Ted's angry face.

Mary jumped up. 'Ted, whatever...?' But he cut her short.

'Have you read it?' he bellowed, shoving the letter into his wife's hands.

Mary focused her eyes on the uneven loopy writing and read. Then she gasped, her hands coming up to cover her cheeks. 'What a terrible thing to do! Oh, Rose, how could he take up with someone else when he's promised to you?'

'You're well rid of him,' Ted exclaimed. 'I'm famished. What's to eat?'

'I'll be down in a minute.'

When Ted was safely out of the room, Mary turned to Rose. 'I can't believe it's true. You and Harry were so happy together and so in love.'

'I know, Mam. I can't believe it. I don't know what I've done wrong.'

'Wrong!' Mary retorted angrily. 'You haven't done anything wrong. He's lost his senses.'

Tears trickled down Rose's cheeks and

Mary brushed them away. 'I best go and see to tea.'

'I don't think...'

Mary said soothingly, 'Sweetheart, you'll need all your strength to get through this.' Her hand on the doorknob, she turned to Rose. Her voice gentle and reassuring, she said, 'Rose, you are young and pretty and in time you will meet another young man.'

Rose's shoulders drooped. She didn't want anyone else. Only Harry. Her heart leaden, she stared about her bedroom, seeing her pretty patchwork quilt, the pink dressing-table set her grandma had crocheted many years ago and the gleam of the mirror out-shining the faded wallpaper. None of these lifted her spirits and nor did the lingering scent of her treasured bottle of Evening in Paris, the perfume Harry had bought her. 'For you, Rose, the most beautiful girl in Yorkshire, with all my love.' How she had cherished those words spoken with such passion. Now they didn't mean anything. Just cheap words, that left her with a bitter taste in her mouth.

Slowly, she got to her feet. 'Oh, Harry, how could you when I love you so?' she whispered. It was unreal. She couldn't believe it was true. She picked up the letter from the bed where her mother had left it. The words blurred before her eyes. Then something flashed into her mind. Could it be a joke written by someone imitating Harry's handwriting? Tomorrow was Saturday. She would call on Harry's mother to see if she had received a letter. Feeling a slight touch of optimism, she went downstairs.

Next morning, Rose was up early to see Mrs Carter before she went shopping. She took the bus, an extravagance, but for once she didn't care. An icy wind blew as she walked down Burleigh Street. She pulled up the collar of her coat, once a sparkling cherry red, now faded to a brownish red. Knocking on the door, Rose waited, hopping from one foot to the other, as the cold seeped through her shoes. She knocked again, and after a few seconds, she heard the ritual of shuffling feet and the sound of the bolt drawn back.

Mrs Carter stared at Rose and demanded, 'What do you want?'

'Can I come in, please?'

Mrs Carter folded her thin arms across her scrawny body, clutching a grey-coloured cardigan, and pursed her lips. She didn't move. Rose stood her ground.

'I can say what I have to say with your neighbours listening,' she inclined her head to the next door where two women were standing on the doorstep, 'or I can say it in private.'

Begrudgingly, the older woman moved aside to let Rose in. They faced each other in the cold, cheerless kitchen that smelt of boiled cabbage and carbolic soap.

Rose thrust the letter at her saying, 'Read this, please, and tell me if it's true or not.'

'I don't know if I should.'

'Please,' Rose insisted.

Mrs Carter took the letter over to the window and squinted at it.

Rose fixed her gaze on a tired print of bygone sailing ships which once graced the River Humber. But it didn't do anything to take her mind off the sick, sinking feeling within her.

Mrs Carter ambled back and shoved the letter at Rose. 'So my boy's going out with a girl.'

Rose gasped, the colour draining from her face. 'So it's true, then.'

'It is. And what's it to do with you?'

'Harry promised to marry me.'

'Never!'

'But he did. I was saving up for when he came home for good.'

'Well, he never mentioned it to me and I'm his mother. He just said he felt sorry for you because you had no one to write to.' Rose flinched as though she had just been slapped hard.

Mrs Carter shuffled over to the door and opened it. 'You'll have ter go. I'm off shopping.'

Rose gave it one more shot. 'Are you sure

Harry's got someone else?'

'Course I am. And don't you come back here any more.'

Dazed, Rose found herself out in the street and the two women were still standing on the next doorstep.

'Are yer alright, love?' one of them asked. Rose felt too choked up to answer and walked blindly away. She walked and walked until she found herself by the pier.

The wind was whipping off the Humber. Two officials, standing near to the sea defences, deep in conversation, gave her a cursory glance as she passed by. Ahead was a couple walking with their arms around each other. They stopped to kiss, locked in a loving embrace. It was more than she could bear; it was like a knife piercing her heart. The pain was excruciating. She rushed on, tears streaming down her cheeks. Rounding a corner, she dug into her coat pocket for her handkerchief, wiped her eyes and fiercely blew on her nose. The wind gusted and cigarette smoke wafted up her nostrils; it was then that she saw him. A man was sitting on a broken bench. He drew in on his cigarette and stared at her. There was something familiar about him, something in the way his eyes focused on her. Then it struck her: it was the drunken man, the airman who had accosted her in the doorway that snowy night on her way home from work. The airman who thought she was someone else.

Her terror must have shown on her face because he said, 'I'm not going to harm you.' His voice was bitter, harsh-sounding. Her first instinct was to run, but her legs wouldn't move.

The man lit another cigarette from the stub of the first one. He blew out a plume of smoke and seemed to be studying her. Still she didn't move. Then he spoke again; this time his voice was surprisingly gentle.

'What are you doing on your own and looking so upset?'

The sting of the wind lashed against her face and she winced. Gazing past the man, into the distance, she remembered that hot summer's day, her sixteenth birthday. It was a Sunday afternoon when she and Harry met. They were promenading on the pier. He trod on the back of her shoe and she had turned round to curse, but he just winked at her. 'Sorry, darling,' he had said. It was like something from an American film. He was so handsome and charming.

'Have you suffered bereavement?' The airman's voice sounded concerned.

Rose had forgotten about him. Suddenly he no longer posed a threat to her. She felt so full of sadness at losing Harry. Her voice faint, she answered, 'I suppose so, in a way.'

'Ah,' the airman said, knowingly, as if he understood. 'Sit down.' He shifted up, gesturing to the space on the bench beside him. She hesitated. She hadn't slept much last night and felt shattered. 'I promise not to bite,' he said. Wearily, on unsteady feet, she sat down next to him. He didn't talk. He just puffed on his cigarette. She glanced sideward at him. His uniform looked as though he had slept in it. He was unshaven and smelt of strong tobacco and stale beer. His dark eyes were red-rimmed; too much drink, she thought. Then she looked again. His lashes were damp. Had he been crying? Hastily she averted her gaze, remembering how he'd mistaken her for someone else. Someone who was dead. Was this why he was here alone, grieving for a loved one? And she was intruding. She ought to go, but she didn't.

Suddenly he broke the silence. 'Do you want to tell me what's bothering you?' She looked at him, questioningly. 'I've nothing else to do.'

'My mother,' she faltered, 'she'll be wondering where I am.'

'I'll walk you home. It's too cold to sit around.' She didn't object.

As they walked through the old town and over Drypool Bridge, they made a strange couple. Rose saw their reflection in a glass-plated shop window, which had escaped bomb damage. She was slender, with large, blue-grey eyes and shoulder-length blonde hair, and neatly dressed. He was tall, with dark, sad eyes and of bedraggled appearance. She wasn't concerned about his appearance because here she was, opening up her heart to the airman. It seemed easier talking to a stranger, telling him the contents of Harry's letter and how devastated she felt. By the time she'd finished her story, they had walked down Hedon Road and past the police station in Crowle Street; nearly home. What did he think of her?

He lit another cigarette, then looked at her. 'Harry's a fool to let you go,' he said quietly.

She stared at him, surprised by his remark. By now they'd reached Hill Street. 'Thank you for listening to me. I feel a bit better now... I'm sorry; I don't know your name.' She blushed, feeling the warm tingle of her cheeks.

'Joe.'

'And I'm Rose.'

'It's nice to meet you, Rose.'

'And thank you again, Joe. I must be going, my mother, she'll be wondering.' She suddenly felt very shy.

A shadow crossed his face, then he said softly, 'It is I who should be thanking you. You'll never know how much.' With that, he turned round and walked away.

THREE

'He looks a bit rough. I've not seen him before.' A dry, hoarse voice sounded in Rose's ear.

Startled, Rose swung round, nearly knocking over her neighbour. 'Sorry, Mrs Fisher,' she exclaimed, catching her breath.

'So yer should be. Who is he?' Vera Fisher loved a bit of gossip. It helped to take her mind off her two sons who had been killed in action, so neighbours didn't take too much offence. And if that wasn't enough, Vera's face was speckled with scars as a result of a bombing raid.

Crossing her fingers behind her back, Rose answered, 'Just someone who was lost and I was showing him the way.'

Vera drew her thick knitted scarf tighter around her thin neck, gave a quirky laugh and said in disbelief, 'Pull the other one.'

Not wanting to get into a deep conversation with Mrs Fisher, Rose muttered, 'Must dash,' and hurried on down the street. Glancing over her shoulder, she saw Vera accosting another neighbour. Now it would be all over the street, her walking home with Joe. All quite innocent, but the gossips would make more of it. They'd sandwich it together and make it into a meal.

She passed the pile of bricks and rubble on the left side of Hill Street where once houses had stood proudly, only to be brought down to destruction by German bombers. Only with her it was Harry who had caused devastation. It hit her with a sudden intensity; what had she done wrong? It must be something so terrible, for Harry, the man she loved, the man who wrote of his passionate love for her, to jilt her for another girl. What had she done wrong? She couldn't stop asking the question. Who was this other girl? And how had Harry the time to meet her when he was supposed to be fighting a war? Her head swam with the unanswered questions. Half-laughing, half-crying, she muttered, 'That'll give Mrs Fisher something real to gossip about.'

Indoors, she leaned her trembling body against the back door for support, her whole being aching with untold misery.

'Is that you, Rose?' her mother called from the kitchen.

She took a deep breath before answering, but her voice wobbled as she replied, 'Yes, Mam.' She slipped off her shoes and hung up her coat. Entering the kitchen, she tried to smile, but her facial muscles refused to relax. Mary was sitting at her Singer treadle sewing machine, which was near to the window to catch the best of the daylight. Hastily she put what she had been working on into a pillowcase and out of sight.

She stood up, looking anxiously at her daughter's bluish, cold face and the stark sadness in her eyes. 'You've been a long time, love.'

Rose just nodded and sat down at the table. Mary went over to the cast iron stove and pulled the kettle, which was resting on the hob top, across onto the banked-up fire. It was a problem to make coal last and to keep warm, so anything that would slow down the fuel consumption was heaped on, like potato peelings, or anything else which would burn. She gave the coals a poke to coax a flame. From the side oven, she took out a plate of bubble and squeak, leftover cabbage and potatoes fried crisp, and placed it in front of Rose. 'Eat this, it'll warm you up. You look nithered.'

While Rose ate, Mary busied herself making a hot drink of cocoa. She could have done this small task in minutes but she spun it out, giving Rose time to collect her composure. Mary sighed inwardly; a broken heart needs time to repair. Sitting opposite her daughter, Mary could no longer bear her daughter's pain. She had to ask.

'What did Mrs Carter have to say?'

Rose stared down into the steaming liquid, then she lifted the cup and sipped. It had a slightly bitter taste. She still longed for sugar in her hot drinks, but going without was part of the war effort. She sighed and, lifting her head, caught the look of concern on her mother's face. Her voice low, she answered, and it was as if she was talking about someone else.

'Mrs Carter confirmed that Harry is going out with another girl. She also said that Harry only wrote to me because he felt sorry for me.' She felt hot tears pricking her eyes.

'She never said that. The cruel woman!' retorted Mary. 'Hasn't she got any heart or sympathy?' She pushed herself up from her chair. Pulling one of Ted's handkerchiefs from her apron pocket she went to Rose's side and handed it to her. 'Don't take on so, love. Mrs Carter's a nasty bit of work. Just wait until I see her. I'll give her a piece of my mind.'

Through her tears, Rose looked at her mother's angry face.

'Don't, Mam. It'll only make things worse. I'll just have to get over losing Harry.' Secretly she hoped that he would come back to her and say it was just a ghastly mistake.

'If you're sure.' But Mary didn't sound convinced.

'Yes, I am. I think I'll start going out and enjoying myself.' Brave words, but harder to put into practice because that was the last thing she wanted to do. But her mother had enough things to worry about and she didn't want to add to them. Her heart still ached with love for Harry. It wasn't something she could stop, not like snuffing out the candle when the all-clear sounded after a bombing raid and it was safe to come out of the shelter.

'Mam, I've got a splitting headache. Do you mind if I go up and have a lie-down?'

'Of course not, love. You go up.'

Rose lay on top of the counterpane, but sleep wouldn't come. Her mind was too full of Harry. What had gone so wrong with their relationship? Restless, she sat up and swung her legs over the side of the bed, her toes touching the bottom drawer of her dressing table. She slid down onto her knees and opened the drawer and stared at the contents of her hope chest.

Here lay two years of the fruits of her scrimping and making do. As well as saving in the bank, she had planned her hope chest, always with a picture in her mind of the lovely house she and Harry would live in one day. Wartime linen, if you were lucky enough to buy it, was utility-made and plain. But Rose, with silks from her late grandma's old needlework box, had lovingly embroidered borders of flowers or cross stitch on pillow-cases and sheets to make it personal just for her and Harry. Hadn't she written and told him so? And she regularly trailed the markets and second-hand shops for any bargains of crockery and cooking equipment. In doing all this, she had denied herself even the basic luxuries. No riding on the bus, no silk stockings when the man at the market had any to sell; she deprived herself of lipstick and cold cream and just washed her hair in rainwater to keep it shiny. The biggest shame of all was not buying any new underwear, resorting to wearing patched underskirts and knickers. She winced at the thought. It had been her dream to have a trousseau of under-garments of satin and lace, soft to touch and glamorous to look at, like the stars in the American films. She shut the drawer and felt utterly miserable and sinking in self-pity. She felt completely worthless.

For most of the weekend, she kept to her room, not wanting to talk about what Harry had done to her. Rose did feel guilty about not helping Mam with the household tasks. On Sunday afternoon, she heard Sally come round to the house. Sally was her best friend since schooldays; she had dark-brown curly hair and a ready smile on her impish face. Mary called upstairs for Rose to come down; she didn't answer, pretending to be asleep. She lay listening to the muffled voices of her mother and Sally. She knew her mother would be telling Sally all about it, and Sally would be sympathetic and caring, and that set Rose crying again.

Time passed, and the house was silent. Rose stirred from the bed and caught a glimpse of her reflection in the dressing-table mirror. What a pathetic sight she looked: her hair was lank and stringy, her eyes were red-rimmed with dark shadows beneath, which stood out more against the dull greyness of her skin. She looked ten years older than her eighteen years. As she stared at the hardly recognizable reflection of herself, anger rose within her; she could feel the bile in her throat.

'Oh, Harry,' she cried, her voice raw, 'look what you have done to me. You've made me a wreck.' Into her mind's eye flashed a picture of another man. Joe.

Joe, who on their first meeting, in his drunken state, had frightened her. On seeing him again, her fear had turned to pity. Forgetting her own sorrow, she recalled him sitting alone on a cold, windswept pier. His whole being was one of desolation and suffering, as if he hadn't the right to live. And yet, he had taken the time to walk home with her, listened to her woes and then disappeared without telling her his troubles. Had he fought in a battle and seen his comrades killed? So many brave men who survived thought they hadn't the right to live. Or maybe he'd lost a loved one?

Rose moved to pour water from the pitcher into the bowl and rinsed her face. The cold

37

water felt cool to her flushed skin and re-freshing. She thought of Joe again and wished she had taken the time to find out what was troubling him.

She turned to look at Harry's photograph, in a silver gilt frame, standing on the dressing table. She sighed heavily. He was so hand-some in his uniform. Every night, before climbing into bed, she had kissed that photograph and prayed for his safe return. But there would be no more kisses, and her prayers would now be for every serving man and woman.

Sally was a true friend. On Monday morning just before 5.30, she knocked at Rose's door. They were on the six-to-two shift with the option to carry on till ten, the late shift, which they often worked, more so Rose. She – her heart sank with despair – had been sav-ing up for when Harry came home. She felt numb, unable to believe that Harry wasn't her love any more, for she could not just turn off her heart like a tap of cold water. Sally chatted all the way to work, not really expect-ing Rose to reply, and for this Rose was grateful. Clocking on in the factory, panic swelled in Rose.

'Sally, don't tell anyone, please.'

Sally squeezed Rose's arm reassuringly, saying, 'I won't breathe a word.'

'What's this then – a secret?' a loud voice

boomed behind the two girls.

Rose nearly tripped over her own foot and was saved by Sally, who was still holding her arm. Quick thinking, Sally propelled Rose forward through into the cloakroom and, as she did so, she glanced over her shoulder and said, 'It's nothing for you to worry about, Brenda.'

For once, Rose was glad of the noise on the factory floor, which made conversation difficult, except for those women who could lip-read.

The noon break was held in a cramped canteen and everyone seemed to be chatting incessantly. Rose and Sally always brought a pack-up of sandwiches whenever possible and bought a cup of weak tea. Rose took out a sandwich, but she didn't feel much like eating. Over the work's tannoy system, the wireless programme *Workers' Playtime* was on full blast, or was it *Itma?* Rose couldn't tell which and she couldn't believe how any-one could talk over such a racket of noise. It was giving her a headache. She bunched her fingers round the mug and sipped the tepid tea, feeling utterly miserable. She gave a fleeting look at the sea of faces around her and, in spite of being surrounded by all these people, she felt so lonely; a deep, gut-wrenching loneliness of despair.

'You've got a long face, Rose,' said Brenda, sitting opposite, munching her sandwich.

Rose glanced across at her. 'Just tired,' she mumbled, and she was, wishing she hadn't agreed to work the late shift as well as this one.

'Oh,' someone else joined in. 'Your Harry home on leave, then?'

Rose felt tears wet her lashes and she bit on her lip.

'Had a row, then?'

'You ain't pregnant?'

She couldn't hold the tears back and fiercely she tried to brush them away.

'Oh, touchy are we?'

'For God's sake, shut up! Can't you see she's upset?' Sally shouted above the taunts. There were more sniggers. Rose scraped back her chair, pushing her way to the cloakroom, but not before she heard Sally's loud indignant voice: 'If you must know, Harry Carter's gone and jilted her for another woman. So put that in your pipe and smoke it.'

It was as if a machine had been switched off. There was total silence in the canteen.

Harry jilting Rose became a two-day diversion at the factory from the worries of war. There were innuendos and comments like, 'She can't keep her man,' which she tried to ignore. It was those who felt sorry for her, the ones who would look at her so sorrowfully, that hurt the most. 'Don't worry, love, you're best off without him,' or,

'Plenty more fish in the sea.' She knew they were being kind, but she found their sympathy harder to cope with.

Rose came to bless Sally for being her best friend. She just wouldn't take no for an answer.

'When are you going to start coming dancing with me?' Sally asked again as the two girls got off the bus on Hedon Road. It was a Saturday afternoon 17th March and the two girls had worked an extra day to help finish an urgent order.

'I've nothing to wear,' Rose began.

Sally giggled. 'Ah, that's where yer wrong. Your Mam has been making you a new dress.'

Rose pulled at Sally's arm, her fine eyebrows arched, and said, 'We haven't any spare coupons, and I know Dad needs new winter boots.'

'Wait and see,' Sally called as she disappeared into her house a few doors from Rose's.

Eagerly, Rose burst into the house, calling as she shrugged off her coat and shoes.

'Mam, I'm home.' But there was no reply.

Rose went into the kitchen. It was silent and in darkness. She flicked on the light switch and went to open the door in the corner leading up to the stairs. 'Mam, are you there?' No answer. She looked round the empty kitchen and then she saw it. Propped up on the mantelpiece was a note. She picked it up and read her mother's hasty scrawl.

Tea's in the oven. Dad and I have gone to see Shadow of the Thin Man *with Myrna Loy and William Powell at the Savoy. Love, Mam.*

Rose smiled to herself. So Mam had managed to persuade Dad to take her to the pictures on one of his rare nights off duty. She ate her solitary meal and felt restless, not tired as she expected to be after working extra. She glanced at the clock on the mantelpiece, and saw there was just time to walk down to the Savoy cinema and meet her parents coming out. She would enjoy hearing about the film.

She wasn't frightened in the blackout with no street lamps, but walking through the narrow confines of the alley, known locally as Ping-Pong Alley, beneath the overhead railway, always gave her the creeps. On reaching Holderness Road, she heard the sound of the siren, warning of an enemy attack. The noise was so deafening, frighteningly so, even though she had heard it so many times before. It couldn't be a raid. All the talk was of the war ending, so surely it must be a mistake?

Ahead of her, further along Holderness Road, she could see that the picture-goers were leaving the cinema and streaming out in all directions. Something made her glance upwards to the dark sky above and she heard the noise of an aircraft. She squinted, seeing nothing, and then it was there just above her head, the enemy plane so low she could see the pilot in the cockpit. She jumped back in fear as the plane dived lower, its machine gun blazing. Then the ground beneath her shook as a bomb exploded. She was flung against a door of a shop as its plate-glass windows smashed into smithereens. Screams filled the acrid air, her eardrums felt like bursting, lights popped and flashed, a kaleidoscope of colours stinging her eyes. Heat whipped around her body and falling masonry rained down upon her, hitting her hard. She lifted up her arms to protect her head and face, closing her eyes in an attempt to ward off her mounting terror. There was an unnatural silence, and then panic broke loose. People were shouting for loved ones and friends. Opening her eyes, Rose saw the carnage all around her and her body went cold at the horror. A woman was cradling an older woman, a man was clawing with his bare hands at a pile of rubble, cries and moans filled the air, and everywhere there was smoke and rising heat.

Her first thought was for her parents. She struggled to her feet; her knees were bleeding, her hair and face were covered in plaster and bits of debris, and her coat was torn. But she was alive. With shaking limbs, she negotiated the path strewn with obstacles of bricks, fallen timbers and broken glass.

She plunged forward. She had to find her parents.

FOUR

In her feverish haste, Rose ran and stumbled over hot strewn debris, crying out her parents' names. She passed people in dazed states and all around was the acrid smell of burning, its fumes stinging her eyes. Then above the frightening noise of crackling, she thought she heard the faint cry of a child. She stopped running for a moment and strained her ears. In the dark confusion of the street she peered, but she couldn't see anything. Then she heard it again.

'Mammy, Mammy.' The cry was faint but she didn't know where it was coming from. An ARP air-raid warden was dashing from the opposite direction towards her. Frantically she caught his arm.

'Help me; I think a child's trapped.'

He looked harassed as he hurried by, not stopping to draw breath. 'Back as soon as I can.'

Rose scrambled over the steaming rubble, calling, 'Where are you?'

The whimpering of the child sounded again. Her eyes gradually became accustomed to the darkness and she could just make out the frightened face of a girl about ten years of age. With horror, Rose saw that one of the girl's legs was trapped by fallen rubble and a huge length of wood. With no thought for her own injuries, Rose dropped to her knees and took hold of the child's outstretched hand. Her first instinct was to give the girl a hug, but she wasn't sure of the extent of the injuries and didn't want to add to them.

'Soon have you safe,' she soothed, and prayed she wasn't deluding herself. She tore a strip of cotton off her petticoat and gently she wiped away the coating of dust and muck from the girl's eyes and face.

Hastily she looked over her shoulder to see if the warden or anybody was around to help, but there was so much chaos around her. Twisting back to the girl, she could see the unhealthy stark white of her face and that she was too quiet. The thud of Rose's heart pounded so hard in her chest it hurt as she bent forward to feel the girl's pulse.

Relief swamped her as she realized the girl was not dead, but must have slipped into unconsciousness. Moving carefully, not wanting to disturb the debris of brick and mortar so that it wouldn't fall on the girl and cause her further injury, Rose inched towards the plank of wood. She couldn't see much and under her breath she cursed, wishing she had a torch. Yet she had her own willing pair of hands; she put all her strength into lifting the plank but it wouldn't budge. Wiping the sweat and grime from her brow, she noticed that one end of the plank was weighed down by rubble. Slowly and painstakingly, she clawed away at the fallen rubble, at the same time keeping her neck craned so that she could see the child's face.

She saw the girl's eyelids flicker and then her eyes opened and the pale face became distorted with terror. 'Mammy, Mammy,' the girl whimpered.

Rose said soothingly, 'Hello love, I'm Rose. What's your name?'

'Shirley. I want my mammy.' She began to sob and the debris shifted slightly.

Rose felt as though her heart had leapt into her mouth. As calmly as her chattering teeth would allow, she said, 'Shirley, love, you must keep perfectly still or the rubble will fall on your face. Try to think of nice things, like your favourite book.' All the time Rose was talking, she had never stopped shifting the rubble. Just a bit more and then she might be able to ease the heavy plank clear off Shirley's leg. Her bare hands were cut and bleeding, but she toiled on. Gradually, the wood began to loosen. If she was to shift it away from Shirley, she would have to reposition herself with her back to the girl. First she put a hand under the wood to see if she could feel exactly where Shirley's leg was. Shirley moaned with pain and Rose didn't want to cause her any more distress. Gently she manoeuvred her arm under the wood until her fingers touched Shirley's leg and she felt the sticky dampness of blood.

Shirley cried out, 'It's hurting.' Soothingly, Rose said, 'Soon have you free, love.' Carefully she slid her arm out and with all her strength she began inching the timber away from Shirley's leg. Abruptly the wood gave an almighty belching sound as it slithered and crashed over fallen debris. As the pressure was released from her leg, Shirley let out a piercing scream. For a second, so exhausted, Rose just fell back onto her heels. At the sound of Shirley's cry, she looked to see that the girl was straining forward to touch her injured leg. Rose jumped to her feet and was by the girl's side.

'I'm bleeding,' cried Shirley.

Rose put a comforting arm about her shoulders and felt the shake of the thin body in shock. Hastily, Rose tugged off her torn coat and wrapped it around the child to try and keep her warm. The girl began to sob and clung to her in such a vice-like grip of panic that Rose found it difficult to breathe. Without delay, she would have to give Shirley's injured leg some attention. She remembered watching her father when he was learning the first-aid routine and she now forced her mind to recall it. As she whispered words of reassurance to Shirley, a man's voice said in her ear:

'We'll take over now, miss.'

Shirley's grip slackened and Rose turned to see the ARP warden who had passed her earlier. He was with another man. Weary and drained of energy, Rose sat on the floor surrounded by debris, watching as the two men worked quickly to make Shirley comfortable. Soon they had her secure on a stretcher.

The first man handed back her coat, saying, 'Are you a relative?'

'No.'

'Are you all right, miss?'

With a jolt, it was then that Rose remembered she was supposed to be looking for her parents. Breathlessly, she stammered, 'Mam and Dad, I've got to find them. They were at the pictures, coming out.'

'They could be up nearer the Savoy, helping.' He eyed her bleakly, not wanting to raise her hopes or crush them. 'Minor injuries are being treated across at the church hall, others at the infirmary. But try down there first.' He indicated in the direction of the cinema. 'But miss, your hands and knees need first aid, so don't delay.'

Rose looked down at the dry, caked blood on her knees, which ached with stiffness.

For the first time, she was aware of the soreness and stinging of her hands, but they didn't matter: she must find her parents.

Half-running, half-limping, she hurried along the road towards the cinema, all the time calling her parents' names, stopping to ask if anyone had seen them.

Panting, out of breath, she rested for a moment to survey the chaos around her, looking for signs of her parents, but they were nowhere to be seen. Her stomach knotted with panic. What if... Hot tears rolled down her cheeks.

'Oh, please, Lord,' she whispered, 'not my mam and dad!'

A woman in the WVS uniform took hold of her arm, saying, 'Who are you looking for?'

'My parents. They were here at the pictures and I can't find them.' She was shaking so violently that she couldn't control her sobbing.

The woman put a sympathetic arm around her, saying, 'What's your name?'

'Rose Ellerby.'

'Now Rose, I am Mrs Butler and I'll take you across to the church hall. There we may be able to find where your parents are.' Rose allowed herself to be led like a child, her emotions raw, her inside churning at an unbelievable speed.

In the hall there was a sort of ordered bedlam. Rose stood on the threshold surveying the scene while Mrs Butler made enquiries at a makeshift official desk. People sat huddled on wooden chairs, nursing mugs of steaming liquid, and a few casualties were lying out on the floor with first aiders in attendance. It was then that she saw him.

'Dad,' she called across the noisy room, her hopes rising. But the man didn't turn round and so she started to pick her way through the maze of chairs and bodies towards him, when Mrs Butler caught her arm.

Rose tugged free. 'Dad's over there,' she said, giving Mrs Butler a cursory glance. By now the man had stood up ready to move on to another casualty. Rose's heart sank. It wasn't her father. She started to shake again.

'Sit down, my dear. You're in shock. Now drink this while it's still hot.' Rose clasped the thick white mug of hot, sweet tea and sipped. She had drunk half the mug of tea when Mrs Butler returned. Rose looked up into the comforting, professional face. Her heart pounded as she waited, praying Mrs Butler would say the right words. She held her breath.

Her voice clear, Mrs Butler said, 'Now, my dear, your parents are at the infirmary. Your father is not injured but your mother has a suspected fracture of the wrist and a back injury.'

At the news that her parents were alive, huge relief shot through Rose's body.

'I must go to them.' She tried to jump up, but Mrs Butler's restraining hand stopped her.

'It's not safe for you to be walking the streets and besides, you are in no fit state to do so. Now you sit tight and I'll arrange for transport to take you to the hospital.' She gave Rose a sympathetic pat on the arm and went back to the administration desk.

After half an hour's wait, Mrs Butler beckoned to her. 'Rose, your transport's here.'

Thanking her, Rose made her way to the door. Outside, the night air smelt rancid with burning and smoke. Fires still smouldered and the occasional flame spurted. A crew were clearing a fallen wall, checking for anyone trapped and for signs of life.

'Rose,' called a masculine voice.

She turned, surprised to see Joe, the airman, standing by an old van. At the sight of the big man, she felt a welcome sense of security. 'Joe, what are you doing here?'

'Helping to take the injured to hospital.' His voice sounded tired and she noticed his crumpled uniform was covered in dust. He opened the van door for her and she climbed into the passenger seat. In the back, sitting on sacks, were a young couple, arms protectively around each other. Sitting next to Joe, his presence gave her comfort. She glanced at him as he concentrated on driving in the blackout. She wanted to talk to him and she said the first thing which came into her mind. 'I thought you'd gone back to base.'

He didn't answer for a few seconds, as if he was having difficulty in choosing his words. 'I've been to visit my son who's evacuated in Lincolnshire...' His voice trailed.

She stared at him. It had never occurred to her that Joe was married and had a family. She recalled their first disastrous meeting and his mistaking her for someone called Ellie. But this wasn't the time to ask. She saw the tears glistening in his eyes. She wanted to touch his arm to offer him sympathy, but it wasn't the thing to do when he was driving.

They reached the infirmary and Joe slammed on the brakes, jumped down and opened the van's back doors for the couple to get out. By now, Rose was standing on the forecourt.

'I'll come with you,' offered Joe. Together they went to the reception desk.

'My mother, Mrs Mary Ellerby, was brought in earlier.'

The receptionist, checking her list, said, 'She's down the corridor in casualty.'

But she wasn't. Rose felt the panic rise, choking her, and she couldn't get her words out.

Joe took command, catching the attention of a nurse. 'Mrs Mary Ellerby, was brought in earlier, can you tell her daughter,' he indicated Rose, 'where she is, please?'

The nurse checked a wall chart. 'If you go up the stairs, she is in the first ward.' Rose felt the gentle strength of Joe as he took hold of her arm and steered her in the right direction.

FIVE

Rose's heart sank at the sight of her mother's fragile figure cocooned in a bed of white sheets. Her right arm was in a plaster cast up to her elbow, and her back was supported by several pillows. The face peeping out from the depths of the pillows was as stark as the bedding, except for the dark-blue bruising on her right cheek.

'Oh Mam,' Rose cried, hurrying to the bedside.

Ted, sitting by Mary, put a finger on his lips to restrain Rose. But Mary opened her eyes and smiled at her daughter. Rose bent forward to kiss her mother tenderly on the forehead and then she gently took hold of her mother's hand on her uninjured arm.

A look of concern swept across Mary's face and her voice croaked, as she whispered, 'Rose, what have you done to your poor hands, and your coat?'

'Mam, it's nothing to worry about. A good

scrub in carbolic and a dab of iodine and they will soon heal, and my coat was past its best.' She tucked her hands out of sight in the folds of the coat and pulled her skirt over her sore knees, asking softly, 'How are you feeling?'

'Tired.' Even as she spoke, Mary's eyelids drooped.

A nurse bustled up saying, 'Time for patient to rest. You may visit tomorrow afternoon.'

'It's a long walk home,' Ted muttered. 'We could stay and be no bother.' The nurse gave him a frosty stare. At this point, Joe, who had been standing by the door, approached.

'I've got the van outside. I'll take you home.'

Rose flashed him a grateful smile, and said, 'Thanks, Joe. We'd appreciate that.'

By the time they arrived at Church Terrace, the night had turned to the earthy grey of morning. Lingering still in the air was the smell of charred wood doused by water. Rose shivered as she stepped from the van onto the pavement. Joe was about to drive off, but Ted caught his arm, saying, 'Come on in, lad, and have a cuppa.'

Indoors, Rose took the kettle off the hob top and poured the warm water into a bowl to clean her hands. She refilled the kettle and placed it on the now blazing fire. Ted had given it a good rake and put on a few pieces of coal and it flared up instantly.

'You see to yourself, Rose, I'll mash the tea,' said Ted.

She glanced in surprise at her father. He always said that making tea and such domestic things were women's work. She supposed that her mother's and his near miss with death had made him realize just how precious life is to be bothered with petty things. As they had been leaving the infirmary, they had overheard a conversation between two officials, that the bombing raid on the patrons leaving the cinema had resulted in twelve fatalities and numerous injuries. Rose shuddered with relief; her parents were safe, but her heart went out to those bereaved families.

Joe, his greatcoat now discarded, sat at the kitchen table, his eyes bleary with fatigue. He couldn't remember when he'd last slept. He thought of the long journey to Lincolnshire, changing trains, cold, draughty stations and having to stand squashed on crowded trains. But worst of all was his son, Peter. The little boy, only five years old, hadn't seen Joe for over a year. So when Joe, unshaven and looking travel-weary, arrived at Peter's billet, the boy had hidden behind his foster mother and refused to talk to him. When he was finally coaxed round by Joe producing a bar of chocolate, Peter had asked for his mother. He had failed his son.

'Bread and cheese do you, lad?'

Joe, broken out of his depressing thoughts, stared at Ted, for a moment forgetting where he was. Then he answered, 'I don't want to take your rations.'

'It's the least we can do for all your help. Isn't that right, Rose?'

Rose, coming back into the kitchen from the scullery, caught the drift of her father's words. 'Of course it is.' She sat down at the table, opposite Joe.

For the very first time Joe really looked at Rose. She shone with warmth despite her recent trauma. Her fair hair freshly brushed was like a halo around her lovely face, and her skin, newly washed, was pink and glowing. Her perfume... He laughed, he couldn't help it. Her bluey-grey eyes stared, not sure of him. Ted, busy slicing bread, also looked at Joe.

'I'm sorry,' apologized Joe, 'but I was thinking out loud, what a refreshing scent carbolic and iodine make after being on a train crammed next to sweaty bodies.'

As if they understood, both Rose and Ted nodded in agreement and the atmosphere, tinged with sadness and worry, lightened a little.

Joe tucked into his sandwich. 'By, this is tasty, beats black paste any day.' After drinking two mugs of strong tea, he craved a cigarette. He rummaged in his trouser pocket and withdrew a squashed packet, offering it to Ted.

'Nay, lad, I'll have me pipe, but you carry on.'

He offered the packet to Rose. She shook her head and smiled at him. Joe liked it here in this warm, welcoming kitchen with these good people. He had been starved of love and friendship for so long that he'd forgotten what it was about. Meeting Rose was his good luck in more ways than one. Maybe someday he would tell her.

Ted was talking to him. 'So you've been on a train journey recently, Joe?'

'Lincolnshire to see my son, he's evacuated there.'

'Best place till this damned war finishes. Is his mam there as well?'

Joe, despite the heat of the room, felt a chill touch his heart. He swallowed hard and gulped. He must come to terms with it for Peter's sake. He spoke slowly. 'My wife was killed in a bombing raid on Venture Street along with our unborn child.' He heard Rose gasp. He couldn't meet her eyes, not wanting to see the sympathy. Instead he lit another cigarette and inhaled fiercely, but he couldn't stop the trembling within him. He could feel Rose watching him and he wanted nothing more than to bury his face in the softness of her body and weep. The ticking clock filled the room, making his head ache.

Ted broke the silence. Scraping back his chair he got to his feet. Joe, thinking he had outstayed his welcome, said, 'I must be going.' But he wasn't sure where to. His billet had been taken when he'd gone to see Peter, and he hadn't had time to search for another one.

'Nay, lad,' said Ted, 'too late to be travelling. We all need some shut-eye. You bed down on our couch. Rose will rustle up some blankets.'

Joe stared at the older man in surprise. 'Do you mean it?'

'Of course I do.'

'You're very kind.'

Rose left the kitchen and soon returned. 'Joe, I'll show you to your room.' He followed her to the front room. She gave him an apologetic smile. 'Sorry, but we've only two spare blankets and a counterpane. The rest were given away to help people who had been bombed.'

He eyed the inviting made-up bed on the settee. 'It looks comfortable and the way I feel, I could sleep on a clothes line. Is it all right if I have a quick wash?'

'Yes, in the scullery. There's water in the kettle. Is there anything else you need?'

He looked at her for long seconds, engulfed in loneliness. He longed to hug her, to feel her warmth next to his, to bring some respite to the onslaught of his mind and body. It had been almost a month since his wife had died and months since he had last seen her. How he'd wept for her loss and for the unborn baby he never had the chance to hold in his arms. He must stop torturing himself. Also he must return to see Peter and tell him of the loss of his mother and comfort him as best he could.

'Are you all right, Joe?' Rose's anxious voice broke into his sad thoughts.

'Sorry, Rose, my mind was wandering. Thanks, everything's fine.'

'Goodnight, Joe,' she said softly as she left the room.

For a few moments, Rose leaned against the closed door of the front room. She couldn't get out of her mind the despairing, haunted look in Joe's eyes. How he was suffering, grieving for his lost loved ones. Upstairs in the privacy of her room, she knelt down and prayed. She thanked God for her mother's life, when so many had been taken, and asked for comfort for the bereaved. Once in bed she couldn't sleep, her mind too full of the recent events. The trauma, all too vivid, wouldn't go away. Over and over again replays of events crowded her thoughts and she could still hear the screams of the frightened and injured. She wondered how Shirley, the girl she had rescued, was faring. Her last thoughts, before drifting into a restless sleep, were of Joe, who had suffered so much.

She was woken up by the sound of loud knocking on the front door. She lay for a moment wondering what day it was. Then she sat up with a jerk. She groaned, pushing back the bedclothes, and then she remembered her mother in hospital, dear Mam lying injured and hurting. Work, for once, would just have to wait.

There came a tap on her bedroom door. 'Rose, it's me, Sally.' She crept into the room, her face tight and anxious-looking. 'Oh, Rose, your poor mam.'

Sally hugged Rose so tightly that Rose could feel the soreness of her ribs, which she hadn't noticed last night. Freeing herself from her friend's hold, she said, 'Sally, will you tell the foreman I won't be in? When Mam comes home I'll have to look after her for a while.'

'Don't you worry, girl. One wrong word from him and I'll sock him.'

Clutching her aching ribs, Rose laughed. 'You're a tonic, Sally Wray.'

'Anything I can get you? A cream cake, box of chocolates, shampoo?'

Rose laughed again. 'I wish.'

When Sally had gone, Rose would have loved to turn over and go back to sleep, but there was a lot to do. She washed and dressed, and felt rather fragile and in need of a cup of reviving tea. On reaching the bottom tread of the stairs and about to push open the door, she heard Joe's voice. Her heart lifted a notch to know he was still here.

Joe and Ted sat at the kitchen table with the big brown teapot between them. 'Morning, love,' said Ted as he lifted the pot to pour her a mugful. 'Toast's on oven top.'

Rose acknowledged both men, feeling amazed at the domestic transformation of her father.

As she ate her breakfast, she looked across at Joe. He was clean-shaven and had lost his dishevelled appearance. In fact, in a rugged kind of way, he looked quite handsome.

'I've been down to the phonebox and rung the infirmary and they say Mary's had a comfortable night.' Ted sucked in his breath, trying to hide his emotional state. 'Doctor's going round the ward this morning and if she's stable, she can come home this afternoon.' With this, Ted got clumsily to his feet and went out into the backyard.

Rose stared after her dad, feeling close to tears herself. She looked down at the piece of toast on her plate, suddenly losing her appetite.

'I've got the van for the rest of the day,' Joe said. Rose glanced at him, glad of the distraction. Joe continued, 'There's just enough petrol to get us to and from the infirmary to bring your mam home in style.' He grinned a little sheepishly.

'That's kind of you, Joe,' she replied, her voice strained with worry. 'Mam will take badly to being laid up. She likes always to be helping and doing for others.'

Joe spoke with sincerity. 'What I've heard about your mother, she sounds a survivor. She'll be up and about in no time. You'll see.'

They arrived at the infirmary in good time, giving a lift to a woman whom they saw crying at a bus stop, desperate to see her injured young son. The doctor was still doing his rounds so they stood in the crowded waiting room.

It was a relief to learn, from the sister in charge, that because Mary had someone at home to care for her and her own transport, she was being discharged.

'Arrangements will be made for a district nurse to call and re-dress your wife's back wound.' The ward sister addressed Ted. 'And an appointment will be made to have the plaster cast removed.'

Ted, his voice full of emotion, said, 'Thank you, Sister.' Pure joy flooded his face as his beloved Mary was wheeled into the waiting area, ready to go home.

Once home and Mary safely ensconced in her chair by the fireside, Rose said to Joe, 'You'll stay for tea?'

'I would love to, Rose, but I have to get the

van back to the depot and...' He paused, with a faraway look in his eyes. 'I've got to go and see my son before I return back to base.' He was stationed on an aerodrome in North Yorkshire, with the ground crew, mainly on fire and rescue duties.

Ted shook hands with him. 'Thanks for your help, lad. When you're home, call anytime, you'll always be welcome. Ain't that right, Mary?'

Mary, looking frail and tired, said, 'Yes, Ted.'

'I'll walk with you to the van,' Rose said. She slipped on her best coat, the only one she had now. In silence they walked to the van parked at the kerbside then Joe turned to her, and Rose saw once again the desolation in his eyes. Inside she wept for him. He held out his hand to shake hers, but on impulse she flung her arms about him and hugged him close.

'Take care,' she whispered. Then as they drew apart, she felt the soft warmth of his lips brush her cheek.

She watched the van disappear from view, and still she stood, her hand caressing her cheek, feeling still the tenderness of that brief kiss.

SIX

Rose shopped, queued, cooked and cleaned. Most of all, she spent time looking after her mother. So with her loving tender care, Mary gradually became stronger in body and spirit.

'The terrible shock of seeing innocent people slaughtered before my eyes,' Mary said to Rose, as they sat by the fireside. 'I'll never ever forget that. But life goes on.'

Ted was a gem. When he wasn't working during the day and fire-watching at night, he was being attentive to Mary. One night he brought her a bottle of milk stout. 'This will build you up,' he said. Settling down to read Mary snippets of interest and humour from the local newspaper, he said, 'I see General Patton and his tanks are heading towards the Moselle. And a girl at the Electrical Lamp Factory was fined £8 for being absent from work and late six times into the bargain.' He glanced at his wife's solemn face, careful not to read out anything that might remind her of that terrible night. He put on his most jovial voice. 'Now, this is the best. Five hundred Dutch children sang as they came into Paragon Station. That would have been worth listening to.' To his delight, Mary answered:

'I love to hear children singing.'

Ted knew why Mary was downhearted. Partly it was because of the bombing raid and her injuries, but the main reason was because their Freddie hadn't been allowed compassionate leave. If his mother's injuries had been more severe or life threatening, then it would have been granted. Ted sighed heavily; war was so fruitless.

On the Saturday afternoon of that week, Sally called round. Mary was resting and Ted was going down to Mr Reilly's allotment to see what vegetables were ready for picking.

'Might be a cabbage or two,' he said, as he pulled on his boots, shrugged into his coat and jammed his cap firmly on his sparse head of hair.

'Or onions,' Rose added hopefully. After queuing for hours, all she had managed to get for Sunday dinner was a ration of liver. It worried her as food was getting scarcer, but she didn't want to relay her fears to her mother, though Rose suspected that her mother knew.

'Talk about tightening belts, any more cut-backs and we'll slip through,' remarked Sally. 'And you'll soon have an eighteen-inch waist.'

Rose touched her waist; lack of food wasn't why she'd lost weight. It was the loss of Harry.

The two friends settled down by the fireside. 'I'll mash a pot of tea when Mam wakes up.' Sally fidgeted with her hair, which Rose knew was a sign that something was bothering her.

'Out with it, Sally,' she commanded.

Sally sighed. 'It's old misery-guts at work. He wants to know when yer coming back. Said we've all to make sacrifices. The insensitive old sod,' she finished, pulling a face.

'I thought it was too good to be true. I've had a word with Mrs Fisher. If I do the early shift at the factory and give Mam her breakfast before I go, Mrs Fisher will then come in and help Mam to dress and do a bit of dinner. I'll be home from work in time to cook the tea.'

'Mam said she'll help with the shopping,' said Sally.

Back at work, Rose found that her life had become a kind of juggling act. With the help of Mrs Fisher and Mrs Wray, and her dad's input, she managed to keep the household ticking along nicely, though she never stopped marvelling at the sacrifices women made, their endless time and energy, to keep a family clothed and fed in such austere conditions forced on them through war. On Saturday afternoon, Rose picked up a good tip from a woman in the butcher's queue: 'To make butter go further,' the woman explained, 'put it in a dish and add a little milk and whip it up so it becomes nice and creamy.' Rose tried it, and it spread a treat on a slice of new bread. She licked her lips; it tasted good too.

Throughout the weeks while Mary was incapacitated, Rose felt too tired to think about a social life. The dance dress, which Sally had hinted at, hadn't been mentioned. Tonight, Rose was ironing. She'd persuaded Mary to go with Ted down to the local pub, the Dockers' Arms. Mrs Fisher popped in to say she'd heard they had a supply of milk stout in. Mary admitted she was becoming fond of stout; it gave her energy levels a good boost.

Sally came in to see Rose. 'Heard anything about your Harry?' she asked innocently.

'He's not my Harry,' Rose replied hotly, but she couldn't betray her true feelings. 'It's daft, I know, but I can't stop loving Harry. I can't just cut off my feelings, even though he's jilted me.' She lowered her eyes, and continued ironing.

Sally eyed her friend thoughtfully, and said, 'You ought to be more like me, I love 'em and leave 'em. Best way. Gosh, Rose, at eighteen you should be out there enjoying yourself. The only reason I'm in tonight is cos I've no money. Come pay day, I'll be out there living it up.'

As if she hadn't heard a word Sally said, Rose whispered, 'What about my hope chest?'

Sally stared at her friend, puzzled for a moment. 'Oh, you mean all that fancy underwear you've got in the bottom drawer of your dressing table?' She giggled. 'Now you can wear it and give some poor sailor or airman a treat. That Harry doesn't know what he is missing.'

Rose, looking shocked, said, 'I couldn't do that.'

'Well, it will only rot if you don't.'

'But Harry might come back,' said Rose, ignoring Sally's face-pulling. She folded the last item of ironing and replaced the flat iron on the hob top. Not wanting to expose any more of her secret thoughts about Harry, Rose quickly changed the subject. 'Let's have the wireless on and find a good play to listen to.'

But it was the news that crackled on the old wireless set. A presenter was speaking about war – what else? thought Rose – but as she listened to the man's words, she exclaimed to Sally, 'Do you think the war is really going to end?'

'I dunno, but it's hard to turn your back on the news on the wireless and in the newspapers. People whisper about it at work, but nobody really says it will. It's tempting providence.' She drew in a long breath, and then said, 'Come on; let me find some cheerful music.' She pushed Rose to one side and began fiddling with the tuning knob.

Just then, the back gate of the yard creaked open. 'They're back early,' Rose remarked. She glanced out of the kitchen window to see a man in army uniform. 'It can't be!' She rushed to open the kitchen door. 'It *is* you. Oh, Freddie! Mam will be so pleased to see you.' As she hugged her brother with joy, she felt his weariness. She stepped back to let him in and was shocked to see how thin and gaunt he was. Until then, she always had the mental picture of Freddie with the broad, smiling face, his soft brown hair, and ready to crack a joke. Now he looked tired and worn out. That's what war does to you. Gone was the care-free lad who had taken her with him on adventures; they had had such fun together. He didn't mind that she was five years younger than him, letting her tag along on those balmy sunny days of long-forgotten summers. Down the five lanes, or the Cinder Trod, as it was locally known, passing the railway track on one side and the cemetery on the other side of the fencing, on to Barmston Drain to swim in its cool waters, fish for little silver tiddlers or just to dangle your feet in the water. Those were halcyon days and would they ever return?

'Hello, Freddie,' said Sally, all smiles.

But Freddie only gave her a cursory nod. He looked round the kitchen. His voice gruff, he said, 'Where's Mam and Dad?'

'Corner pub, do you want to go?'

'No, I just want to sit by the fireside.' He flopped into an easy chair and closed his eyes.

Sally gave Rose a quick glance, saying, 'I'll go and tell your parents.'

Rose put the kettle on to boil. There wasn't much food in the pantry, nothing to make a substantial meal for a battle-weary soldier. She glanced at Freddie and wasn't surprised to see him sleeping. She bent down, unlaced his boots and eased them off and moved them, and his kitbag, to the far corner of the room.

Five minutes later, Mary and Ted came hurrying into the kitchen. 'Freddie,' cried Mary, her voice full of emotion.

At the sound of her voice, he opened his eyes and said, 'Hello, Mam, how yer doing?'

'Much better, son, but I thought they wouldn't let you home.'

Freddie winked at his dad, and said, 'I worked my charm on them.' Mary's face took on a worried expression, her voice conveying her anxiety. 'You aren't absent without leave?'

'Of course not! I came over with a consignment,' but he didn't say what, 'and I was granted a 24-hour pass. So how about a cup of tea and a bit of something to eat? I'm famished.'

'Rose,' Mary said, 'in the pantry, behind the bread bin, there is a tin. Bring it out, please.'

'Spam,' said Rose with surprise, as she came back with the tin. 'I didn't know we had this.'

Mary, now more like her cheerful self, said, 'I always ice something away, just in case.'

All four sat round the kitchen table, tucking into Spam sandwiches, and Ted produced a bottle of stout for Freddie.

Next morning, Rose was first up and nipped down to the allotments where Mr Reilly kept a few chickens. She was in luck. When she told him about Freddie being home to see Mary, he willingly gave her one of the three eggs which he had collected earlier. He knew that the Ellerby household could do him a favour, when he needed one. Mary, when fit, usually did his family a bit of sewing.

When Rose arrived back home, Ted and Freddie were up, sitting at the kitchen table drinking tea, and discussing the war. Not that Freddie could say too much about where or what his unit was engaged in, except to say that they had Hitler on the run.

Rose listened, as she fried the egg for Freddie, sandwiching it between two thick slices of bread. She joined them at the table and steered the conversation to what she thought was a more positive topic. 'Freddie, when the war ends, will you go back into the buses?' He had been a corporation bus driver before the war. She watched as he licked his lips, savouring every tiny morsel of food. Ted, leaning back in his chair, also watched him and Rose wished she could have got an egg for him.

Freddie's eyes dulled as he answered, 'To tell the truth, sis, I'm exhausted by driving. This bloody war spoils everything and there are things I'd rather forget.'

'Oh, I didn't mean to upset you. Anyway,' she added cheerfully, trying to keep the conversation light, 'when you come home you'll find a nice girl to settle down with.'

'Now you're talking. You get them lined up for me.' They all laughed and just at that moment, Mary came downstairs.

'Why didn't you wake me, Ted?' She came and gave Freddie a kiss on the cheek. 'Did you sleep well, son?'

'Yes, Mam, it felt like heaven to sleep in a real bed.' He had slept well, but not well enough to take away this terrible feeling lodged within him that refused to go away. If the truth be told, he didn't want to go back to his unit. He was tired of war, its senseless killing of innocent people, which seemed to make no discrimination whichever side you were on. And then there was the destruction of homes and cities. It had been a shock to him when he arrived at Paragon Station to see the devastation of Hull city centre. Familiar landmarks were gone, like the family store of Hammonds and the tall Prudential

Building. Streets that he had run through as a boy were smashed to smithereens by bombs. Unintentionally, he voiced his thoughts out loud.

'It's no different here than it is in Germany; all the destruction and we are supposed to be winning the bloody war.'

They all looked at him, aghast by his outburst.

It was Ted who spoke. 'Aye, lad, that's as maybe, but we've all had to make sacrifices and no one ever said war was fair. The sooner it's over the better.' He got up and went into the scullery for his coat and cap, and then he came back into the kitchen. He stood by Freddie's side and put a hand on his shoulder, saying, 'You take care, son, and come back safely to us. That's all I ask.'

Freddie gulped, as he looked up into his father's watery grey eyes, ringed with heavy lines. His voice was gruff with emotion, as he replied, 'Thanks, Dad.'

As her father left for work, Rose jumped up to clear away the table. Freddie stretched out his legs and yawned. Mary, who up until then had remained quiet, said to Freddie, 'Go back to bed, love, if you're still tired.'

He put his arms behind his head, flashed his mother a smile and said, 'I want to spend all day with you and I'm here to look after you while Dad and Rose are at work.'

Mary's face lit up. 'I'd best get dressed.'

Rose followed her mother upstairs to help her. 'Once I get this plaster off, I'll be as good as new,' Mary commented.

Rose wanted to say something to her mother about how Freddie had changed, but a glance at her mother's happy face and she didn't.

Instead, she voiced her thoughts to Sally, as they went to catch the bus to work. 'You saw our Freddie; did you think he was different?'

Sally glanced at her friend, and she thought of her older sister's husband, who was in the navy, and answered, 'They lose their sparkle, especially when they're missing home.'

They joined the bus queue, and Rose replied, 'It's not the same for our Freddie; he's not got a wife or a girlfriend. He's put on a brave face for Mam.' She was silent for a moment and then she said, 'I think he hates the war and all that killing. Then, don't we all?'

SEVEN

The day arrived for Mary to have the plaster cast removed. After a bumping bus ride, no luxury of a van driven by Joe this time, Rose was guiding her mother through the infirmary door, when a childish voice cried out, 'Rose!'

Holding Mary's arm steady, Rose half-turned to see that hobbling towards her was Shirley, the girl she had rescued from the rubble of the bombing raid. Close on her heel was Mrs Butler, the WVS lady, who had helped Rose to find her parents.

Shirley flung her arms about Rose, crying, 'My fairy angel. I told my mam about you.'

Rose glanced over Shirley's head to Mrs Butler, and smiled. Then gently she disentangled herself from Shirley, saying, 'This is my mam. She was hurt as well.'

Mary held up her plastered arm. 'Mam,' Rose introduced, 'this is Mrs Butler, the lady I told you about, who helped me to find you and Dad on that night.'

'You do grand work. When I'm better, I'm going to do more to help with the war work.'

By now they were all in the reception area for outpatients. Mrs Butler, who looked very smart in the WVS uniform of grey-green and wine-red, costume and hat, seemed tired.

'We could certainly do with more volunteers, Mrs Ellerby,' Mrs Butler said, glancing at her watch. 'When I've seen to Shirley, I've another family to call on.'

'Where's Shirley's mother?' asked Rose.

'At home with my new baby sister,' Shirley exclaimed, proudly.

Rose looked at her mother, now seated

with Shirley by her side, both chatting. 'Me and Mam could take care of Shirley and see her safely home if you are pressed for time.'

Mrs Butler's pinched face creased with relief. 'Would you be so kind, dear?'

A thoughtful look flashed across Mrs Butler's face. 'If you ever have time to spare, call into the office. I would be glad of a pair of willing hands.'

It was towards the end of April before Rose found the time to call into the WVS office, situated in the city centre, to see Mrs Butler. She was busy with a client and so Rose sat on an uncomfortable wooden chair to wait. It was at her mother's insistence that she came. Mary was now physically fully recovered, though the scar of that terrible night would always be with her.

'You just have to get on with life,' Mary had said, matter-of-factly.

Rose was trying to, but Harry was constantly in her thoughts and she still longed for him. Was this other woman in the forces, someone who he might see on a regular basis? Her thoughts were interrupted...

'Rose, how lovely to see you.' Mrs Butler was extending her hand in greeting and then ushered her into the small, cluttered office. The desk was covered in files and documents. 'Sit down, my dear.'

Rose sat on the uncomfortable twin of the

chair in the waiting area. Her voice filled with enthusiasm as she said, 'I've come to help!' She watched the tired eyes of Mrs Butler light up.

'My dear girl, you couldn't have come at a better time,' Mrs Butler said, yanking a file free from the pile on her desk. She flicked it open and read the title, 'Community Hall Project'. She stared at the page for a moment, as if she was trying to remember what it was about. 'Ah, the committee is trying to negotiate funds for it.' She looked up, meeting Rose's bright eyes. 'I believe there's a redundant church hall we may be able to use, but it will need some renovations and a lot of elbow grease. The idea behind the concept is to offer social help to the lonely, bereaved, and those in need. When this war finally ends, many people will need to rebuild their lives and indulge in a little light relief from time to time.' Now she looked anxiously at Rose. 'What do you think, dear?'

Rose, who had been listening intently, said, 'I think it is a wonderful idea and I would be willing to help.' Suddenly, she thought of Joe. Would he welcome such a venture?

'Excellent,' said Mrs Butler.

Rose felt a sense of pride and she knew instinctively it was something she wanted to do.

Back home, she was telling her mother about the project as she laid the table for tea, when Ted burst into the kitchen. He didn't stop to take off his boots and jacket as he usually did when coming in from work. He was waving a newspaper and saying in an excitable, blustering voice, 'He's gone and topped himself!'

Both Rose and Mary stared open-mouthed at Ted. 'Who, Dad?' asked Rose bewildered.

'Why, Hitler of course! You know what this means?'

It took a second for Rose to grasp the meaning. 'You mean the war's going to end?'

'Aye, sooner rather than later,' said a jubilant Ted. 'I could murder a drink.'

'After tea, we'll go to the pub,' said a delighted Mary. Rose stared in surprise at her mother, for it was very rare for her to suggest going to the pub. But the wonderful feeling that the end of the war could be near was a great cause for celebration.

Ted, now minus his jacket and boots, put his hands in his pockets and muttered, 'Empty.'

'Don't worry, Ted; I've put by something for just this special occasion.'

The pub was thronged with rowdy, happy people. Someone was belting out tunes on the old piano; Mrs Fisher was dancing with the coalman. Sally was there with her mam and dad. She jumped up from her seat and said:

'You can both squeeze on here, Mr and

78

Mrs Ellerby. I'll stand up with Rose.'

A man produced a bottle of whisky, declaring, 'I've been saving this since 1939.' Shots were poured out and a toast was performed. 'To the end of the war and to peace! May all our brave lads and lasses come home safely!' Everyone raised their glasses.

'Isn't it exciting,' said Sally, as she and Rose joined hands with a circle of people to sing 'Auld Lang Syne'.

Later, as Rose lay in bed, her head throbbing with drinking whisky and the jubilant sound of the celebrations still ringing in her ears, she thought of Harry and his homecoming. She didn't think she could face him. He had been her sweetheart for two years and now he'd found another. Hugging her arms around her body, she ached with uncertainty. Deep in her heart she still longed for him. She was fooling herself. She knew she must move on, but how? Nothing made sense and she felt worthless. Burying her face in the pillow, she sobbed.

Helping others became Rose's salvation. Hard work, long hours at the factory and the setting-up of the community project left Rose little time to dwell on thoughts of Harry. But one day she was waiting on the edge of a crowded pavement for a horse and rulley to pass by, when on the other side of the street she saw him. Her heart gave a wild flutter. Oh Harry! She remained transfixed, her legs immobile. She was pushed forward and a woman caught her sharply in the back with her shopping basket. This jolted Rose back to her senses. Once on the opposite side of the street, she looked in the direction where she thought she'd seen Harry, but he was nowhere in sight. It could have been him, she wondered. And what if it was him and they had come face to face? What would she say?

Stepping forth, she concentrated on the task in hand. She was on her way to visit Shirley's mother, Mrs Betty Duncan. Rose was working the two-to-ten shift. With production at the factory slowing down, they didn't need to work an extra shift.

'War's coming to an end,' forecast the foreman. Rose hoped he was right.

Betty was finding it difficult to cope with her baby and her other three children: Shirley and her two brothers. Betty had flatly refused to have any of her children evacuated, though she had been tempted when Shirley was injured in the bombing raid. The family lived in Wyke Street, in a two-bedroomed terraced house. The front door was in need of painting and at some time the windows had been shattered and hastily repaired; but then most homes suffered some defects.

Rose knocked. She could hear the baby crying inside. She knocked again and still no answer. She turned the knob and the door opened. She called out, 'Betty, it's me, Rose.'

'Come in,' a voice shouted above the noise of the crying baby.

Stepping in, Rose closed the door behind her to find herself in a dark passage. She edged past the pram, which almost filled the passage width. At the end of the passage, the door was ajar and she entered.

Betty, a cigarette dangling from the corner of her mouth, was standing at the kitchen table scraping butter on bread with one hand and tucked under her other arm was the baby. The other three children were also standing around the table, hungrily waiting for their breakfast before the dash to school.

'I've been up all night, with this one,' Betty said, as she bounced the baby on her hip. 'She's teething.'

'Let me take her,' Rose offered.

Betty gave her willingly. 'There's her bottle on the hob. That'll keep her quiet.'

With the baby in her arms, Rose looked around for a chair. There was only one in the room, an old rocker.

Betty followed Rose's gaze around her kitchen and said matter-of-factly, 'No coal so I chopped the chairs up for the fire.'

'We grow more if we stand,' piped up Shirley.

Rose smiled in acknowledgement. 'You certainly look a healthy bunch.' And they did.

'They never go hungry,' said Betty. 'Though it's a problem most of the time, my money's like a piece of knicker elastic.' The boys giggled at the reference to the unmentionables.

With the children safely off to school and baby fed, changed, and sleeping in her pram, Betty slumped in the rocker and Rose made her a much-needed cup of tea. Passing the cup of hot liquid to the older woman, Rose put forward her suggestion:

'Betty, I'm here to help, not to interfere in your home or life.'

Betty cocked a wary eye at her. 'I don't need charity. I can manage. It's just I'm so tired.'

'It's not surprising. You're a marvel looking after four children single-handed. If you're willing, I'm offering to take baby out for a walk in her pram and do any shopping for you while you have a rest. Catch up on your sleep.'

Betty sat up. 'Do you mean it, Rose?'

'Yes, I do. I don't have to be at work until this afternoon.'

'I'd love a bath and to wash my hair,' sighed Betty.

Rose eyed the iron kettle on the hob top. 'Will you have enough hot water?'

'I've got the copper on to do a wash, I can use that.' Betty's tired face lit up with enthusiasm. 'It'll be bliss. In a hot tub all on me own. No bairns to pester me. Not that I don't love 'em.'

'You deserve a treat. Now what about shopping?'

'I've five shillings in me purse and I get me weekly rations from the corner shop. Get what you can from the butchers, but try and get me a bit of fat to render down. Me bairns like a bit of dripping on their bread. And the little one's called Daisy, after my mam, who was killed in the first air raid.'

'Oh, how sad, but Daisy is a lovely name. Now don't you worry about the bairns coming home for their dinner. I'll see to it and make sure they get back to school. You have a couple of hours' sleep.'

With her hands firmly on the handle, Rose felt strange pushing a pram, a new experience for her, but she felt proud to do so. When she parked it outside the butcher's shop a woman peeped in to gaze at the sleeping baby, and commented, 'Lovely bairn.'

It was all unfamiliar to Rose, shopping for children. She hoped to get something they would like to eat, dinner time being their main meal of the day. She turned to make sure that Daisy was safe. Mrs Butler had stressed to her that with other people's children, their safety was paramount at all times, and Rose was mindful of that.

The woman in front of her in the queue turned and nudged her, saying, 'Sausages!

Butcher's got sausages.' Rose glanced ahead at the queue of patient women and a few old men and prayed there would be enough for her.

When she reached the counter and it was her turn to be served, she smiled at the big florid-faced man in his faded white overall coat. 'Sausages and a piece of fat to render, please.'

Wordless, he weighed out four sausages of different lengths and wrapped them up in newspaper and added the fat. Then he spoke: 'Elevenpence.'

She opened Betty's purse and counted out the coins.

At the greengrocer's, she could only get a small turnip and a quarter stone of potatoes. At the corner shop, she bought plain flour, a packet of dried egg powder, butter, a loaf and a jar of mixed fruit jam; though what kind of fruit the jam was made of was hard to define, but jam sandwiches were always a favourite of hers when she was a child, and still were. When she came out of the shop, Daisy was restless. Rose guessed she was ready for a feed and needed her nappy changing. Releasing the brake on the pram she was ready to set off when a voice croaked in her ear.

'I hope yer aren't going to pass yon brat off as my Harry's.'

Rose looked round to see Mrs Carter. The older woman looked flustered with her eyes wild, her grey hair trailing from beneath her hat, which was askew, and dried-up food was stuck on her chin. The cool tone Rose was going to use turned to one of concern.

'This is Daisy, one of my friend's children. You don't look well, Mrs Carter.'

'Mind yer own business,' and with her nose in the air, she shuffled off.

Rose stared after her, wondering if there was anything she could do to help. She would mention Mrs Carter's distressed condition to Mrs Butler. If Mrs Carter was ill and needed assistance, she probably might accept help from someone other than Rose.

By now, Daisy was demonstrating just how powerful her lungs were. Rose moved at a rapid pace, and reaching the house she manoeuvred the pram over the step and into the narrow passage. Not wanting to disturb Betty, she swiftly lifted the noisy baby up into her arms and went into the kitchen, thankful to spy on the hob top a bottle of feed Betty had prepared in readiness. Rose sank onto the rocker, and cradling Daisy in her arms she let the baby latch on to the teat, listening to her sucking greedily.

Rose nuzzled the soft downy hair on Daisy's head and felt a dreamy sense of peace. Motherhood was beautiful and she wondered if she would ever experience having a child of her own. Her chances of ever finding love again were limited, what with so many young men killed in the war.

Now Daisy was fed, changed and fast asleep, Rose laid her down in her pram. Daisy seemed to prefer sleeping by day and staying awake at night. No wonder Betty was exhausted and especially with her having three other children to look after. She glanced at the clock on the mantelpiece; she'd better get a move on if she was to have dinner on the table for the children coming home from school. It might help Betty if they stayed for school dinners for a day or two? In no time, the children were home, coming in the back door so as not to wake up Daisy.

'What we having?' demanded Billy, the youngest boy.

'Toad in the hole,' Rose said, with pride.

'Sounds horrible.'

Hands washed, they stood at the table in expectation. Rose placed the plates on the table. 'Sausages and Yorkshire pudding, turnip and mash.'

'Gravy as well?' added Billy, cheekily.

Rose enjoyed looking after the children, even if only for a short time. The next morning she was at a home confinement, fetching and carrying for the midwife, as well as looking after twin boys. The boys, aged two, were at the adventurous stage, opening and closing cupboard doors and emptying the contents of the flour tin, and they proved quite a handful. But the moment of enchantment for Rose was when the midwife let her hold the newborn baby girl in her arms. The twins, looking like cherub angels as Rose had washed and changed them into clean clothes, sat either side of their mother as she nursed her newborn daughter.

'You're talking a lot about babies,' exclaimed Sally, as they went for their tea break at work later that afternoon. 'Hope you are not getting broody.'

Rose, serious-faced, replied, 'Do you think I'll get left on the shelf now?'

'Rose Ellerby, you ain't even nineteen yet. Some good-looking lad will snap you up.'

'Do you think so?'

'Yes. Now me, I'm gonna have a good time and have load of fellows, go dancing every night till I drop.'

As they walked back to the factory floor, Sally grabbed Rose and whirled her round and then trotted out the Military Two-step.

'Now then, less of that larking about. The war's not over yet,' rebuked the foreman.

'Misery-guts,' muttered Sally under her breath.

Rose laughed; Sally always could lift her spirits. She wished at times that she could take life less seriously. Perhaps when the war was over?

The next day, Rose was up earlier and had finished her shift by two o'clock. Then she went straight to the WVS offices to help to sort out second-hand clothes for the needy, and after that she was book keeping. She was hemmed in in a cramped corner of the warehouse and had the ledger balancing on her knee. She dipped the pen in the inkwell and recorded the date at the top of the page: 8th May 1945.

She didn't get much further because she heard such a commotion. The door to Mrs Butler's room opened and Mrs Butler appeared pink-cheeked, eyes aglow.

'Rose,' she called, as if Rose was in the next building. 'It's over! Mr Churchill said the war is over!' She came and grabbed hold of Rose, pulling her to her feet.

Rose gasped, not sure if she had heard right, and said, 'What did you say?'

'My dear girl, the war is finally over.'

'Oh, how wonderful,' Rose cried. And before she could stop them, tears of joy began to run down her face and a great tide of relief swept through her. The two women went out into the street, where other women who worked nearby were dancing the conga. Rose and Mrs Butler joined on to the joyful line, which snaked along the pavement. The street was rapidly filling up with people, as the news began to reach every corner of Kingston upon Hull. Church bells, which had been silent for so long, began pealing; traffic came to a standstill, boats' and ships' hooters sounded on the River Hull and the Humber Estuary.

At last, peace had come. Now it was a time for jubilation. The war in Europe was ended; no more fighting and the troops would be coming home. And so would Harry. Rose felt her body stiffen as reality hit her. Disentangling herself from the dancing line, she took refuge in a shop doorway. All she could think of was that she was no longer Harry's sweetheart. And it hurt.

EIGHT

Rose shrugged her shoulders; she wasn't going to let being jilted by Harry Carter blight her life. If she hurried, she would just have time to slip home and see Mam before going to work. She found the jubilant but breathless Mrs Butler, to let her know why she was leaving early.

Everywhere she went, Rose met joyous people who wanted to dance with her. She joined in the spirit and let herself have a few twirls, but the dancing reminded her of happier days with Harry, and she wasn't supposed to be thinking of him. Excusing herself, she hurried on. Passing a pub, with its doors flung wide open, coming from within she heard a man's baritone voice singing a song of victory, reminiscent of the First World War.

Arriving home, Rose opened the back door and called, 'Mam, it's only me.' In the kitchen, she found Mary and Mrs Fisher sitting by the fire, smoking cigarettes. Rose smiled; it wasn't often she saw her mother smoking and both ladies were holding a glass of dark-red liquid. 'What are you drinking?' Rose asked, sniffing and peering into her mother's glass.

'I'm not sure, love. It's some concoction Mr Reilly makes up from berries.'

Rose hugged her mother and Mrs Fisher. 'Isn't it good news? The war is ending and peace will come again.' She was just going to say about Freddie coming home, when she recalled that Mrs Fisher had lost her two sons.

'Praise to God,' said Mary. 'It'll be a relief to have those dark days behind us.' She pulled herself up from the chair. 'You'll have a drink, love?'

Rose glanced at the clock on the mantelpiece and then eyed the suspect drink offered. 'I won't, but thanks, Mam. I've got to go to work. I'll see you later.'

'I'll try and rustle up something special for tea,' Mary said, eyes shining with happiness.

When Rose arrived at work, everyone was in a celebration mood. Sally came rushing up to her, flinging her arms around Rose's neck.

'Ain't it marvellous, we've beaten the Jerries. And we don't have to work.'

'Come from high up,' grumbled the foreman. 'Nowt ter do with me.'

'Come on, Rose,' said Sally, releasing her arms from her friend. 'We're going to the city centre to join in the fun.'

In Victoria Square, the noise was deafening, but oh so happy. It was as if everyone from Hull was there. No one seemed to mind the downpour of rain, for it couldn't dampen spirits. The crowd stretched all around the bombed buildings, as far as Rose could see. Suddenly, she was swept off her feet by two sailors. They swung her high in the air and she was glad she had her clean undergarments on. She shrieked with the thrill of the excitement; it was exhilarating, like being on the waltzers at Hull Fair before the war. All too soon, she came down with a bump and the two sailors seized on Sally. The next thing Rose knew she was in a line of women dancing the Palais Glide. The crowds cheered and parted so that the women had freedom of movement. They danced so fast that Rose lost her turban and her hair cascaded onto her shoulders in blonde waves.

Then a sailor grabbed her round the waist, saying in a Cornish accent, 'My, you're a smasher.' And with that, he kissed her full on the lips. It took her breath away and made her ready for another. But he moved on, delighting in sharing his favours.

Rose stood still, feeling bereft, and in the midst of all the jollification, of all the happy people around her, she suddenly felt alone. She hadn't been kissed like that in a long time. Not since Harry. Before she could stop them, tears rolled down her cheeks.

Wildly, she looked for Sally and saw her dancing with a soldier and enjoying herself. Rose squeezed through happy crowds of laughing men, women, children, soldiers, sailors, airmen and people from all walks of life. She went to sit on the steps near to Queen Victoria's statue, not caring that the stone was damp. Next to her was an old man who was puffing on a thin, hand-rolled cigarette. Rose sniffed and blew her nose and felt utterly miserable.

'I've nowt to look forward to,' the old man next to her said.

Rose glanced at him, not certain if she had heard him properly, and said, 'I beg your pardon?'

The old man repeated his words.

'Why's that?' asked Rose.

'Me old woman died in a raid and me son was killed in action.'

Rose turned to look at the man more closely. His body was thin and emaciated, his eyes were dark and sunk into the sockets and she noticed that as he put the cigarette to his dry, cracked lips his hand shook. He looked as though he was in need of a good meal. 'I'm sorry to hear that. Have you any other family?'

'None that care.'

'Tell me about your son.'

He looked at her in disbelief and gulped, 'You want to hear about my Cyril?'

'I've got all the time in the world to listen.'

His voice was croaky. 'I'm right proud of him,' he began. 'He drove tanks in the desert. He could show that Rommel a thing or two.' His voice began to gather a fierce energy. Rose listened attentively, thinking at least she had her parents and her brother. She didn't interrupt him, he seemed happy, in a sad sort of way; perhaps it was his means of releasing grief. Though how did you come to terms with the loss of the only members of your close family?

'I had a grand letter from his chief.' The man patted the breast pocket of his jacket, indicating that he had it close to his heart. 'Said how Cyril had died a hero, fighting to make the country a better place for mankind. Aye, he did.'

The old man's eyes held a faraway look. Rose sat in quiet respect by his side as he absorbed his thoughts and his precious memories. What else did he have?

All around them, the jubilation continued.

After what seemed a decent interval, she spoke.

'I'm Rose Ellerby; I live with my mam and dad in Hill Street.'

The old man stared at her, as if seeing her for the first time. 'I'm Alf Norton, I live in Burleigh Street.'

'Pleased to meet you, Mr Norton,' she said, politely.

He stared at her, weighing her up; liking what he saw and felt, he said, 'Call me Alf.' Conversationally, she asked, 'Do you know Mrs Carter?'

'Aye, Ida Carter lives a few doors down from me.'

'I used to go out with her son, Harry.'

'You went out with Harry? Are yer sure?'

'What a funny thing to say.'

'It's just that you don't strike me as his type.'

'I don't understand.'

'Oh, sorry, lass, it was just my stupid opinion. My old woman always said it'll get me in t'trouble.'

'I don't mind, tell me?'

The old man rubbed his rough chin and looked embarrassed. Finally, Alf conceded, 'You're a nice lass, not the sort Harry used ter hang around with. Some of the lasses were a bit rough. He was a bit of a wayward lad, though I put it down ter his mother. She suffocated him and I suppose he rebelled.'

'I saw Mrs Carter the other day and she didn't look well.'

'She does look a bit off colour. It's the war. It wears yer down. Happen she might pick up when Harry comes home.'

'He's not been home recently?'

Alf pulled his pouch from his jacket pocket to roll a cigarette and she was amazed to see his arthritic fingers move with such speed, no trembling, as he evened the tobacco along the thin oblong of paper. He rolled it expertly, struck a match and lit it, and inhaled deeply and coughed. Clearing his throat, he answered, 'His mam would have been blathering about him if he had.' His rheumy eyes searched Rose's face. 'Still sweet on him, are you?'

She blushed. Was it that obvious? 'I was his girl for two years and we were supposed to be getting married, but...' Her throat tightened and she fought back those infuriating tears.

'Minnie, me old woman, bless her, she always said things happen for a reason. But I'd be blowed if her and Cyril's deaths makes sense ter me.'

Alf now looked utterly miserable and Rose's gloom quickly dispersed and her heart softened towards the old man.

'Mam's cooking something special for tea and she's sure to do enough for four. You can come and eat with us and chat to Dad.

95

He'll like that.'

Alf's eyes, a watery shade of grey, suddenly took on a sparkle. 'Are yer sure, lass? Don't you want to stay and enjoy yourself?'

From where she sat on the steps with Alf, Rose could see a host of legs, some bare, many with trousers, dancing and swaying in all directions. A church choir was singing and people clapped to a band.

'I think I've had enough excitement for now.'

She got to her feet and Alf creaked to his. She scanned the crowd for Sally, but couldn't see her; no doubt she would be enjoying herself and Rose could catch up with her later.

The meal stretched to five; Mrs Fisher was invited. When Rose and Alf entered the warm, cosy kitchen, they were greeted by a delicious aroma of something baking in the oven. Rose explained to her mother how she'd met Alf, and about the sad loss of his loved ones.

'You are welcome, Alf. Ted will be glad to have a man to chat to,' Mary said, pulling a stool out from under the table for him.

'Why, if it ain't Alf Norton! You're a stranger.'

Mary and Rose both turned to stare at Mrs Fisher, who had just entered the house.

'Vera, fancy you still going strong.' Alf

arched his bushy eyebrows in mock disbelief.

'I'll have none of your lip!'

'How do you know each other?' Rose asked curiously.

'School. Right from infants ter leaving. He used to pull my pigtails.'

Rose looked at Mrs Fisher's cropped grey hair and found it hard to imagine her with pigtails, and even harder still as a schoolgirl. She smiled to herself, as the two old folks began reminiscing and catching up on life and its tribulations.

'My, my, we're having a party, are we?' Ted burst into the kitchen, grinning from ear to ear. He seized Mary and gave her a big kiss.

'Ted!' she said, blushing like a young girl.

'Dad,' Rose said, 'this is Alf Norton. He and Mrs Fisher were at school together.'

Ted about-turned to where they were sitting at the far end of the kitchen table. 'How do, Alf.' He shook hands with him. 'It's a great day. To think, no more fire-watching and such like. I'll be able to sleep easy in me bed again.'

'Aye, I'm glad it's over. War brings heart-ache,' Alf said sadly. Mrs Fisher patted his arm.

'I'm about to dish up, Ted,' Mary said as she stirred the gravy in the pan.

'I'll just have a quick wash, love.'

They were all seated around the kitchen table and Mary was cutting the golden brown crust of a large meat and potato pie. The aroma was mouth-watering and tantalizing and the meat looked succulent and tender. In answer to the questioning glances from her husband and daughter she said, 'I've had two tins of best stewing steak iced away for over a year. It was my share-out from the parcel the Yanks sent us for sewing garments for a show they put on.'

'Good for you, love,' said Ted with a twinkle in his eye.

'Now what's he up to?' Rose whispered to her mother.

They didn't have to wait long to find out. The meal over and they'd all eaten their fill, Ted produced a quarter bottle of whisky. 'Just enough for a tot each.'

Glasses filled, Ted coughed and stood in front of the mantelpiece. 'Let's raise our glasses.' They all stood up. Proudly, Ted puffed out his chest. 'To the end of the war and a time for peace. And may all our armed forces return home safely.'

'Amen to that,' they all chorused.

That weekend, the residents of Hill Street and the little terraces off, prepared for the biggest street party ever, to celebrate the end of the war in Europe, and peace.

'I remember the King and Queen's coronation, such a grand do,' Mrs Fisher reminisced.

Rose baked dozens of fairy buns and

whisked up jellies and Sally prepared potted meat sandwiches for the children, while Sally's mother was in charge of the grown-ups' feast.

Mary borrowed white sheets to cover the assortment of tables loaned from anyone willing. Someone had hung an ancient-looking Union Jack from their bedroom window and there was coloured bunting stretched across the street. Rose and Sally stood outside admiring the scene.

'Look, Bernie Smith's pulling out his piano. We're in for a sing-song and dancing,' Rose said. Immediately, she thought of Harry. Damn him.

She'd heard a whisper that Harry was home and she supposed he would be with his new sweetheart. Soon, any thoughts of Harry were swept away, as she was far too busy serving the children's food and organising games, musical chairs and pass the parcel.

Later, as Bernie belted out hot jazz numbers, a group of sailors from Alexandra Dock, drawn by the music, descended on Hill Street. Rose found herself partnering sailor after sailor and she didn't stop dancing all night. Much later, Bernie, fortified by the bottle of rum the sailors had brought him, played soft, romantic music. Rose slipped quietly away.

NINE

With the homecoming of the men from the war who needed their jobs back, women had to look for alternative employment, especially the single ones. Rose voiced her thoughts to Mary. 'I'm thinking of asking Mrs Butler if there is a job for me in the WVS organisation.'

Mary, sitting at her machine, looked up from her sewing and commented, 'That's a good idea, love. You've a flair for helping folks sort out their lives. Look at the way you brought Mrs Fisher and Alf together, two lonely people who've found friendship.'

'That was just a fluke, Mam.'

'No, Rose, you did a kindly act.' She snipped a thread with scissors.

It was then that Rose noticed the garment her mother was sewing. 'What a pretty dress.' It was of cornflower-blue silk with a cleverly panelled skirt, which made it look fuller. Her mother certainly had a way with the wartime restrictions of less material, which was still in force. Suddenly, Rose felt envious, wishing she had the chance to wear such a beautiful dress to a dance with someone she cared about. Sighing inwardly, her bright voice belying her emotion, she asked, 'Is it for someone special?'

Mary kept a straight face though she was bubbling within. 'Yes, for a very special person.'

'Lucky her.'

'You think so?'

Rose hadn't known her mother was taking in dressmaking. She supposed the extra money would be handy for replacing household articles damaged in the countless bombing raids, like crockery and cooking utensils, when such items would become available again. She felt a tinge of guilt, for she still had her hope chest, but she didn't want to relinquish it just yet.

As soon as she was working again she would help with the household replacements, and she would take great delight in buying new material for a winter coat for her mother and herself.

Mary rose, pushing back the chair, and reached for a coat hanger, slipping the dress onto it. She held it up, saying, 'Every seam, every buttonhole, every tuck is stitched with love and it is priceless.' Her face broke into a wide smile at the puzzlement on her daughter's face. Unable to hold back any longer, she said, 'It's for you, Rose.'

Rose remembered Sally telling her about the dress. But that was before Mary had been injured in the last bombing raid and since then, Rose had never had the chance to go to a proper dance.

'Oh, Mam!' She went to fling her arms about her mother, but Mary stepped back.

'Whoa. Let me hang it up.' The dress, safely on a hanger, was hooked on the picture rail. Rose then hugged her mother, nestling her face against her soft cheek.

Mary, her voice tinged with uncertainty, blurted, 'When do you think our Freddie will be home?'

Rose hugged her mother closer. She had been thinking the same, but didn't like to say, not wanting her mother to worry. Gently, Rose eased back to look into Mary's face. Trying to keep her tone light, she said, 'You know our Freddie, he'll just turn up. Surprise you.'

'Do you think so?'

'Yes, so don't worry. Just make sure you've something special put aside for him to eat. To make a fuss of him, he'll like that.' Rose's words did the trick. Already she could see the look in her mother's eyes as she planned her son's homecoming.

The next morning, Rose was in Mrs Butler's shoebox of an office. She was standing because the only chair, apart from Mrs Butler's, was piled high with files and documents. Mrs Butler, usually so efficient, was looking hot and flustered. But nevertheless, her good manners always prevailed.

'Hello, dear, I didn't expect to see you this morning. Changed your shift?'

Rose explained about the men coming home from the war who now needed jobs. 'Mrs Butler, I was wondering if there might be a job here for me?'

The older woman eyed her thoughtfully. 'I could certainly do with your help.' She waved her arms to take in the mountain of paperwork. 'I have so much administration work to do that I'm neglecting other duties. The community project, for example.'

'The building has had a clean-up,' Rose reminded her.

'Yes, I know, but the whole idea is for it to be a meeting place for people who are in need of friendship and help to rebuild their lives. I'm afraid the committee haven't yet secured funds to have it up and running.'

But, within a month, a benefactor from Tucson, America, businessman J.C. Mennett, had donated a considerable sum of money for the community project to go ahead. It seemed that his only son, while serving as a pilot in Britain, was on a short leave, missed his train back to base and was stranded on a deserted country station just outside of Hull. Mrs Butler's husband, on night-watch duty, took him home and gave him a bed for the night.

'It was quite a common occurrence,' reflected Mrs Butler. 'Geoffrey often brought stranded people home so I didn't think anything different of the young American airman.'

Rose was impressed, especially now the project could finally get on its way. Often when about town, she saw men huddled on street corners, women tired out, queuing and still having to make ends meet. Despite the ending of the war, the restriction on rations had not been lifted; in fact they were tighter and there was talk of bread being rationed.

'People need light relief,' reflected Rose to Mrs Butler. Rose now worked full-time with Mrs Butler and though her wages were lower than at the factory, she enjoyed the work more. It gave her satisfaction to see people's faces when she helped to solve a problem for them. Like the simple task of finding two pairs of wellington boots for twin boys whose only footwear was boots with the toes cut away to accommodate their growing feet.

The community hall was a redundant church hall, which had been used to store equipment, and before that it had been a meeting room. Rose, with Mrs Butler, was taking a tour of the premises. Rose felt a little nervous; her heart seemed to be beating faster. Was it doubt or fear? Or was it both? It was one thing to clean up a building, but to be responsible for getting it up and running was quite another. No easy task.

As if she could sense Rose's thoughts, Mrs Butler turned and said, 'Rose, I have every confidence in you and your ability to carry out this project.'

For a moment, Rose stared at Mrs Butler, then a smile lit up her face and she exclaimed, 'I can do it. And I will. Thank you, Mrs Butler, for having faith in me.'

'That settled, we'll get down to business.'

From her handbag, Rose withdrew her pencil and the notebook she had made from odd bits of scrap paper held together by string. She wanted to visualise what each room could be used for. She glanced around the room once used as a makeshift kitchen. Still in place were a stone sink and tap, a small gas oven with two ring burners on the top, an old wooden table with a broken leg, and a set of cupboards with doors off their hinges. Next to the kitchen was a small ante-room, empty except for a broken chair. She made a note that the room could be used for intimate gatherings or if anyone wanted to speak in private.

Mrs Butler popped her head round the door and said, 'Rose, I have to go. I have a meeting to attend. I'll leave you to lock up.'

Rose had been so intent on her work that she had almost forgotten Mrs Butler's presence.

'Yes, all right,' Rose said. She went into the

larger room; it would be great for entertainment. Rose closed her eyes and hummed a tune, imagining couples dancing. Then she saw a picture of a couple dancing close together looking into each other's eyes. It was her and Harry.

Suddenly the outside door blew open, sending dust motes scurrying around the room, invading Rose's nose, tickling it and making her sneeze several times. That brought her back to reality; though, in her heart, she knew that she wasn't really over Harry Carter.

Within days, Rose recruited volunteers to brighten up the rooms, to paint the walls with whatever materials could be donated. Battleship grey was the only colour on offer at the moment. She trawled the big department stores to see if they had any tins of distemper. She managed to secure a tin of pre-war sunshine yellow and someone else had brought in a tin of vivid red. Rose and her faithful band of volunteers, armed with old bits of net curtain and anything that would make a pattern, set to work, transforming the dull walls into a lively, welcoming room.

A week later, on a Saturday dinner time, Rose was meeting Sally for a quick snack in Kardoma teashop on Whitefriargate.

'Over here, Sally,' Rose called to her friend.

Sally came bustling up. 'I'm glad you got a table, 'cos supervisor's a stickler for time-keeping so I can't be late back.' Sally was now working at Woolworth's and loving it. Like Rose's job, hers was a complete change, too.

'It's a good thing I've ordered, then,' said Rose. With that, the waitress came with a tray carrying a pot of tea, fish paste sandwiches and chocolate cake.

Sally's eyes widened at the sight of the cake. 'It's our own special recipe,' said the waitress proudly. 'And these are the last two portions.'

Between mouthfuls of food, Sally asked Rose, 'Are you coming dancing with me tonight?'

'Sorry, but I'm working.'

'Working on a Saturday night,' Sally said, spluttering bits of chocolate cake onto the tablecloth, which she hastily swept aside.

'I've got my first social evening at the community hall. You're welcome to come.'

'No fear. I like a bit of action.'

'We could go to the pictures during the week. That's if there's anything on that we fancy.'

'I fancy a Betty Grable.' Sally glanced at the clock on the far wall. 'Got to go.' She put some coins on the table, her half of the bill. 'Bye.'

With her friend gone, Rose sat a moment, going over in her mind the arrangements she'd made for this evening and hoping that she hadn't missed anything out.

Suddenly a masculine voice said, 'Can I join you?'

Stunned, Rose looked into the handsome face of Harry Carter, his dark-blond hair falling over his rakish-looking eyes. She glanced beyond him, expecting to see his lady friend.

Harry noted her glance and said, 'I'm on my own.'

Two women on the next table stopped their conversation to see what was going to develop.

Conscious of this and not wanting to draw unwanted attention, Rose replied, somewhat stiffly, 'Please do.'

Harry sat down and signalled the waitress. 'Would you like something to eat, Rose?'

'I've eaten, thank you.'

He ordered meat and potato pie and a pot of tea. 'Ma's not up to cooking,' he commented. 'So what have you been up to, Rose?'

Rose, who desperately wanted to escape, didn't think her legs would carry her. She felt like one of the jellies she'd made for the victory celebrations; one slight move and she would wobble over and slide off her chair. She gripped the table edge with both hands. Harry didn't seem to notice her plight, or he chose to ignore it, and she couldn't think how to answer him.

Just then, the waitress appeared and placed the plate of food in front of Harry and the teapot and cups next to Rose. But she didn't make any move to pour. Harry glanced across at her expectantly, but Rose remained still.

'I'll pour,' he said. 'There's nothing like a good cup of tea.' He tucked in, hungrily. Then suddenly he laid down his knife and fork. 'You haven't said what you've been doing.'

A wave of anger swept through Rose and she retorted, 'What right have you to ask me what I have been doing? It's none of your business, Harry Carter.'

'It was a mistake,' he blurted.

'What was?'

He looked sheepish and scratched his square jaw. 'The other woman, it was never serious. It's you I love.'

Taken aback, Rose stared in bewilderment at him. This was the last thing she expected to hear. 'I don't understand. You sent me the letter.'

'Sorry, mates egged me on and I guess I'd had too much to drink at that time. Forgive me?'

'It's not that easy.' Her heart longed for him to come back to her, but her head told her otherwise. How could she ever trust him again?

Uncertainty must have shown on her face

because he said quickly, 'I can take you out tonight?'

'I'm working,' she stated blandly.

'Tomorrow night, then?'

'I'm not sure.'

His face took on a sad expression as he said, 'It was hard at the front, seeing mates die in front of my eyes. Please, Rose.'

Now Rose felt guilty. 'I suppose,' she said, 'we could go out, but just as old friends.'

He grinned. 'The pictures okay? Pick you up at seven.'

'No.' Her voice was so loud that the two women on the next table looked at her. She moderated her voice. 'I'll meet you under the clock at Paragon Station.'

'Great,' Harry enthused. He reached across the table and was about to take hold of Rose's hand, but she snatched it away.

Quickly, she got up from the table. 'I must go,' and without a backward glance and with her head held high, she marched out of the cafe.

Harry stared after her retreating figure, and then he winked at the two women on the next table, who had been watching, and said with confidence, 'She'll come round.'

TEN

Rose didn't have time to dwell on Harry because she was so busy with the first social evening at the community centre. She had managed to secure the help of a three-piece band, piano, drums and a clarinet. All three musicians were retired, but could still thump out a good tune. The food was a bit scant but it was difficult because of the ongoing rationing. She would have to have a rethink on that score. Alf and Mrs Fisher came and so did Betty and her husband, who had managed to get a babysitter for a couple of hours.

'First night out since Bob came home,' Betty enthused. But secretly, she and Bob were like strangers and she felt a frump. Four children to look after didn't leave her much time for herself, and Bob seemed distant, preoccupied with his thoughts. She tried to get him to talk about his experiences in the war, but he wouldn't be drawn. They sat awkwardly next to other couples who were also trying to rekindle their marriages after years apart, but didn't know how to go about it. A few men just sat smoking and staring into space.

It seemed, when Rose spoke to them, that

they were content to just do that and listen to people chatting around them. A couple of young girls came and stood on the threshold and then disappeared. Rose guessed they were looking for the younger element. She made a mental note to persuade Sally to come next time and bring her friends from Woolworth's.

It was getting on towards ten and the evening was winding down, just a few of the men who were in no particular hurry to move on lingered, when in walked Joe.

'Joe,' Rose cried with delight. 'What a wonderful surprise.' Impulsively she kissed his cheek. It was clean-shaven and smelt fresh. She stood back to admire him. 'You do look smart in civvies.' She had only seen him in his uniform and usually, because of circumstances, he'd always looked dishevelled. Now he wore a dark-blue pin-striped suit, light-blue shirt and tie.

Joe reddened slightly. 'It's my demob suit.'

'Cup of tea?' She saw his hesitation. 'Sorry, I've nothing stronger.'

'Tea will be fine.'

They sat in a quiet corner at a small card table, both with their hands clasped around their mugs of hot liquid. Rose suddenly felt shy, but she remembered one of her jobs was to be supportive to ex-servicemen. 'How long have you been home?' she asked brightly.

'Last night. I slept at a mate's and today I've been searching for lodgings. I want to get Peter back as soon as possible.'

'You've found somewhere?'

'Aye, Crowle Street with a Mrs Mitchell, she's a widow and her family are all married.' Rose nodded. She knew with so much bomb damage, you were fortunate to have a whole house. In Joe's case, with having Peter, a woman on the premises might make things easier for him. 'Joe.' Their eyes locked. She felt the sudden flare of heat rise within her. 'I'm always here if you need help at any time, even if it is just to talk.'

'I appreciate that, Rose.' He unwound his hand from his mug and reached out to touch hers.

Rose felt the warmth of his fingers, strong, sturdy and sensual, sending a tingling sensation through her body.

'So this is what you mean by working.' Harry stood before them, breathing out fumes of strong beer as he spoke.

Rose jerked back in her seat and Joe slowly removed his hand.

'Harry, I didn't expect to see you,' she blurted out.

'Obviously not,' he sneered.

She felt annoyed with him, but nevertheless she said politely, 'Harry, this is Joe, he's just found a home for him and his son. Joe, this is Harry.' She hesitated, then said,

'A friend.'

Harry came to stand next to Rose, putting a possessive arm about her shoulder. He gave Joe a curt nod.

Joe got to his feet, saying, 'Excuse me, I've things to do.'

Rose watched him go. Joe was a good friend. She looked down at the table where Joe's mug of tea sat half empty.

'Have you finished here, then?' Harry said in her ear, tightening his hold on her shoulder.

Slowly, she rose to her feet and twisted from his grip. 'I've just to tidy up.'

'I'll help you and then I'll walk you home.'

'Oh Harry, that is kind of you.' She warmed to him, feeling a slight thrill of her old feelings for him returning.

As they walked, Harry talked about the war, his pals, and the devastation. She guessed he needed to get things off his chest. But who would listen to Joe? Would it be Mrs Mitchell? Or would he bottle it up? She thought of the first time she had seen him, drunk and grieving, and she decided to go and see him, just to make sure that he was all right.

By now they had reached Hill Street and Harry was still talking. For a while, she had forgotten his presence until he interrupted her thoughts of Joe.

'How's your mam and dad?'

She glanced quickly at him, and then answered, 'They're fine, thank you.'

'I could come in and say hello.'

She hadn't mentioned to her parents about seeing Harry. She felt a slight sense of panic tighten in her stomach. Things were moving too fast for her. She didn't want to rush and let it all blow up in her face. Perhaps that's what had been wrong with their relationship before, she had been too willing to fall in with his demands. If he truly loved her he would respect her wishes. Besides, they hadn't been out properly yet. She turned to him; her smile sincere, she said, 'If you don't mind, Harry, I won't ask you in tonight. Another time.'

'I suppose so,' he retorted glumly.

She thought of the cheerless house at Mrs Carter's and could see why Harry was in no hurry to go home. But she couldn't thrust Harry on her parents, not until she had told them. They'd need time to get used to the idea of Rose and Harry together again. And so did she.

Suddenly, he pulled her into his arms, his mouth rough and eager on her lips, his hands caressing her body. She smelt the grease on his hair and felt the taut muscles of his body pressing close to hers.

'Rose, I want you,' he whispered. He pinned her against the wall, his breathing heavy. He groped up her skirt. She felt his hot, clammy hand on her thigh.

Unable to move and shocked by his behaviour, she cried angrily, 'Harry!'

Abruptly breaking away from her, he muttered thickly, 'I can't wait for ever.' With that, he turned and hurried away.

Rose stared after him and hastily rearranged her clothes and wiped her lips. She was not sure about his parting words. Did he mean he wanted them to marry soon? Her head was spinning with all kinds of notions as she slipped into the backyard before anyone saw her. Harry had never revealed that side of his nature to her before. He was always the smooth and funny type. Maybe that was what the war had done to him. Would she get used to it?

Indoors, her parents were sitting in their chairs on either side of the fireplace, drinking cocoa. They both looked up as she entered the kitchen.

'How did it go, love?' asked Mary.

Rose took a deep breath to steady her racing pulse, smiled, and said, 'I think it was a success for a first one, but I need more people to come, and I need to arrange more food.'

'How was the band?' asked Ted. It was through his contact that Rose had got the band.

'They turned up trumps, Dad.'

'You look a bit flushed, Rose,' Mary said.

'Don't you overdo it.'

'I won't.' She went and sat on the arm of Ted's chair. 'Joe came this evening. He's got lodgings for him and his son in Crowle Street.'

Ted's face lit up. 'That's great. Tell him to come round anytime. He's always welcome.' Rose knew she must tell them about Harry now or she wouldn't sleep tonight. 'There's something else I need to tell you both.' Mary looked quizzically at her daughter. Rose slipped off the arm of her father's chair and went to stand at the table, her hands firm on the back of a chair. She drew a deep breath. 'I've met Harry again. And we're walking out again.'

Neither parent spoke. They just looked dumbfounded at their daughter. Then anger crossed Ted's face as he spat out, 'What's brought this on?'

Rose told them of their chance meeting in the cafe and how he had walked her home tonight.

Still Ted didn't look convinced and said, 'Can't say I like the fellow.'

'What about the other girl?' Mary asked.

'He realized it was a mistake and it's me he loves.'

'Oh, Rose,' cried Mary. 'Is it what you really want?'

Rose thought of all the times she wished for it to happen, for Harry to realize his error and come back to her. 'I think so, Mam,' she whispered.

Mary then spoke. 'Ted, you will just have to bury your feelings and do what is best for our Rose.' Ted grunted in reply. Then he lumbered up from his chair and turned his attention to banking up the fire with ash and slack in readiness for stoking up in the morning. Mary began putting away her knitting. Rose escaped to the seclusion of her room.

In her room, she flung off her clothes and not even bothering to wash or brush her teeth she crept into bed. She buried her face deep into the pillow and wept. What for, she wasn't sure.

She met Harry the next night as arranged, but she didn't enjoy the film. It was a comedy which failed to make her laugh, though Harry did. He seemed surprisingly relaxed.

A few days later, Sally caught up with Rose on the way home from work. She put her arm through Rose's, saying, 'You look gloomy.'

'I was just thinking about the effect of war on people.'

'I thought you'd be happy seeing you and Harry are together again.'

'How did you know?'

'The whole street knows. You've been seen.'

Rose laughed. 'I always knew he'd come back to me.'

'He was a daft fool to leave. So when's the wedding day?'

'We've only just started walking out again, but I've got a feeling Harry doesn't want to wait too long. But we'd have to get somewhere to live first.'

'Can't you live with his mother?' Sally added mischievously.

'Never.'

'Your parents, then?'

'I love Mam and Dad, but I'd rather Harry and me start life together in our own home.'

'How about getting them to build you a house?' Sally pointed to a group of children playing houses among the rubble of the bombed buildings. 'Can I be your bridesmaid?'

Rose laughed, saying, 'Of course! Only don't breathe a word yet to my parents or yours.' Sally pretended to zip her lips.

A few weeks later, Mary said to Rose, 'Bring Harry for tea on Sunday.'

'Thanks, Mam, that'll be lovely. Harry's been longing to see you both again.' Rose had been waiting for such an invitation from her mother. Now Harry would be pleased.

Then Ted piped up. 'You can invite Joe as well.'

Rose stared at her father; she didn't think it was a good idea. Not for Harry's first visit. Besides, Harry had made it plain that he didn't like Joe.

Mary came to the rescue. 'Not this time,

Ted. We'll have Joe another time.'

'I can't see why not,' Ted grumbled, picking up the newspaper, rattling it as he opened it.

On Saturday night, she and Harry went dancing. Harry was generous with his demob gratuity money and liked to splash it around. At the interval, he sneaked out to the pub across from the dance hall and downed four pints of beer in quick succession. It was a bet with another chap to see who could drink the most in the least time. Of course Harry won. But drinking so much in such a short time had upset his stomach and given him a headache.

'What time is it?' Ted asked. It was Sunday tea time.

Rose glanced at the clock on the mantelpiece. 'Ten past five.' The invite was for Harry to come at 4.30 for tea at five o'clock, so they could have a social chat and for Harry to renew his acquaintance with Mary and Ted.

'He's late,' said Ted, giving Rose a disapproving glance.

Mary glossed over Harry's lateness by saying, 'Maybe his mother's ill.' She began fussing over the sandwiches, hoping they didn't curl up too much. She'd done a trade with Mrs Fisher, swapping a packet of Gold Star cigarettes for a small tin of salmon. Mary had blended the salmon with vinegar and salt and pepper, and to make it go further she mixed in mashed potatoes left over from dinner.

Rose escaped to the front room. She pulled aside the curtain to watch for Harry's approach. The terrace was quiet, empty; only a cat poked about looking for titbits. Everybody would be indoors eating their tea. Wind blew dust about and Rose shivered. She went over to the fire burning brightly in the grate and held out her hands to catch the warmth. It was a treat to have a fire in the front room and she knew her mother must have been very frugal with the coal rations in order to do so, and all in honour of Harry, to make him welcome. She glanced at the clock on the sideboard: 5.20 pm.

'Come on, Harry. Where are you?' she cried out loud, agitation whirling within her. Over at the window again, she lifted the edge of the lace curtain and there he was, sauntering down the terrace. She rushed through into the kitchen calling, 'He's here.'

'About time,' Ted groused. 'My stomach thinks me throat's been cut.'

'Ted...' Mary gave her husband a knowing look.

Rose was at the front door and opened it before Harry could knock. She smiled brightly, saying, 'Harry, come in out of the cold.' She really wanted to say, *You're late*, but he looked quite sullen. 'Everything all right?' she asked

'Missed the damned bus and had to walk.'

He shrugged out of his heavy overcoat and handed it to Rose. She hung it on one of the row of wall-hooks.

'Come through and see Mam and Dad.'

Ted was standing with his back to the fire. He was wearing his best trousers, his shirt was old, but the frayed collar had been neatly turned by Mary and he'd put on his Fair Isle pullover. It strained a bit across his stomach. Ted held out his hand to Harry.

'How do, lad.'

Harry took the proffered hand. 'Fine, Mr Ellerby,' he replied. He glanced at the tea laid out on the table; his stomach heaved and his demob suit felt tight.

Mary, her print pinafore discarded, was wearing her best navy dress with the white lace collar. 'Sit yourself down, Harry. You must be starving.'

Rose pulled out a stool for Harry. She had taken great pains with her appearance. She wore a skirt, which Mary had turned inside out, and it looked like new. It was slim-fitted, green with tiny specks of multi colours, and she'd teamed it with a pretty white blouse. Her hair was swept up in a shining wave at the front and sides and hung loose at the back. She smiled at Harry, but he seemed not to notice her.

'How's your mother?' she asked, for something to say.

He stared at her as if she'd said an alien

word. An awkward moment passed before he replied. 'She's all right.' He sat down, pushing his legs under the table.

'Well, this is cosy,' said Mary brightly as she set down the big brown teapot on the table.

Ted helped himself to a sandwich and began munching. Rose picked up the plate and offered one to Harry. 'Take two,' she said. 'Pass the piccalilli, Dad.'

It was time to cut the cake. 'Mary's famous for her ginger cake,' Ted said with pride.

She smiled, cutting thick wedges. 'Tuck in and I'll pour more tea.'

After tea, the two men retired to the front room for a smoke. 'You're quiet, Rose,' said Mary as she swished the soda round the bowl of washing-up water.

'It seems strange, Harry here again.'

Mary glanced sharply at her daughter. 'Are you having second thoughts?'

Rose paused before answering, 'He seems the same yet different. I know the war and fighting must have affected him deeply, but there's something I can't quite put my finger on.' She looked in earnest to her mother. 'Does that make sense?'

'You're right about the war affecting him and others. Give it time and don't rush into things, like getting married too soon. Let him settle back into his job and find his feet.'

Both women were silent now. Harry was pressurising her, not to marry, but to make love. And that was something Rose couldn't discuss with her mother. She would have to find a quiet time to talk with Sally.

'There's something bothering me, Rose.'

Rose, so lost in her own thoughts, stared at her mother's concerned face and said, 'Mam, are you feeling unwell?' Gently she eased Mary into a chair. 'Tell me what it is.'

Mary gave a long sigh and dabbed her eyes on her apron. 'It's our Freddie.'

Rose felt herself go cold. 'Mam, has something happened to him?'

'I don't know. That's just it. I've had no news from him for ages.'

'What does Dad say?'

'He thinks I'm worrying about nothing. But I know something is wrong. I can feel it.'

'What did Freddie say in his last letter?'

'You read it. What did you think?'

Rose unscrambled her mind and said, 'He didn't say much, as I recall, only that he was still in Germany and helping.' She thought for a moment. 'I suppose he couldn't say what *helping* meant. But don't worry, Mam. If anything was wrong, we would have heard.' Rose hoped she sounded reassuring.

ELEVEN

A few days later, Rose called at Sally's house and asked her to come for a walk.

'Blimey, you're keen,' exclaimed Sally, surveying the cloudy, blustery sky.

'I need to talk to you, in private,' Rose whispered, not wanting to be overheard.

'In that case, I'll wrap up warm.'

The two girls, arms linked, were about to walk down the terrace, when Mrs Fisher came out onto her front doorstep.

'Where're you two off to?'

'Just for a walk,' Sally said, smiling sweetly.

'In this weather?' Mrs Fisher scoffed.

The girls continued at a brisk pace. Once round the corner they slowed down and both went into fits of giggles.

'I swear she's a mind reader,' said Sally. 'She can smell when there's something of intrigue about.'

Rose didn't speak until they were going over Southcoates Bridge.

'It's Harry.'

'I guessed it would be. He's not packed you in again?'

'No, it's just the opposite.'

Sally puffed, 'That is a relief. So what has

he done?'

Rose replied, 'Nothing so far.'

Sally gawped at her friend. 'Do you mean what I think you mean?'

Rose nodded. 'And I don't know what to do.'

'Do you want to?'

Rose surprised herself by her quick response. 'No.'

'Don't. He can't force you.' Then she looked aghast. 'He hasn't, has he?'

'No, not forced, but he's making it pretty obvious.'

'How soon are you going to marry?'

'That's just it. He's not mentioned getting married.'

'Be cautious, Rose.' She could have added, he broke your heart once, he could do it again.

Rose hugged her friend. 'I feel better for talking to you.' And they both chanted, '*Friends forever*' as they linked little fingers.

Shivering, Sally said, 'Come on, it's cold. Let's go home.'

Back in Church Terrace, the girls said goodbye with a promise to have a night out. It was with a happier frame of mind that Rose went indoors. Her cheeks were glowing after the exhilarating walk and her mind was clearer. She wasn't going to give in to Harry's demands.

'It's only me,' she called cheerfully as she

shrugged out of her coat and hung it up on the peg on the back door. She went through into the warm, welcoming kitchen and stopped. There, sitting on the chair by the fire opposite her father, was Joe. And sitting cross-legged at his feet was a little dark-haired boy, about five, trundling a finely crafted wooden train.

Her eyes lit up. 'Joe, this is a lovely surprise.'

He got to his feet, his arms outstretched and she went to him and hugged him. 'And this must be Peter.' She dropped down to the child's level. 'Hello, that's a great train.'

The boy looked up into her face; his brown eyes were clouded, his bottom lip wobbled and he said in a small voice, 'Uncle Sam made it for me.' Over the top of Peter's head, her eyes met Joe's and she saw the raw anguish etched on his face.

'They're staying for tea,' Mary said. 'Though it's only bubble and squeak, but I've made some fairy buns and I need someone to help me decorate them. Will you help me, Peter?' He scrambled to his feet and onto a kitchen chair, eager for diversion.

Joe sank back in his seat, relief flooding his body. He had been at his wits' end. Peter was so unhappy at leaving his foster parents, Sam and Moira Burns; he had sobbed every night since Joe had brought him home. Mrs Mitchell was kind enough, but she tired easily. Joe had come to the Ellerby home in desperation and he was so grateful for the warm welcome, and to see Rose, a wonderful warm-hearted girl, lifted his heart. Rose perched on the arm of Joe's chair and looked across at her father. Ted was suddenly immersed in his newspaper. She said quietly to Joe, 'If I can help in any way with Peter, you have only to ask. You can always come along to the community hall. I've started a weekly playtime for young children on a Saturday morning so parents can go shopping or whatever. Bring Peter along.'

Joe reached out and took her hand. She felt his rough, calloused skin and the strength of the man. 'I'm grateful to you, Rose. Can I talk to you when you've time? Just to mull over things and see about Peter's schooling.'

'I'll be happy to. How about tonight? I'm free. Harry's meeting up with some workmates.'

'Tonight.' He looked towards Peter.

'I'm sure Mam and Dad will keep him entertained for an hour or two.'

A voice behind the newspaper piped up, 'He can sleep the night if he gets tired.' Ted lowered his newspaper and eyed Joe. 'A night out will do you the world of good. And our Rose, in her official capacity, will soon sort you out.' He gave a broad wink and returned to his newspaper. Rose and Joe just stared at each other and then both burst out laughing.

Later, after tea, Rose and Joe went out. They cut down Ferries Street and on to Hedon Road, in the direction of the town. It was the best part of the day, the cold wind had dropped and the temperature risen. The summer evening was warm and balmy, the sky a swirl with fleeting clouds. Now that the war was over, people lingered on doorsteps, gossiping, trying to keep up the camaraderie of the war years, and wondering when the food rationing would cease.

They moved along at a steady pace, Rose doing most of the talking. She knew she was chatting too much, but it was to cover up her feelings of embarrassment. How could she have been so forward, saying to Joe that she was free to see him tonight? It was in her official capacity, she told herself, part of her daily routine, helping and supporting lone parents to settle their children. It was especially difficult for evacuees separated from their parents in their most formative years. Her work was mostly on a practical basis, like schooling, grants and contacting the relevant departments of power and helping to fill in forms, which some people found overwhelming. But more personally, she was there to listen, and to give a comforting hand or hug. A hug, Mrs Butler had informed her, was not strictly in her guidelines. Though, with a twinkle in her eye, Mrs Butler had said, 'Rose, you are to be commended on your excellent work. I've had positive feedback from grateful people, and from our superiors.'

'You all right, Rose?'

Rose, realizing that she had stopped talking, looked up into Joe's concerned face. 'Sorry, I was thinking about work.'

'And I'm going to add to your overload.'

'No, I'm only too happy to help.' She felt her cheeks redden. Ahead was a public house. Gently, Joe took hold of Rose's elbow. 'In that case, we'll talk in comfort.' Pushing open the door, he steered her through.

Inside, the landlord leaned on the bar, listening to the radio with two other men, chortling at some joke being aired. The room itself was war weary, in need of refurbishment. Its walls were smoke brown and peeling, and the leather seats of the chairs and stools were cracked and split and impregnated with stale beer smells. In the stone fire grate was a small pile of logs, in readiness for a cool night. Rose decided that in spite of the downtrodden appearance of the pub, she could feel the lingering memories of times past, of sing-songs around the upright piano, now silent, and of men in uniform and women, laughing, welcoming the short respite from the duty of war.

Rose settled at a table near to the window and Joe went to the bar. He came back with a half pint of beer for himself and a port and lemon for her. Placing the glass in front of her he apologized. 'Sorry, that was the only alternative to beer.'

She replied, 'It's good of you to treat me, Joe.'

'My pleasure,' he said. For a moment he stared thoughtfully into his beer, then he raised his head and looked straight into her eyes. 'I do have an ulterior motive.' Her insides gave an unexpected quiver. He continued, 'I've to start back at my old job at the flour mill on Monday. I would rather spend time with Peter, to see him into his first day at school, but it's not possible. I need the stability of a job to pay my way and provide treats for Peter.'

All the time he was speaking, their gazes held. Rose found her voice.

'You want me to take Peter to school?'

'That's if your work schedule will allow.'

Monday mornings were usually hectic in the office with problems that had mounted up over the weekend. She would go early and leave Mrs Butler a note as to the reason for her absence.

'I'll be happy to take Peter to school.' The tension around Joe's mouth relaxed.

'Rose Ellerby, I could k...' he stopped. 'Sorry, not the right thing to say to a girl who's walking out with another chap.' Instead he patted her hand. 'I can now go to work with an easy conscience.'

Rose wished that he had kissed her. She

wouldn't have minded in the least, though she wasn't too sure about Harry minding. He'd developed an obsessive streak. 'Will Peter need anything from home before I take him to school in the morning?'

Joe stroked his chin thoughtfully and Rose couldn't help noticing his strong, firm fingers.

'He's wearing his clean clothes and I've made arrangements for his school dinners. He just needs a friendly hand to hold.'

To Rose's surprise, tears sprang into Joe's eyes. She recalled Peter had lost his mother and Joe, his wife. How sad for them both, and difficult for them to readjust to living together again. Instinctively she moved closer to Joe and put a comforting arm about his shoulder and whispered, 'It'll be fine, Joe, don't worry.'

He swallowed hard and said, 'It's good to have a friend like you, Rose.' And with that he turned his face to hers and kissed her on her cheek.

His lips felt warm and tender, sending an unbelievable current of sparks through her body. The intimacy of his nearness filled her with pleasure. Then, remembering she was here in her official capacity, she said, her voice trembling, 'I'll always be here for you, Joe.' He looked questioningly at her, then she added, 'And for Peter.'

A voice interrupted. 'Do you mind if we sit

at your table?'

A man and a woman stood before them. Rose glanced about, surprised to see the pub was full. She hadn't noticed people coming in. 'We're just going,' Joe said and took hold of Rose's hand, which felt quite a natural act.

'Sorry,' said the young man. 'Didn't mean to drive you and your girl away.'

Rose looked wide-eyed at Joe, but he just grinned.

Outside, the sky, a navy blue, twinkled with stars, a crescent moon glowed and a breeze gently drifted, smelling of the river. So busy looking up, Rose missed her footing and caught her shoe against an uneven pavement, the result of bomb damage. Joe steadied her, saying, 'Tuck your arm through mine.' He had on an old jacket of Melton cloth, thin and worn smooth with age, but comforting. Rose experienced a wonderful sense of being secure so close to Joe, as they walked towards home in companionable silence.

On reaching Church Terrace, Rose said, 'Come in and see if Peter has settled.'

'You and your parents are very kind,' Joe said, and instinctively he touched her cheek. It was just a fleeting, tingling touch, and she blushed.

'We do what we can to help,' she said, softly, her eyes searching his. For a few moments, their gazes were locked. She broke the spell, saying, 'We'd better go indoors.'

Entering the kitchen, Mary whispered, 'He's sound asleep. You go up, Joe, and have a peep at him. It's the room on the right.'

He slipped off his shoes and trod up the stairs silently. He paused on the tiny landing, then seeing the door ajar he pushed it open wider and went in. Inside the room a night-light burned and he could see Peter curled up on a small camp bed at the foot of the single bed. Joe went down on his knees and kissed his son's forehead. Peter whimpered and sucked on his thumb in his mouth. A lump stuck in Joe's throat, swamping him with overwhelming love for his son; his motherless son. No wonder Peter was confused and unhappy. Losing his mother, then settling with foster parents, only to be uprooted and brought back to what? A man who had only a rented room and was out to work all day. He was Peter's dad and he loved him dearly, but Peter didn't return his love. Joe found this hard to bear though he understood why: he was a stranger to his own son. Given time, he hoped to overcome this and together they would survive. That's why his friendship with the Ellerbys was important to him and not just because of Peter. It was because he respected and admired them and felt at ease in their company. They were friends whom he could trust to chat over day-to-day happenings.

Once more he kissed his son's forehead,

whispering, 'Sleep tight, little fellow, and I'll see you tomorrow.' He straightened up and noticed the room, its femininity, the alluring trace of scent. This was Rose's room. He felt an urge to touch everything, to be close to her. He shook himself. What was he thinking of?

Downstairs, he could see that Ted and Mary were tired, though Mary tried to stifle a yawn. Rose was busy ironing a fresh blouse for work. He would have loved to have stayed, to be part of this family scene, but he didn't want to overstay his welcome.

'I'd best be getting off. Thank you for looking after Peter.'

Rose smiled across at him. 'Don't worry, Joe; I'll see him safely to school. I'll see you out,' she offered, about to rest the iron back on the stove.

Joe was quick to reply. 'No, don't let me stop your ironing.' He knew if she saw him to the door, his willpower would disintegrate, because the desire he felt right now was to kiss her tender, parted lips.

Outside, Joe paused to light a cigarette. He didn't feel like going back to his lonely room. He looked at his watch: nine-thirty. If he hurried, he would catch Billy Collins at his local pub. Billy had already started back working at the flour mill and he would be able to give Joe the latest happenings because things would be bound to have changed somewhat since before the war years.

He found Billy having a game of dominos with three other men.

'How do,' he said. The men nodded, not taking their eyes off the game. Joe pushed his way through the tight knot of drinkers to the bar and ordered half a pint. While he waited, he glanced about to see if there was anyone else he might know, but the room was too crowded to see. Someone moved aside and through the gap he saw a man's face: Harry Carter sitting at a table talking to someone Joe couldn't see. The gap widened and Joe saw that Harry Carter had his arm around a woman's shoulder. A woman in her late twenties, heavily made-up and showing lots of cleavage. Then he saw her place a hand on Harry's knee in an intimate way. The gap closed and the scene disappeared. He would have liked a closer look at Harry and the woman; perhaps it was an innocent encounter, but his gut feeling told him otherwise. Already Harry had once deserted Rose. Rose, who was a beautiful, warm, caring person, a woman to be cherished. Would Harry Carter, the man Rose loved and wanted one day to marry, cherish her, respect her and be true to her? He'd better, Joe thought angrily, or he will have me to contend with.

TWELVE

Peter clung tightly to Rose's hand as they walked down the street to Hill Infant and Junior School. Rose remembered it well from her schooldays. It was a Victorian building with high windows so that the pupils could not see out and be distracted from their learning. The tall iron gates had long since disappeared to help the war effort.

Entering the playground, she glanced down at Peter and felt a surge of pride at his well turned-out appearance. Joe had put a lot of effort into it. Peter's neatly cut hair was just visible from beneath his cap. His well-pressed grey trousers hung just below his bony knees and he wore hand-knitted socks, which covered his calves and were held in place by elastic garters. His thick-soled black boots were highly polished, the frayed cuffs of his wool jacket had been neatly repaired, his shirt was new, dove-grey twill, and his tie was a knitted effort. Rose wished she had a camera to take Peter's picture, though she would always remember how he looked on this day, his first schoolday.

She felt his stiffening as they were directed to the headmistress's office.

'I don't want to go,' he whimpered, his bottom lip quivering. She squeezed his hand gently and whispered, 'You'll be fine, Peter. I'll come and see you tonight and you can tell me all you have done.'

The headmistress, long past her retirement age, was thin with grey hair and grey, fatigued skin. The strain of war had taken its toll on her and Rose could sense that she had no energy left to welcome in a new pupil. The cluttered office smelt musty and damp. Peter sneezed, and the headmistress tutted. Rose quickly pressed her handkerchief into his hand. After taking Peter's particulars, the headmistress rang a bell on her desk. A girl appeared. It was Shirley and Rose felt an instant surge of relief.

The headmistress rapped, 'Shirley, show Peter Tennison where the cloakroom is and then take him along to Miss Green's class.'

Rose watched the two children go and stood for a few seconds before realizing she'd been dismissed. The headmistress, pen in hand, was writing in a ledger.

Later, as promised, Rose went to see Peter on her way home from work. When she arrived, she was met with great enthusiasm by Peter, who was in the company of Mrs Mitchell's daughter and her two children. Rose was invited in to the homely kitchen where the aroma of freshly baked bread tantalized her nostrils and her grumbling stomach. She couldn't remember when she had last eaten.

'I'm going to school again,' Peter's young voice piped up. 'I'm a big boy now.'

Rose ruffled the top of his head, saying, 'Good, do you want me to take you tomorrow?'

Before Peter could reply, Mrs Mitchell's daughter, Maureen, interjected, 'I collected him after school so I might as well take him in the mornings with my daughters.'

Rose found herself saying, 'That's kind of you.'

The other woman stared Rose full in the face as she said, 'I'm doing it to help Joe.'

Mrs Mitchell, sensing an atmosphere, said quickly to Rose, 'A cup of tea, lass?'

'Thank you,' said Rose, politely, 'but Mam's expecting me home.'

Rose hadn't seen Peter or Joe for some time, though she heard from her parents that they were both doing well. Rose's workload was increasing. As well as the office work and helping clients, her main responsibility was for the progression of the community hall. So, as well as her days, her evenings were also taken up with work, which didn't please Harry.

'Always an excuse,' Harry grumbled, 'you'll just have to make time. You're invited for a special meal. I've something important to tell you.' They were having a quick cup of tea together in a cafe in town before Rose went off to do her evening shift at the hall. Rose felt her heart give a lurch. Carefully she put down her cup on the saucer and said, 'That sounds intriguing.' She glanced at Harry's face, but he wasn't giving anything away.

Hammering filled the community hall. Rose had managed to secure a couple of dozen wooden chairs, but they all needed attention. She'd asked Harry to help but he said he had to meet a mate, though he might get back in time to walk her home. She was in the kitchen putting assortments of crockery in the cupboards, thinking about the invitation to Mrs Carter's for a meal. Rose hadn't seen Mrs Carter since the time they'd had that confrontation in the street, before Harry came home. All she got from Harry when she suggested coming down to see his mother was that she wasn't well. Perhaps she was feeling better now.

She was carrying a pile of cardboard boxes into the hall.

'Let me take them, Rose,' said a warm, masculine voice.

She turned her head to see Joe and her heart quickened as she said, 'This is a nice surprise.'

'If I'd known you could have done with help, I'd have come sooner.'

Rose blushed faintly. 'I thought you had

enough on with Peter and your work.'

'I can always spare time to help you, Rose. Peter's fast asleep and Mrs Mitchell's keeping an eye on him. I just felt like a bit of company.'

Soon the helpers drifted and only Joe and Rose remained. Rose was sweeping up the bits from the floor and Joe had just finished stacking the mended chairs securely.

'Let me,' he said, coming up to Rose to take the brush from her. He reached out and his hand clasped over hers as she held the brush handle. His heart somersaulted and he yearned to take her in his arms and kiss her.

'What's this, then?' A male voice rasped.

Rose jerked away from Joe to see Harry in the doorway. Joe cursed under his breath.

'Hello, Harry, have you come to walk me home?'

'Yes, get your coat.'

Joe didn't move, but watched as Rose hurried to the cloakroom.

'What do you think you're doing with my girl?' snarled Harry.

'Just helping out.'

'Well, don't any more.'

'Why not?'

'She's mine, so you keep away from her.'

'I'm ready.' Rose turned to Joe and said, 'Thanks for your help.'

Joe nodded, saying curtly, 'Goodnight,' and strode from the building.

Her heart heavy, Rose locked the street door, wishing that Joe and Harry could be friends.

Suddenly Harry gripped her arm, his fingers digging into her flesh. 'I don't want you to have anything to do with him,' he snarled.

She shook off his arm. 'He's a friend, he was only helping.'

'I know his type and his helping. You just keep away from him, understood?'

Rose glared at him.

On Thursday, Rose walked to Harry's house. Work had been hectic and she wasn't yet ready for Mrs Carter and her barbed remarks. But if the woman hadn't been well, maybe she'd mellowed. Either way, Rose wasn't looking forward to the visit. Perhaps it was Harry's way of making the peace between her and his mother, though Harry seemed more on the aggressive side than the peacemaking side. She was finding it difficult to deal with his obsessive behaviour and it was having a strain on their relationship. She tried to make allowances for him; after all, the trauma of fighting in war did unbalance some men. She saw it daily in her work. She admired the women who often told her of the miseries they suffered and had no option but to carry on for the sake of their children. Then she thought of Joe and how he'd suffered, losing his wife and unborn child, and now caring for his son, though he had turned to drink at first and then pulled himself around. He had told her it was her doing, knowing her and her parents, which had been his turning point. Why couldn't it be the same for Harry? She sighed; she would have to try harder to please him.

She knocked on the door of the Carters' house. The door opened with a jerk, startling her.

Harry stood there. 'About time,' he said abruptly.

'I'm not late.' She shrugged off her coat, hanging it on the peg at the back of the door, and followed him through into the kitchen where the most delicious savoury aroma assailed her nostrils. She was surprised because Mrs Carter had never been much of a cook and to the best of her knowledge neither was Harry.

In the kitchen a woman bustled over the stove with her back to them. Rose was taken aback. Mrs Carter was more rounded than when last she had seen her and looked different. The woman turned round, her cheeks flushed with heat and her smile ready.

Then a thin voice piped up, 'You're here then.' Seated in the far corner of the room sat Mrs Carter, thinner and scrawnier than ever.

'This is my Aunt Aggie,' introduced Harry.

'Pleased to meet you, love, heard such a lot about you. Now, you look perished. Sit yerself down and I'll dish up.' Rose glanced at Harry, trying to read his expression. Was his aunt being here something to do with what he had to say to her?

The piecrust melted in Rose's mouth and the meat and vegetables were tender and tasty. Aunt Aggie chatted, cheerfully. She came from a village near Beverley and was a widow. Mrs Carter stared vacantly and toyed with her food, while Harry just shovelled it in.

Aggie was saying, 'We'll clear away, then have cake and a cuppa and then we'll talk.'

Rose helped Aggie, Mrs Carter just sat and Harry disappeared into the backyard.

At last, tea and cake was served and they all sat round the table. 'Our Ida's not well,' began Aggie. 'And I'm taking her home to live with me so I can look after her.'

Rose swallowed the hot tea, burning her throat, making her cough. Harry frowned at her.

'Can you get me a drink of water, please, Harry,' she croaked. Begrudgingly he did.

She sipped the cool water and then looked at Aggie, sensing there was more to come.

Aggie continued, 'As I was saying, that leaves our Harry.'

Rose looked at Harry; he seemed able to take care of himself. Then it dawned on her: was Harry going to live with Aggie as well; was he going to jilt her again?

'Our Harry's going to take over the rent and this will be his house. So it stands to reason, makes sense for him to wed. He needs a wife to care for him.' Aggie smiled at her nephew.

Rose sat stunned. Things were moving too fast for her to grasp the full meaning.

Aggie turned to Rose. 'You're bonny, lass, bit thin though. When you wed our Harry and give up that horrible job, you'll be fine.'

Still Rose couldn't speak. Harry moved his chair closer to Rose and slipped an arm around her waist and gave her a hug. 'I can't wait,' he whispered in her ear, 'to get you into bed.'

Rose felt cold inside as the reality clicked in. She pulled herself away from Harry's clutches. It had all been decided without any consultation with her about their future together. Harry had never thought to discuss it with her first. He just assumed she would fall in with his wishes. And she definitely wasn't going to live in this house.

'What do you say, love?' said Aggie. 'You've fallen on your feet.'

At last Rose found her voice. 'I'll have to talk it over with Mam and Dad.'

'What's there to talk over?' demanded Harry. Panic filled Rose; she felt trapped. Then a voice in her head said, *You know what to do.* She scrambled to her feet, nearly knocking over the chair, and announced, 'I'm not going to marry you, Harry Carter.'

With three pairs of startled eyes staring at her, she fled the kitchen, pulled her coat off the peg and rushed from the house. She galloped down the street, like the best horse in a race.

Out of breath, Rose arrived at Church Terrace and went straight to Sally's house because she knew Sally's parents were having a night out at the pictures. Up in Sally's bedroom, Rose poured out her heart, saying how she didn't want to marry Harry. She didn't love him any more and told her friend what had transpired at the Carters' house.

'I don't want to marry him and live in that awful house,' she finished.

While Rose had talked and got everything out of her system, Sally had remained quiet. Now she spoke. 'I'm glad you've seen sense at last. This other woman, the one he was having the affair with when he wrote you that letter; it was her who chucked Harry over. She was married and her husband was coming home.'

Rose felt her body go cold as she gasped, 'A married woman! But he said he loved me.'

'Poppycock. The only person Harry Carter loves is himself.'

Back home, Rose told her parents what had gone on at Harry's house and that she didn't want to marry him. She didn't mention what Sally had told her about his affair with a married woman. Rose shuddered with humiliation at her own trusting naivety.

'Do you still love him enough to live elsewhere?' her mother was asking.

Rose came out of her reverie and replied with such revulsion, 'No, I don't.'

Mary glanced at her daughter in surprise, but before she could say anything, Ted, rising from his chair to get a spill from the jar on the mantelpiece to light his pipe, said, 'Never trusted the fellow. You're well shut of him, lass.' Rose started to sob and Mary gathered her close and wiped away the tears.

'Don't take on so, sweetheart. It's better to find out before you married him that you don't love him. It wouldn't have been a good marriage.'

Later, as she lay wide awake in her bed, Rose thought of her lucky escape from Harry, though it didn't make her feel any happier. She felt a failure. And Harry had only thought of her as second best. She was nineteen now, would she be left on the shelf? Perhaps that was her destiny, not to marry and have children, but as her job decreed, she was here to dedicate her life to looking after others. With that thought on her mind, she fell into a fitful sleep.

Hours later, loud banging on the front door jolted Rose awake. She raised her head and glanced at her bedside clock: two in the morning. Her first thought was that it was a bombing raid and a neighbour was knocking them up, thinking they had not heard the siren. But as she tumbled from her bed, rubbing sleep from her eyes, it dawned on her that the war was over.

The banging came again and a drunken voice shouted, 'Open up!'

'Oh no,' Rose groaned. There was no mistaking Harry's voice. She dashed from her room onto the landing, hoping Harry hadn't disturbed her parents. But her father was already up.

Trousers pulled over his pyjamas, Ted ordered, 'You stay put, lass, I'll deal with him.'

'Tell him I'll meet him in the cafe tomorrow after work.' The least she could do was to give Harry an explanation. She sat on the edge of her bed, listening to Harry's incoherent ramblings and her father's firm, no-nonsense voice. Eventually, Harry went. Ted came back upstairs and Rose heard Mrs Fisher's bedroom window close with a thump. Rose gave a big sigh: now all the neighbours would know her business.

The next morning when Rose arrived at work, she found a note on her desk from Harry. *Don't bother me any more. I never loved you, you cold fish.* Tears stung Rose's eyes as she read his hurtful words. It had been written in anger; even so, it upset her.

She didn't have time to brood over Harry and their second break-up because the day was busy and chaotic, more than usual. It wasn't until she had her coat on and was leaving the building that it struck her hard.

'Rose!' Sally called, as she headed across the road to her friend.

'Oh, Sally!' Rose burst into tears. Her friend's arms went around her, hugging her. Sally held Rose close, letting her cry, both girls oblivious to the stares of people passing by.

Gradually, her tears spent, Rose gave a weak smile. 'I'm the biggest fool,' she said, and showed Sally Harry's note.

Sally tossed it back. 'He's only saving face. Tear it up and chuck it away. Come on, let's get home. Shall we walk or bus?'

'Walk, please. It'll give me chance to be more cheerful before I get home. Mam and Dad have enough to do without worrying about me. Our Freddie hasn't written for a while.'

'Freddie,' Sally said, with a twinkle in her eyes. 'He's a good-looking man. Pity I'm no good at letter writing, but when he comes home, maybe he might walk out with me.'

'That would be wonderful,' Rose enthused. 'He needs someone to have fun with after the awfulness of fighting a war.' She linked her arm through Sally's and the two girls strode out.

Passing war-torn streets of crumbled devastation, the two young women came across a group of boys tending a fire on a ruined site. The tantalizing aroma of potatoes baking in skins drifted, and they were drawn to the fire, as if puppets pulled on strings.

'Have a warm,' said a smoky-streaked-face lad. 'But we ain't got any spuds to give yer.'

Rose and Sally both laughed and Rose asked, 'Can I chuck some waste paper on your fire?' The lad shrugged indifferently. Rose threw Harry's note into the heart of the fire and watched as the flames curled around it and greedily ate it up, its ash mingling with other debris.

She turned to Sally, saying, 'That's it. Now I can really get on with my life.'

'Atta girl,' cheered Sally.

THIRTEEN

A few days later, Rose decided to go and see Joe and Peter. She was interested in hearing how Peter was getting on at school and to see how Joe was. She knocked on the door of the house in Crowle Street and it was opened by a girl of about six, one of Mrs Mitchell's granddaughters.

'Hello, I've come to see Joe and Peter.'

The girl opened the door wider and Rose entered, following through to the kitchen, and there a cosy scene greeted her: Joe was seated next to Maureen, Mrs Mitchell's daughter, and they were deep in conversation and seemed unaware of her presence. But Peter, on seeing Rose, rushed to her and flung his arms about her. Hugging him close, feeling the comfort of his thin body against her, she buried her face in his tousled hair. Here, in this warm kitchen, she felt an outsider, and now that she was here, she only wanted to escape.

'Rose!' exclaimed Joe, scrambling to his feet. 'I haven't seen you for a while.'

'I've been busy,' she babbled, feeling foolish. 'I was passing so I thought I'd see how Peter was settling in at school.'

'He's fine. Aren't you, son?'

'I've drawn a snowman,' Peter said enthusiastically, and dashed from the room.

'You'll stay and have a cup of tea?' Mrs Mitchell invited.

'Thank you, but no, I've only popped in for a moment.'

Peter came back into the room to show Rose his coloured chalk picture on a small slate board. She felt a lump stick in her throat and she fought to keep her tears at bay. Peter had drawn a snowman encircled with a mammy, daddy, and a little girl and boy: a family scene. She couldn't meet Joe's eyes. She took a wild guess at what he and Maureen had been discussing. Joe was a widower with a son, and Maureen was a widow with daughters; it seemed natural that they should become one family.

Peter was pulling at her arm. 'Rose, do you like it?'

She looked into his earnest face, dropped down to his level and cupping his cheeks in her hands, she kissed his forehead.

'It's wonderful,' she whispered.

She turned to go and Joe was by her side. 'I'll see you out.'

On the doorstep she couldn't meet Joe's eyes. Was he going to tell her about him and Maureen? So she was surprised when he said, 'I was sorry to hear you and Harry had broken up.' When she looked at him questioningly, he said, 'Sally told me.'

She stood awkwardly and shrugged. 'It wasn't meant to be, me and Harry.'

'Everything all right?' Maureen appeared, placing her hand possessively on Joe's arm.

'Must go.' Rose turned, her shoulders hunched as she hurried away.

The sky was dark, no moon to light her way, no guiding star. Rose felt utterly wretched and miserable. She knew she should feel happy for Joe and Peter; after all, they had suffered so much. But if Joe married Maureen, he wouldn't need her friendship. And she would miss Joe's companionship, more than she cared to acknowledge.

She didn't go home, not wanting her

parents to see her in such a state of desolation. Instead she made her way to the community hall and let herself into the empty building. She stood in the centre of the big room and in the gloom, lit only by a single electric bulb, she closed her eyes. In her mind, she heard music, dance music; the beautiful, haunting melody of 'I'll Be Seeing You' filled her head. Her eyes still closed, she slowly danced, her feet moving rhythmically, her body swaying. As she danced around the deserted room it suddenly came to her. She would organize a dance for the New Year, to welcome in 1946.

Breathlessly, she sank down onto a chair. Could she do it? Already she was organizing a Christmas party for the children and to organize another event so soon afterwards would be hard work. Could she do it?

'Yes I can!' Her voice echoed around the empty hall, startling her.

Next morning in the office, Rose announced her intention to Mrs Butler.

'Good heavens, Rose. Don't you think that you have enough on? And besides, we have no extra money to spare. I can't see how you can possibly organize another event.'

Rose stuck out her chin and Mrs Butler recognized the determined sign.

'Well, you have my blessing and I'll do what I can to help, but I cannot guarantee anything.'

Rose's first piece of good luck came via Alf Norton. She was telling him and Mrs Fisher her plan.

'I've a friend who plays the bagpipes,' he announced. 'He owes me a favour.'

On Tuesday afternoons after school, Rose held a recreation class, mostly for children and a few mothers. Today they were busy making decorations for the Christmas party; coloured tissue paper twined around wire hoops to create hanging garlands, and Father Christmases made from wooden clothes pegs using bits of off-cuts from worn-out garments. Shirley and her mother, Betty, were working on a banner. Its background was a blackout curtain and the words *A Merry Christmas* were outlined in blood-red chain stitch filled in with blobs of cotton wool. Rose paused by their table.

'What's on yer mind?' Betty asked, looking up.

Rose pulled up a chair and launched into her idea. 'I'm planning a party for grown-ups on New Year's Eve. Would you have the time to make a banner?'

'Of course we can, can't we, Shirley?' Her daughter nodded in quick agreement.

Later that evening, tired but happy, Rose was relaxing at home. Mary was making a hot drink, when a sharp rap sounded on the back door. Ted, glancing up from reading the paper, said, 'I'll go.' He knew that with every unexpected knock, Rose thought it might be Harry.

But it was Joe. He was out of breath with running.

'Sorry to trouble you, but it's Peter. He's ill and fretting for you, Rose, can you come?'

Without hesitation, Rose was on her feet. 'What's wrong with him?'

'Came home from school soaked and caught a chill and now he seems feverish.'

She pulled on her coat, and followed Joe out, running to keep up with his long strides.

Mrs Mitchell was sitting in a chair, her heavily bandaged ankle resting up on a foot stool. She smiled weakly. 'Sorry, I'm no help.'

Not even stopping to take off her coat, Rose followed Joe through the latch door in the corner of the kitchen and up the narrow walled staircase into the bedroom. It held two single iron bedsteads, a chest of drawers and a small wardrobe, a chair and a stool.

In one of the beds, Peter moved restlessly about. Rose touched his forehead. It was burning up.

She turned to Joe, saying, 'Bring me a clean flannel and a basin of cold water and ask Mrs Mitchell if she has a Fenning's cooling powder.' Rose stroked Peter's hot cheeks, saying soothingly, 'I'm here, sweetheart,' and the little chap clutched at her hand.

Joe came back with the water and the cooling powder. 'First,' said Rose, her coat now discarded, 'we'll strip off his clothes and sponge him down.' Gently, together they administered to Peter's needs and then gave him the cooling powder.

Finally, Peter slept, his little body clad in clean pyjamas and between fresh sheets. Rose held his hand, listening to his now much steadier breathing.

Joe came up with two cups of cocoa. Rose accepted hers and sat back on the chair.

'I'll stay the night,' she said, glancing back at Peter. 'Just in case he wakes up and needs me.' She turned back and saw the relief in Joe's eyes. 'But I'll have to let my parents know.'

'I'll go,' he said, gulping down his drink.

Rose resumed her vigil, watching over Peter. It seemed the most natural thing to do.

In no time at all, Joe returned. Her mother had packed her an overnight bag.

'She'll be here first thing in the morning to look after Peter so you can go to work.'

Rose got to her feet, stretched her stiff body, and was just about to settle back down on the chair when Joe said. 'You can have my bed. I'll take Mrs Mitchell's. She's sleeping downstairs in her chair.' Rose glanced at Joe's bed.

'I can change the sheets,' he offered.

'No need.'

Later, after bathing Peter's forehead with

cool water and making him comfortable, Rose slipped into Joe's bed. As her head touched the pillow, she caught a faint whiff of the scent of Joe's hair. She hugged the blankets close around her and her mind thought thoughts that she shouldn't be thinking.

With careful nursing, Peter made a full recovery and soon returned to school, none the worse for his bout of fever. In fact he made much of his illness, telling pals in the playground that he had his own special nurse called Rose.

Joe took Rose to the cinema as a thank-you, though she couldn't recall what the film was about for she was more conscious of Joe's nearness. They sat in the back row, his arm around her waist; he drew her close and she snuggled up to him, turning her lips to his, and they indulged in the art of kissing.

Leaving the cinema, they strolled hand in hand.

'Shall we do it again?' Joe asked.

'I can't, Joe.' The happy look on Joe's face faltered.

Quickly, Rose explained, 'I'd love to, Joe, but the New Year's Eve dance is taking up my time. You'll come to it, Joe?'

His face relaxed. 'Wouldn't miss it,' he said, and kissed her lightly on the cheek. She squeezed his hand, pleased their friendship was still intact though not sure where it would lead. She was careful not to mention

Maureen's name and neither did he.

A few days later, Rose came home from work to find her mother sitting by the fire, reading a letter, looking a bit mystified.

'What is it, Mam?'

Mary glanced up. 'It's good news from our Freddie. He says he'll be home in January.'

Rose sighed with relief. 'That's good news. It will be lovely to have him home for good.'

'He says he's bringing someone with him,' Mary said, 'but he doesn't say who.'

'It could be another soldier. Perhaps one who's lost his family?' Rose said.

'Oh dear, how sad,' Mary sympathized. 'I'll sort the front room out for him to sleep in.'

So for the next few days, happy at the thought of her son finally coming home, Mary cleaned and dusted, washed and ironed everything in sight. First was Freddie's small box-room, which had only space for a bed and a chest of drawers. In the front room she pondered over the settee; would it be comfortable enough for Freddie's friend to sleep on?

Christmas 1945 was a quiet affair. What with the parties in the summer to celebrate the end of the war, food supplies were short and besides, Mary wanted to have a welcoming home celebration for Freddie and his friend.

Alf Norton and Vera Fisher both came for

Christmas dinner.

'Now, I'll tell you straight,' Vera said, 'Alf is my lodger, he sleeps in the back bedroom and has use of my front room on weekends, and I cook and wash for him.' With that, she sat heavily on a chair, smoothing her best dress of pearl-grey silk rayon over her knees. Alf, in his best dark suit, stood awkwardly.

There was dead silence. Then Mary said, 'It's nice to have company. Sit next to Vera, Alf.'

Ted had somehow procured a rabbit. 'It's in lieu of payment for a favour I've had done for a friend,' he told Mary, his tone suggesting that she asked no questions. He sharpened the knife ready for cutting. Rose brought the steaming dishes of vegetables to the table: roast potatoes, carrots and cabbage, and a jug of rich gravy.

Afterwards, they all sat in the front room. Ted poured out the sherry and they toasted the king as they listened to his broadcast. Rose sat quietly, thinking about Joe; he and Peter were having their Christmas with Mrs Mitchell and family and that included Maureen. It seemed ages since they had spent time together and she yearned for Joe's touch, his nearness.

On Boxing Day morning, Rose was at the community hall, organizing the children's party for later that afternoon, when Shirley arrived with her two brothers.

'I thought your mother was coming to help?' Rose asked.

'Can't because baby's crabby and Dad's shouting,' Shirley said.

After a tea of potted-meat sandwiches, jam tarts, and jelly, washed down with lemonade, they played games. The two favourites were pass the parcel, because the winner won a chocolate bar, and hide-and-seek. By the end of the afternoon, Rose was exhausted. From time to time, she kept looking towards the main door, in the hope that Joe might walk in.

She walked home alone, passing houses with lights (no more blackout) shining through windows to reveal happy family scenes. A great tide of loneliness swept through her body.

How she longed to be loved and to love someone. It was Joe she wanted. She always felt happy in his company, but did he just see her as a friend or more than a friend?

'Penny for them?' A voice cut into her thoughts.

'Sally, I didn't see you.'

'You were miles away. Now, tell me then?'

Rose anchored her beret more firmly on her head and gave a big sigh.

'It's nothing, really, just thinking: will I get a boyfriend or be left on the shelf?' She didn't mention Joe.

'You're too pretty for that, but you have to

get out more. Come with me to Hollis New Year's Eve Dance. Think of all those brawny-armed men who work in the timber yard.'

Rose sighed again. 'I can't.'

By now the two girls were turning the corner into Crowle Street and Sally pulled sharply on Rose's arm, causing her to halt. A man behind collided with them.

'Now then, you two, what's this?' boomed the authoritarian voice of a burly police-man. 'No fighting in the street.'

Sally replied, cheekily, 'We weren't, constable. I was just trying to make her see sense.'

The constable eyed Rose. 'You're the young woman from the community hall.' Rose nodded. 'I've got just the man for you. He's locked up in my cell.' Rose looked alarmed.

'No need to worry, lass. He's only there because he's homeless. He got a bit drunk so I've locked him up for Christmas.' His grey eyes twinkled. 'I've just come to feed him.' He tapped the paper carrier bag under his arm. 'Come and have a talk to him.'

Both girls followed him into the unusually quiet police station, not sure what to expect. They waited in the tiny reception. On its wall was a huge poster showing a big, colourful, hungry-looking beetle of foreign origin which, if not caught, could destroy crops. The constable signed in, then lifted up the flap of the wooden counter and went

161

through into the cell area, whistling as he went. The duty policeman looked up from the report he was writing before going off duty, but didn't speak to them. Rose shivered, feeling Sally, who stood close to her, mirror her shivering too.

The constable returned. 'Come through.' He lifted the flap for them then and led the way down a short corridor to a small, square-shaped room with a high, barred window and drab walls of an undefined colour. In the room were an oblong wooden table and four chairs. On one of these chairs sat a young, dishevelled-looking man, wearing a crumpled demob suit. His fair hair was long and in need of a cut, his hand shook as he drew on a cigarette, but it was his hollow, sunken eyes that made Rose gasp. Although she had seen that bleak look many times these past few months, it never failed to move her. It was as if they, the ones returning from the war, were the ones who had lost their loved ones and all hope of the future. She was desperately trying to think of what to say to him that didn't sound trite. When suddenly:

'Well, if it isn't Frank Belfield!' exclaimed Sally.

Blankly, he stared at her.

'You're my Cousin Jim's friend. Was,' she amended. 'He went down, all hands lost,' she mumbled, tears suddenly filling her eyes. Frank lowered his gaze.

'I'm sure my Aunt Gertie would like to see you. You know, with you and Jim being friends,' she finished, a little unsure if she was saying the right thing. He didn't look up.

The silence filled the room; Frank's family had all perished in a bombing raid on Hill Street.

The constable, who had left the room, returned with four steaming mugs of tea, and beef sandwiches and two mince pies for Frank.

'So you know Frank?' he asked. The girls both nodded. 'Well, he's due out in the morning.' The constable supped his tea, leaving his words hanging in the air, waiting.

Sally spoke first. 'I could come in the morning.' Then she addressed Frank. His mouth full of his sandwich, he stared at her. 'Would you like to see Aunt Gertie? I think she would like to talk to you about Jim. You know, about the old days.'

He finished his eating, pushed back his greasy hair from his eyes, and said, hesitantly, 'Do you think she would?'

'I'm sure she would. She misses Jim.'

Rose sat back, watching this touching scene and feeling deeply humbled. Sally was a good friend, the best. Then she remembered her official position and perhaps the reason why the constable'd invited them in to see Frank.

She sat up and said, 'Sally can bring you along to the WVS office and I can try and fix you up with temporary lodgings, until you can find something permanent.'

He nodded in response.

As Rose and Sally walked home, Sally was very quiet, not like her usually talkative self. Rose squeezed her arm.

'It's my turn to say a penny for them,' she said.

Sally, her face serious, her voice low, began, 'All through the war I was determined to enjoy myself. Not to let Hitler get the better of me, but I feel ashamed now. I never once gave the lads like Frank a second thought. If I did, I assumed they were enjoying the fighting, seeing it as an adventure. But it wasn't. Frank is homeless, with no family, no job; and he came back to Hull to nobody. But I'm going to alter that. I'm going to be his friend. He can count on me.' With that, she marched off to her house, leaving Rose speechless.

FOURTEEN

With the organization of the New Year's Eve dance, Rose didn't see Sally until two days later. The WVS office was not far from Woolworth's, where Sally worked. She came in her dinner break, with a smarter looking Frank. He was clean shaven; his hair was cut, slick and in place with Brylcreem. His suit was brushed and pressed, he wore a clean shirt and a tie, and his shoes were polished to perfection. His eyes were still sunken with dark smudges and he had lines around his mouth; the war and its aftermath had taken its toll on him.

Rose led them both to a corner of a large room which was used for storage. She didn't have an office of her own, but had made this corner her own office space. They seated themselves on packing cases and Rose produced her clipboard and pencil and smiled at them both. She addressed Frank first.

'You are looking much better. How are you feeling?'

Frank's voice was flat and nasal, as if he had a bad throat or smoked too much. 'Not bad, thanks.' He pulled a packet of Woodbines from his jacket pocket and offered it to both girls. They shook their heads. He lit up and, drawing on the cigarette, he inhaled and unwound.

'I've not got long,' said Sally, glancing at the clock on the far wall. 'Frank is lodging with Aunt Gertie for now.' She blushed. 'That's until things become more settled.'

Rose raised an eyebrow, and then asked, 'What can I do for you now, Frank?'

'The factory where I used to work has gone, bombed to smithereens. It was a shock, I can tell you. I didn't expect to see such devastation. Not here. I didn't realize. I should have done, what with Mam and Dad and the bairns all gone. But I thought if I could get my old job back, I could make it. But...' His voice trailed away.

Rose said, 'The first thing to do, Frank, is for me to take down all your relevant details.'

Sally jumped up. 'I'll have to go, I can't be late back,' she said apologetically to Frank.

'But...' Frank began, but Rose put a steadying hand on his arm.

'I'll look after you,' she said, and Sally flashed a smile of gratitude.

Later, that evening, Sally called to see Rose at home.

'Thanks for helping Frank. He didn't understand about claiming his gratuity. It'll tide him over until he gets a job.' She hesitated, then said, 'I want to ask you something, but you might think I'm daft.'

Sally blushed and Rose thought how pretty she looked in her warm, cherry-red coat and navy beret. She felt dreary beside her glowing friend, but she smiled at her.

'Go on, what?'

'Can Frank and me come to your New Year's Eve dance?'

'That's the best news I've heard for ages. I need some young blood.'

Sally went away happy. Rose flopped back on a chair and looked around the empty kitchen, her sense of loneliness acute. Her parents were visiting friends and Rose had welcomed the quietness, until Sally came. Sally and Frank: together their names sounded special. Aloud she said softly, 'Rose and Joe.' She smiled, loving the ring of their two names together. Where was Joe now?

She glanced down at the sheets of paper, which had fallen to the floor, and retrieving them she placed them on the table. She fiddled with the wireless set. A good murder play would give her a jolt, but all she could tune into was a comedy sketch programme, which didn't make her laugh or lift her spirits. There was only one thing to do. She grabbed her new midnight-blue coat with matching scarf and beret, and slipped on her shoes and went out.

In the street she breathed in the cold, clear night air, filling her lungs with its crispness. Digging her hands deep into her coat pockets, she walked down the silent street. She was in no particular hurry, no particular place to go, and no particular person to see, so she told herself. She walked on and nothing stirred in the eerie stillness.

Suddenly, the quiet of the night was broken by the laughter of a man and a woman, and children talking. Rose stopped in the shadow of the shop on the corner of Crowle Street and looked in the direction of the voices. She saw Joe, the street lamp illuminating the joy on his face. Her heart in turmoil, she held her breath as she watched the happy family group enter the Mitchell house. She let out her breath; it froze on the night air and she retraced her steps. Had she been deluding herself and reading more into Joe's friendship? But she couldn't ignore the stirring of her heart and the ache in her body for him. But could he ever be hers?

For the time leading up to the New Year's Eve dance, Rose kept busy. Work and helping others was her solace. She had managed to engage, for free, the same band as before, plus three new recruits. These three young men, who had been well known in the dance band circuit prior to the war, were eager to start playing again. The six-piece band now consisted of pianist, drummer, clarinet, saxophone, bass and trumpet players. Rose sat in on one of their rehearsals and enjoyed listening to their great sense of rhythm.

On New Year's Eve, Rose sat before her dressing table mirror. Determined to look her best, she applied a light dusting of powder and a pretty pink lipstick, a Christmas gift from Sally. She brushed her blonde hair until it shone and swept up the sides with tortoiseshell combs and piled the top of her head with a wave and curls. She'd seen this glamorous style at the pictures. She eased on her fully fashioned stockings, taking care not to snag them and causing the thread to run and ladder. She wore the lovely blue dress that her mother had made. She slipped on her new court shoes, a gift from her parents, then stood up and surveyed her appearance in the mirror. In the soft light, the sadness in her eyes didn't show too much. She looked hard at her reflection, gave a half-smile and flicked off the light.

Downstairs, her parents greeted her appearance with approval.

'Rose, you look so beautiful,' Mary said, her eyes shining with pride.

'Yes you do, love,' echoed Ted.

Rose looked at her parents hopefully, saying, 'You're not coming to the dance?'

Mary glanced furtively at Ted and made pretence of counting her knitting stitches. She answered, 'Dad and I, well, we've got something else on.'

Rose stared at her mother, wondering what the secrecy was about.

Ted stood up, knocking his pipe out on the side of the fire grate. 'You go off and enjoy yourself, love,' he said, giving her a wink.

Rose sighed. She felt baffled by her parents' odd behaviour, but she didn't have time to dwell on it. She put on her coat and tied on a headscarf, to protect her hair from the elements.

Arriving at the hall, Rose looked around with satisfaction and joy. It was festooned with paper trimmings and coloured balloons, left over from an American base camp. Draped across the top of the makeshift stage was a banner, wishing everyone a *Happy New Year for 1946*. Rose just stood in the middle of the hall, her eyes brimming with tears of joy. The change to the room was unbelievable. It was something special to share with everyone who had endured the severity of war, at home or away. The government had announced a plan to rebuild homes and workplaces but Rose knew that the most delicate area of rebuilding was breaching the gap of loved ones who had been separated for such a long time. Reconstruction of their lives together was difficult. Many were like strangers, never seeing their children grow up, and for some, their lives would be forever broken.

A voice interrupted her musing.

'It looks smashing, Rose,' said the jovial voice of Ray, the piano player, who had just entered the hall. He came to stand by her side.

'More than I hoped for. But you're right. It is smashing.' They both laughed. The rest of the band started to arrive and they began to assemble their instruments and tune up.

Soon people began arriving, bringing small contributions to the buffet and soft drinks. There was no alcohol, but no one seemed to mind. Rose watched couples, who seemed shy at first, take to the dance floor, but it only took one couple to swing onto the floor. The band struck up a lively tune, Glenn Miller's, 'Little Brown Jug', and the floor rocked as the dancing feet of couples swung into action. Rose stood on the end of the dance floor, watching in fascination as the couples relaxed, lost in the rhythm of the dance steps. Sally was there with Frank and another young couple, and Rose watched as Sally pulled Frank onto the dance floor. He trod on her toes, but she only laughed. Betty and her husband, Bob, arrived late, both looking very unhappy and ill at ease with each other. Rose went to greet them, her arms outstretched, saying, 'I'm so glad you could both come.'

Betty's bottom lip quivered as she bit back a tear. 'I'm sorry we're late. Baby played up at last minute, she's teething.'

'She's spoilt,' muttered Bob. 'She gets more bleeding attention than me.'

Betty ignored her husband and said, 'I forgot to bring the corned beef sandwiches.'

Bob, still angry said, 'I wanted to go for a pint.' Betty's bottom lip started to quiver again.

Quickly, Rose cut in, 'We've a bottle of Sarsparilla.'

'I suppose that will have to do.'

Rose dashed into the kitchen. The bottle was coated in dust and she wasn't sure how old it was. She gave it a rub with a damp cloth and just hoped that the contents were still drinkable. She poured out a glassful and a lemonade for Betty. Back in the hall, she ushered the now silent couple to a table, where two other couples sat talking, and introduced them. Rose glanced at Betty, noticing how tired and drawn she looked and hoping that as the evening progressed, she would begin to relax. All through the war, Betty had carried on under immense hardship, but remained cheerful, and full of determination to keep her family together and not to give in. Now, it was as if her candle had been snuffed out.

Mrs Fisher and Alf Norton came in. Vera was wearing an attractive dress of pale gold, and her hair was neatly curled. Alf had on his best dark suit and blue shirt and tie. Rose showed them to a table and provided them with a glass of lemonade each.

She didn't see him approaching. She turned straight into Joe's arms. Gently, he pulled her closer, his warm breath caressing her cheek as he whispered, 'You look beautiful, Rose.' He held her so close that she could feel the beat of his heart; or was it her heart?

'Joe, I didn't know if you would come. I thought, Maureen ... you and she...?'

'You do think wicked things,' he said. 'I'll explain later.' He held her at arm's length and admired her dress.

'Give him a twirl, Rose,' a cheeky voice

called out. Rose obliged and laughter rang out.

After a few greetings, Joe manoeuvred Rose to the relative privacy of the kitchen. They stood, arms entwined around each other, not wanting to let go. Rose stared into Joe's honest brown eyes, feeling the strength of his body against hers, and her whole body surged with love for this man. She lifted up her chin and parted her lips, her eyes still on his. He lowered his face to hers and gently kissed her lips. Then he drew away from her, saying, 'I have good news to tell you, Rose.'

Still basking in the warmth of his body and the tenderness of his kiss, she looked dreamily at him. Then she mentally shook herself.

'Mrs Mitchell is going to live with her daughter, Maureen, and she has put in a good word with the landlord for me to take over the house to rent.'

'But I thought you and Maureen–'

Joe put a finger on her lips. 'It's always been you, Rose, but I couldn't say so when you were with Harry.'

'I never think of him now. Your news is great and...' she began, shyly, but was interrupted by Vera Fisher coming into the kitchen. 'Is there any grub tonight? I feel faint.'

Rose blushed and, turning to where the food was in readiness to be taken out to the buffet table, didn't see Vera wink at Joe. After the food came the spot prizes for dancing and Rose was so much in demand that she and Joe never got the chance to have a dance together. Once or twice she caught his eye across the dance floor.

Later, Rose was in the kitchen tidying up, when Joe walked in.

'Rose, I'm having a wonderful night. I didn't think it was possible for me to begin to enjoy life again. And it's all thanks to you.'

Tongue-tied, she picked up a teacloth. But Joe whipped the cloth from her hands and with an exaggerated bow said, 'Please may I have this dance, Rose?'

How could she refuse him? As Joe and Rose went out onto the dance floor, the band struck up with the last waltz before the end of the old year. Encircled in the embrace of Joe's strong arms, the touch of his body next to hers, Rose felt giddy, as if she was intoxicated. Joe drew her closer, her cheek resting on his chest; she felt the quickening of his heartbeat. She knew without doubt, she loved Joe and wanted to spend the rest of her life with him. Looking up into his warm, brown eyes she saw her love and feelings were returned.

Midnight came and Rose couldn't believe how time had passed so quickly. The piper, in full dress of the MacGregor clan, made his grand entrance to the tune of 'Auld Lang Syne'. Everyone joined hands in a circle and sang. In the distance, the boats and ships on the River Hull and Humber Estuary sounded their hooters, and churches, for the first New Year since before the war, rang out their bells.

'Happy New Year,' everyone chorused. Joe swept Rose into his arms and his lips sought hers, sealing their love with a passionate kiss.

'Will you marry me, Rose?'

She only had one answer: 'Yes!'

Later, as Rose lay in bed, reliving the most amazing evening of her life, she listened to the steady breathing of the little boy sleeping in the camp bed at the foot of her bed. Now she knew why her parents had not come to the dance; they had been looking after Peter, Joe's son. Once she and Joe were married, Peter would become her stepson. She loved the little boy and wanted to be a real mother to him.

She felt so blessed and happy, and her happiness would be complete when her brother, Freddie, came home for good.

FIFTEEN

The telegram arrived on a cold and frosty January morning. Mary opened it and immediately burst into floods of tears. Rose snatched the telegram from her mother's trembling hands and read: '*Will be with you tomorrow. Freddie.*'

'I can't believe he's finally coming home. My boy,' Mary marvelled, wiping away her tears of joy on the corner of her apron. 'Wait till I tell Ted.'

Rose hugged her mother, and she let out a sigh of relief.

'Oh Mam, it will be lovely to have him home for good.' She remembered her childhood image of her cheeky, playful brother.

Mary pulled away from her daughter, saying, 'I must make a start. Rose, ask Mrs Fisher if I can borrow her baking trays, please?'

The train pulled into Hull Paragon Station, steam billowed and passengers began scrambling, wanting to be the first off the train. The young woman hunched against the window seat, making no move, stared out on the scene. The platform was heaving with bodies striving to see those alighting from the train.

'Daddy,' a child's voice squealed in delight, and a rush of women and children pushed forward, eager to see their loved ones. There were hugs and kisses, and tears of happiness, children swung high by their returning fathers, and laughter and joy filled the crowded station.

The young woman felt a touch on her arm. She turned round and smiled at the tall, travel-weary soldier, and then slowly she got to her feet. They were the last to leave the train. The soldier helped the young woman to step down from the train onto the now quiet platform. She tried to pull her brown, rough woollen coat closer, but the buttons only strained across her heavy figure. Her pale face showed signs of fatigue and her fair hair hung limp in a single plait down her back. She clutched a small attaché case. The soldier hoisted his kit bag up onto his shoulder and gently took her arm to guide her to the entrance. No words were spoken between the couple as they made their way out onto the street in the bustling city centre. In the bus station, they stood patiently in the queue for the number 47 bus.

Once they were on board and seated, the conductor asked, 'Where to, mate?'

'Two to Ferries Street, please.'

The conductor glanced at the woman, and then moved down the bus. 'Any more fares?'

At their stop, the couple alighted from the bus and continued on down Ferries Street into Crowle Street. Here they stopped for the young woman to rest and catch her breath.

'Well, if it isn't young Freddie.' The figure of a woman loomed into view.

Freddie blinked his tired eyes, trying to focus on the woman. Then he recognized her.

'Mrs Fisher, nice to see you.'

'Nice to see you, lad. Your Rose told me you

were coming home and bringing a friend.' Her gaze rested on the pregnant young woman. She sniffed, saying, 'You've kept that a secret.'

Freddie, not wanting to explain anything to the nosey neighbour, took hold of the young woman's arm and said, 'We must be going.'

Mrs Fisher watched them go, tutting as she continued on her way. Crossing over the street, she accosted an acquaintance and began telling her the titbit of gossip.

'Fancy, young Freddie getting her pregnant. I hope he's married her.'

Rose was busy grating a precious bar of chocolate onto the top of a cake to decorate it. This was Freddie's favourite cake. Mary was bending over the fireside oven, checking on the meat and potato pie, the meat from a tin of stewed steak she had exchanged clothing coupons for. As she straightened up, she saw a shadow pass the kitchen window. Her heart fluttered with excitement and she uttered a cry, 'He's here!' Rose spun round, flecking the last of the grated chocolate across the table top.

As Freddie entered the kitchen, Mary dashed to him to fling herself into her son's arms.

'Steady on, Mam. Let me put my kitbag down.' He did so and enveloped his mother into his strong arms. Then Rose darted forward to be hugged by her brother.

Neither women noticed the quiet young woman until Freddie drew her forward, saying, 'Mam, Rose, this is my wife, Elsa.'

Both Rose and Mary were speechless and stared at the pregnant woman. Mary was first to regain her power of speech.

'Freddie,' she gasped. 'You never said.' Her face flushed, she pushed back stray strands of hair. 'You said a friend.'

Freddie said quietly, 'I thought I would surprise you. I met Elsa in Germany.'

'Germany! In the forces?'

'Can we sit down? We've had a long journey. And how about a cup of tea?' Freddie asked.

'Tea,' Mary repeated, looking dazed as if this was too much to take in.

Rose, having regained her composure, took charge. She drew out a chair from the kitchen table for her mother to sit on, while Freddie did the same for him and Elsa. Rose put the kettle on the hob and busied herself with the teapot and cups and saucers, setting them on a tray, placing them on the table. She gave Elsa a quick look, but the woman sat there with her eyes downcast. Rose brought the big brown teapot to the table and poured. No one spoke. She'd forgotten the milk so she went to the pantry to collect the jug.

Rose pushed the cup of tea across the table to Elsa. 'Drink up and you'll feel better.'

Elsa raised her head and glanced at Rose, saying in her native tongue, '*Danke.*'

Mary half rose from her seat. 'Oh my God!' she cried in horror. Her face blanched white, she whispered, 'You're a German?'

For seconds, seemingly hours, the clock on the mantelpiece ticked, filling the silence. Then Freddie, exhausted, slowly got to his feet and slipped an arm around Elsa's trembling shoulders. His voice low, but clear, he said, 'Elsa is my wife. She has suffered the most terrible things and I have brought her here, to my home, to be safe.' Now he looked directly at his mother. 'Are we both welcome?'

Again the clock ticking filled the silence. Mary coughed and cleared her throat.

'Oh, Freddie, you should have prepared me. It's a shock to learn that you are even married, let alone that your bride is pregnant, and German. You've knocked me for six.' Tears filled Mary's eyes and Rose could see that she wasn't sure what to do next.

Rose's professionalism slipped into gear and she sprung to her feet and went to Elsa's side. The young woman also looked in shock. Gently, Rose took Elsa's arm and motioned her to come with her. Glancing reassuringly to her brother, Rose guided his wife from the kitchen to the front room where a bed was in readiness, as they had thought, for Freddie's army friend. The bed was only a make-do on the old sofa, but by the tired look on Elsa's face and the heavy droop of her pregnant body, as long as she had somewhere to rest, this would do.

Rose helped her to struggle out of her coat and to unlace the clumsy boots. Drawing back the bedding, sheet, blanket and counterpane, Rose assisted Elsa to lie down. When she was comfortable, the young woman reached for Rose's hand and said softly, 'Thank you.'

'You speak English?'

'At school,' she replied; her eyelids drooping, she closed her eyes.

Rose watched Elsa's unsteady breathing until it settled and the young woman slept. She turned and closed the curtains. Already, the late afternoon was moving into twilight.

Rose stood for a moment, not sure of her next move. After a few seconds, she braced herself and went back into the kitchen.

Mary was sitting in her chair by the fire, staring into space. Freddie had pulled up his chair to the fireplace and was smoking a cigarette. He looked up enquiringly to Rose, concern etched across his gaunt face.

'She's sleeping.' To her surprise, her big brother let out a sob.

Mary looked up quickly. Her son, her beloved son, had great big tears running down his cheeks.

'I couldn't leave her behind,' he sobbed.

'She would have died without me to care for her. I just couldn't, Mam. She's suffered so much.'

'Oh dear,' Mary sniffed, tears welling her eyes. 'Oh son, don't take on so. We'll look after her, don't worry.' She got up from her chair to take her firstborn into her arms and cradled him like a baby. 'There, there, love. We'll pull through.' Over the top of Freddie's head, she caught Rose's eye and they both knew that there was trouble ahead.

By the time Ted came home from work, Freddie was feeling calmer, having swilled cold water over his red, flushed face, given it a good rub with a soft towel, brushed his hair, and had another cigarette and a strong, sweet cup of tea.

Ted came in all of a bustle. 'Why, lad, it's so great to see you.'

Freddie was on his feet and Ted shook his son's hand and affectionately clapped him on the shoulder. 'My, I never thought this day would come. When you've had a good rest, we'll have a pint together in the pub. Everyone will be so glad to see you home safely.' He glanced around the kitchen, saying, 'Where's your mate?'

Freddie remained silent and so did Mary. Ted looked at them both, sensing something was wrong. Making a swift decision, because there was nothing to gain by delaying telling him, Rose broke the silence.

'Freddie's wife is resting.'

Ted stared at his daughter, not sure if he had heard her correctly. 'Did you say wife?'

'Aye, that's right, Dad. Elsa is my wife and she's German.'

Ted stared open-mouthed at his son and then found his tongue. 'You've brought a bloody German into my house! Have you taken leave of your senses?' he shouted. 'Get her out now!' He slammed his fist hard down on the table, which Rose had set for tea, making the cutlery jump and rattle.

Mary cried out, 'Ted, be careful.'

Amid all the commotion, the kitchen door opened and Elsa stood there, framed in the doorway. Her plait had come undone and her silvery fair hair fell onto her shoulders. Her face was stark white and tears stained her prominent cheekbones, her blue eyes dark and sunk into the sockets.

Her voice little more than a whisper, she said, 'I go now.'

They all stared at her and then suddenly, her body twisted and she slumped forward.

Ted caught her and stopped her from banging her head on the doorjamb. He held the lifeless woman in his strong arms.

'Quick,' Rose commanded, 'get her back into bed.'

Safely back in her makeshift bed, Elsa opened her eyes and stared at Ted and whispered, 'I am so sorry.'

183

Mary moved Ted aside and sat on the edge of the bed and held a glass of water to her daughter-in-law's lips. Rose straightened the bed covers.

Ted took hold of his son's arm and said, 'Best leave your wife to the care of the women.'

The two men went back into the kitchen and Freddie offered his father a cigarette.

'Thanks, lad.' Ted puffed on it, glad of something to do. Staring into the fire as he smoked, Ted tried to get to grips with the situation. He had heard of the Fratting scandal in Germany. It was in the newspapers, German women setting out to snare British soldiers. But he never dreamed that his own son would be taken in by a German woman, and marry her; even less that she would become pregnant. At last he spoke.

'I can't turn the lass out, not in her condition. What is done is done.' He sat reflecting some more, then said, 'It won't be easy having one of the enemies in the house.' He nodded in the direction of Mrs Fisher's house. 'Her sons were both killed by the Germans and half the street was bombed by them with many losses of life.' He shook his head, then continued, 'Do you know what you are up against, son? There will be reprisals because folk will want to take it out on someone.'

Freddie nodded. He had not really

thought too far ahead. His main concern had been getting Elsa to a place of safety. But now, he wasn't sure if this was the right place for her after all.

SIXTEEN

No one in the Ellerby household slept much that night, except Elsa. Clearly exhausted and lacking in physical strength, she slept through supper and the night. Ted, up early for work, lit the fire, banking it with slack, leaving just enough flames for the kettle to boil. Along with everything else on rations, coal was still in short supply.

'You'd think,' he muttered to himself, 'with the ruddy war over, things would get better not worse.' The stairs door creaked and a bleary-eyed Mary came into the kitchen. 'You shouldn't be up, love.'

She let out a big sigh. 'I couldn't sleep. Things kept going round in my mind.' She sat on her chair, clasping her woollen dressing gown closer around her shivering body. 'What are we going to do, Ted?'

Ted thought for a moment, then replied, 'Carry on as normal.'

'Normal!' Mary's voice rose in disbelief. 'How can we do that?'

'We have no choice. What is done is done. Freddie has married a foreigner, an enemy who is expecting our grandbairn.'

'A German bairn! I never thought of that.' She sank further into her chair.

Rose, dressed for work, came downstairs to hear the bubbling and hissing of the kettle and her parents oblivious to it.

'I'll make the tea,' she said. 'Mam, go back to bed, I'll bring a cup up to you.'

'No, love,' Mary sighed, 'I couldn't sleep. I'll make the toast.'

Rose tapped lightly on the front room door and entered. Elsa was sitting up in the makeshift bed. Rose said too brightly, 'Good morning. You're looking better after your sleep.'

Elsa smiled, uncertain, and then said in halting English, 'Very kind, you are.'

Rose's eyes filled with tears and she felt humble on hearing those words. She placed the breakfast tray of tea and toast on the chair next to the bed and opened the curtains. She came back to sit on the arm of the settee and looked Elsa fully in the face.

'You are our Freddie's wife, carrying his child.' She witnessed a sudden flash of fear in Elsa's eyes. She continued, 'You have my respect.' This was out of love for her brother, though why he couldn't have married a British girl, she didn't know. It was going to cause a lot of gossip and backlash. Rose pulled herself up; she must try not to think such thoughts.

'I'll leave you to eat your breakfast and then I'll bring you a bowl and a jug of hot water so you can have a wash.' As an afterthought, she added, 'The lavatory is outside in the yard.'

'Thank you. Freddie,' Elsa fumbled for the words, 'where is he?'

Rose put her hands together, as in prayer, to the side of her left cheek and tilted her head and closed her eyes. A few seconds later when she opened them, it was to see Elsa smiling.

Later, Ted and Rose had gone to work and Freddie was still asleep when Elsa came into the kitchen. Mary, clearing away the dishes, stopped to look at the young woman. She was wearing a plain grey dress, with a white apron tied around her expanding waist. Her colourless face was framed by pale-blonde hair arranged in a single plait, which hung over her shoulder.

Elsa stood uncertain. Trying to think of the word, she stumbled, 'Lava ... lavatory?'

Mary came towards the young woman. 'Of course, my dear, I'll show you.' She led the way out in to the backyard. 'It's next to the coalhouse.' She lifted the sneck and opened the wooden door to reveal a well-scrubbed lavatory pan and seat, with a clean stone floor, its edge patterned with beige-coloured donkey stone. Newspaper cut into identical squares hung tidily from a piece of string. Elsa murmured her thanks.

Mary went back indoors to wash the pots. Elsa soon came back in and picked up the tea-towel and began to dry the dishes. This small gesture lifted Mary's spirits. Maybe Ted was right. They must carry on as normal, though she was dreading Mrs Fisher calling.

Mary, who was about to do the daily shopping, asked Freddie, who was now up, 'Have you a ration book for Elsa?' He looked at his mother in surprise. Mary said in answer to his look, 'I know the war's over, but we're still on rations. Ask Rose how to get one.'

Later that evening, when the family were all together, Freddie had a favour to ask.

'I've to go back to my unit to be officially demobbed and, hopefully, collect my demob gratuity.'

Elsa, who was sitting on the fringe of the group, looked alarmed. 'I come too?' she cried.

Freddie, sensing her anxiety, went to her side and put a comforting hand on her shoulder.

'The journey will be too tiring for you, best stay here.' He looked around at his family's expectant faces. 'Will you look after her?'

Mary responded quickly. 'Of course we will.'

Both Elsa and Freddie looked relieved.

Up early the next morning, Freddie said

to Ted, 'The sooner I go the quicker I'll be back.'

The day eased into its routine, Mary washing up and Elsa drying. There was no conversation between them, but Mary tuned into the wireless and music filled the silence. That task done, Elsa excused herself and went to her room. Mary glanced at the clock: time for a cup of tea before shopping. She called Elsa to come and join her. And, just as Elsa was coming into the kitchen with a garment in her hand, which she was sewing for her baby, Mrs Fisher tapped on the back door and entered, as it was her custom to do.

Her eyes and Elsa's met. Mary, flustered, said in a rush, 'This is our Freddie's wife.'

'Aye, I saw her the day she came.' Taking in Elsa's pregnant figure she remarked, 'It didn't take him long. Is that tea I can smell?'

'Just about to pour, sit down.'

Vera Fisher sat in Ted's chair and turned to speak to Elsa, who was still standing by the table. 'Have you settled in then, lass?'

At this friendly greeting, Elsa replied, 'Thank you, yes.'

Vera stared at Elsa, not believing what she had just heard. 'Say it again,' she said rather loudly, her face hardening.

Elsa glanced at Mary, saying, 'Did I say it wrong?'

Vera was up on her feet. Her eyes blazing with hatred, she screeched, 'She's a bloody

Nazi! A German! She killed my lads!' Before Mary could stop her, she launched herself at Elsa, knocking the young woman onto the floor.

Mary screamed, but Elsa didn't utter a sound, she just cringed in the corner like a wounded animal, covering her face with her hands.

Vera was just about to relaunch herself, when Mary caught her upraised arm and pulled her back.

'Stop it, stop it. You'll harm the baby.'

'Baby!' Vera spluttered. 'A German bastard!' With that outburst, Vera broke into the most terrible, howling sobs.

'What's going on?' Alf came dashing in from next door, out of breath. 'Sounds like somebody's being murdered.' Then he saw Vera, bent double over a chair, sobbing her heart out. 'What's happened?' But Vera was past talking. He glanced round to see the young woman cowering in the corner and Mary, ashen-faced, clutching at her heart.

Mary managed to whisper, 'Take her home, Alf.' He obeyed, but wondered what on earth had gone on in this usually respectable, friendly house. Taking hold of Vera's arm, he gently manoeuvred her from the kitchen and back into her own home.

Mary, getting her breath back, went over to where Elsa was slumped in the corner. At the sight of the fear in her eyes, Mary dropped to her knees.

'Oh, dear,' she cried. Reaching out, she put her arms about Elsa, feeling the uncontrollable trembling of her body; and Mary prayed that the baby was safe.

After a few minutes, Mary reached for a chair and, using it to lever herself to her feet, she said, 'Come on, I'll help you up.' She extended both hands to Elsa and with all her strength, pulled her up and onto her feet. For a while, she just held Elsa close until her body became steadier. Then she said, 'It's best if you go back to bed.'

The young woman didn't reply, nor did she protest as Mary led her to her room. She helped her into the bed and covered her with the counterpane.

Concerned, she asked Elsa, 'Would you like me to send for the doctor?'

Elsa shook her head. 'Water, please.'

After Elsa had drunk her fill and settled down, an anxious Mary sat by her bedside, watching until she was sure that her breathing was regular. She went to fetch her knitting and to continue her vigil by her daughter-in-law's side, the shopping forgotten.

It was late afternoon when Elsa stirred. Putting down her knitting, Mary watched as the young woman opened her eyes and, on seeing her mother-in-law, smiled weakly. Relief flooded Mary, for if anything untoward had happened to Elsa while Freddie was away, she'd have felt responsible. In hindsight, if only she had told Vera about Elsa, that ugly incident could have been avoided. Vera would have vented her anger elsewhere and by the time she had come into contact with Elsa, she would have calmed down.

Elsa pushed back the bedcovers and eased her legs over and placed her feet on the floor.

'Hungry,' she said.

'That's a good sign, you're feeding two.'

Seeing Elsa's puzzled look, Mary said, 'You and the baby.'

They drank tea and ate cheese sandwiches. As they did so, for the first time the question arose in Mary's mind: what must it have been like in her daughter-in-law's homeland? They must have suffered too. She asked, 'Elsa, have you any family?'

She watched Elsa's eyes well with tears; in a voice so sad, but clear, she replied, 'My parents were killed in the bombing, my sister and two brothers were killed in action.' She brushed away her tears, saying, 'I am a lucky one, I have Freddie.'

Mary, feeling her heart contract with sadness, took hold of Elsa's hands. 'My dear, we are your family now.'

Rose felt appalled when her mother told her what had happened to Elsa. But equally, she could understand Mrs Fisher's feelings of hatred. In her mind, Elsa represented Hitler and the whole of the German nation, who were responsible for the deaths of her sons. Rose sat at her desk, in a corner of the storage warehouse, staring into space. She prided herself on being able to help people in distress, but she had no idea how to resolve this problem.

'Rose, anything wrong?' A voice broke into her troubled thoughts.

Startled, Rose turned. 'Mrs Butler,' she stammered. Then it all came out, the whole wretched story. 'And,' Rose finished, 'it has driven a wedge between Mam and Mrs Fisher.' She sighed. 'They have been friends for years, ever since Mrs Fisher acted as midwife and delivered me at birth. What with enduring the war and now this. Oh, I wish Freddie had married a British girl.' She brushed away an angry tear.

Mrs Butler sat down on the old wooden chair.

'Rose.' Her voice was gentle. 'We must look at this logically, the main concern being Elsa and her unborn child. You'd never forgive yourself if anything should happen to them.'

Rose looked up in horror. 'Of course not! I want her to be safe. Elsa is nice. It's just that she's a German, living in our house down a street where half of it is missing, bombed by the Germans, and where many neighbours were killed.' She let out a huge sigh. 'So her presence is a painful reminder. And Mam will have to face the neighbours each day.'

'And you, Rose?' asked Mrs Butler. 'How will this affect your relationship with Joe?'

Rose shifted her cramped body on the uncomfortable chair, feeling ashamed because she hadn't given Joe any thought.

'I'm meeting Joe tonight so I will tell him.' She bit on her lip; how would he react? Joe's wife and unborn child had been killed in a bombing raid, and Peter lost his mother at such a tender age.

As if guessing her thoughts, Mrs Butler said, 'Joe is a good man. He will understand.'

But will he? Rose questioned.

She worked late, going home in the dark, not wanting to see any neighbours. She hurried into the house. Was this how it was going to be, avoiding friends and neighbours, or would they avoid her? It was quiet in the kitchen. Ted was sitting in his chair reading the paper and Mary was at the stove. She turned to greet Rose.

'Hello, love, busy day?'

Rose noticed her mother's drawn face and her heart sank. She tried to think of something cheery to say, but couldn't bring anything to mind. Instead she replied, 'Just the usual.'

Ted looked up from his paper and Rose caught his eye.

'Anything interesting?' she asked.

'Nothing but doom and gloom. You wouldn't think we'd won the war.' Ted shook the paper with great vigour as if to emphasize his point. 'And no meat again for tea. A man needs his strength to work,' he said harshly.

Rose glanced quickly at her mother, who was still standing at the stove, her shoulders slumped, stirring the meagre contents of a pan. Rose's heart leaped in pain for her mother's distress. She went over and put a comforting arm around Mary's waist and was shocked to feel her thinness, which was hidden by the loosely tied, wrap-around apron.

Mary didn't look at her daughter as she spoke. 'I was late going shopping and I could only buy a few veg. There wasn't even a bone to be had.'

'Oh, Mam! Don't worry.' She glanced at the table and saw the half loaf of bread. 'We've bread to fill up on.' Rose made a quick decision. 'Tomorrow, I'll shop before I go to work.'

'Oh, will you, love?' Mary cried with relief. 'I'll dish up now. Call Elsa.'

For the first time since going out together, Rose was not looking forward to seeing Joe. Slowly she made her way down Crowle Street to Joe's lodgings. The sky was a navy blue and the night air smelt chilly and a sprinkling of frost sparkled on the pavements. She tossed words over in her mind, trying to think of the right ones to explain Elsa's presence. The truth: what else could she say?

She arrived at the front door and knocked. Immediately it was opened by Peter, his voice excited as he asked, 'Have you brought me my goodies?'

Her gloved hand felt the paper bag of boiled sweets in her pocket. Affected by his cheerful manner, she replied lightly, 'As if I would forget a promise to you.'

Then Joe was there to admonish his son. 'Now, Peter, that isn't good manners to ask. You should wait.' He kissed Rose on her cheek. 'You are cold. Come and sit by the fire.' Indoors, Joe took her coat and she handed the bag of sweets to Peter, saying, 'These are a whole week's coupons so make them last.'

He quickly popped one into his mouth and his young eyes lit up. 'Thank you, Aunty Rose,' and he hugged her. She felt the comforting warmth of his sturdy little body.

'Guess what I got from school today,' he chattered. He drew her into the kitchen and produced a big red apple. 'It's come all the way from Canada. Teacher's going to draw a map so we know where Canada is. Do you know where Canada is?' His warm brown eyes looked earnestly into her clouded blue ones.

She smiled at his enthusiasm. 'It's across

the Atlantic Ocean so the cargo of apples would have come by ship.' Another question began to form on his lips, but Joe intervened.

'Come on, young man, it's your bedtime,' he said, ruffling Peter's hair.

'But, Daddy, I want–'

'I want, never gets. Bed, I said.'

Not a boy to give up, Peter asked, 'Can Rose read me a story, please?'

Over the top of Peter's head, Joe caught Rose's eye and she smiled a yes.

'Just one story.'

'I've got Rupert the Bear.' Before he could utter another word, Joe steered him away.

The room became quiet except for the clicking of Mrs Mitchell's knitting needles. She was sitting by the fire and Rose turned to her, saying, 'Hello, Mrs Mitchell. How are you?'

She laid her knitting down on her lap and flexed her fingers.

'I'm all right, just a bit of arthritis. Joe tells me you are to marry. You make a lovely family. I wish my Maureen could meet a nice man to settle down with. That's why I'm moving in with her, to look after the children so she can get a job, have a bit of money and then she can go out on a night.'

Rose sat down on one of the kitchen chairs and tried to make conversation, to keep her mind off the problem of telling Joe about Elsa.

'That sounds a lovely idea.'

Mrs Mitchell picked up the socks she was knitting and silence fell again. Rose could hear her own breathing sounding so loud in her head. She wanted to feel calm, but couldn't. She gabbled, 'Have you heard anything from the landlord about Joe taking over the tenancy?'

'No, he said he doesn't make snap decisions.' Rose felt her face go sombre. Mrs Mitchell was quick to notice. 'I'm sure it will be fine. You and Joe will make good tenants.'

'Rose,' called Joe from upstairs.

'Story time,' she said, and called back, 'I'm coming.'

Finally, Peter was settled and Mrs Mitchell made her cocoa to take to bed, saying, 'I like to read in bed.'

At last, Rose and Joe were alone together. They sat at the kitchen table with cups of tea and a piece of spice loaf each.

'What's the matter, Rose?' Joe asked. 'Not having second thoughts?'

Rose stared at him, for a full second, before she grasped what he meant. She reached out and gently touched his hand, feeling its strength, and said, 'No, Joe, but you might.'

He looked puzzled. 'Is there something wrong?'

'Freddie is home and he's married.' Angry tears threatened.

'A wife!' Joe's eyes glinted. 'Lucky fellow.

Surely that shouldn't interfere with us?' He looked into her troubled eyes.

Rose pushed back her chair and stood up. Turning away, she couldn't bear to see the pain that would surely fill him.

'She's pregnant.' Her heart began to pound. To steady herself, she clutched the back of the chair and then took a deep breath. Her voice almost a whisper, she forced out the words, 'She's German.'

'A German woman! But why?' Joe asked.

The tears that earlier threatened flowed and a sob caught in her throat. Joe pushed away his chair and was by Rose's side, gathering her into his arms. Feeling his strength, she clung to him and sobbed.

'Rose, my darling girl,' he whispered, his warm breath fanning through her hair. He held her until her sobs ceased. Then, releasing her, he produced a clean handkerchief from his trouser pocket, and gently wiped her tear-stained face. The handkerchief dropped to the floor, as his fingers slid down her neck, caressing her soft skin. His touch sent tingles down her spine. She knew she didn't want to lose her man. She lifted up her face, her lips seeking his. The kiss was gentle at first, then urgent as passion flowed through their bodies.

'God, Rose, I want you, need you.' Then abruptly Joe pulled away from her. 'Sorry,' he murmured, 'I shouldn't take advantage of you.'

She stared at him, her emotions in confusion. 'Don't you love me?' Her voice trembled.

He reached on the table for his cigarettes, his fingers unsteady as he struck the match, inhaled and let out a plume of smoke.

Tenderly, he spoke. 'Rose, I love you and I want to marry you and for us to be together for always. I long to make love to you, but I don't want to risk you having a baby before we are married. When this house becomes mine and my job is secure, we can marry. I don't want us to start off wrong-footed. And as for your brother marrying a German woman, that's his business, not ours.'

She felt her heart quicken, but her voice was soft and steady as she replied, 'Thank you, Joe, for being so understanding. I love you.'

SEVENTEEN

The dismal month of January dragged on into February and March. Rose was busier than ever. Sally was still avoiding her, and she hadn't seen much of Joe, only the fleeting of meetings and snatched conversations. Joe had a setback; Mrs Mitchell moved in with her daughter, but the landlord said the house was going to a more needy family of six. Not to be daunted, Joe managed to find lodgings in a terraced house in Ferries Street with a Mr and Mrs Stepney, a childless couple in their fifties. Mr Stepney worked in a joiner's shop, and Mrs Stepney suffered from a heart condition, so she wasn't able to offer Joe any of the facilities and comforts afforded by Mrs Mitchell. She would cook their evening meal along with hers and her husband's, but he would have to do his own washing and ironing and keep his room clean. Joe and Peter had the small bedroom at the back of the house with a view of the backways of the terraces running parallel.

Rose arrived at Joe's new lodgings. Its net curtains over the sash windows were grubby and the front step was grimy. Before Rose could knock on the door, it opened and Joe was there, a finger on his lips for her to be quiet. He ushered her indoors. In the dark, smelly room, Rose squinted, accustoming her eyes to the gloom. It was cluttered with heavy furniture.

Joe had taken hold of her arm and whispered, 'They are both asleep.'

Rose was puzzled, wondering who he was referring to.

'Mr and Mrs Stepney, they like a sleep on a Sunday afternoon.' He grinned, mischievously. 'So we have the room to ourselves.'

'Fancy,' was all she could muster and laughed at the situation. Peter, sitting in front of the fire, playing with his toy fire engine, looked up. His sad little face and his eyes lit up when he saw Rose and he hastily scrambled to his feet and into her arms for a hug. She felt the sturdiness of his young body. He was putting on weight. She kissed the top of his tousled head and murmured, 'You're growing up fast.'

'I'm nearly a big boy,' he said proudly.

'I'll put the kettle on,' Joe said. 'Sorry, no cake. Mrs Stepney doesn't bake.'

Rose dropped down on her knees to look at Peter's new shining red fire engine. If things were different at home, she could have invited Joe and Peter for Sunday dinner. But having Elsa there made things awkward... Joe, as if sensing her feelings, said as he brought two steaming cups of tea to the table, 'I am sorry I didn't get to rent Mrs Mitchell's house, but I am still searching. In the meantime, Peter and I have a roof over our heads.' He was silent a moment, then added, 'Next Sunday afternoon, shall we have a stroll to East Park and on the way we can check out the houses?' He glanced at Rose's solemn face.

Rose forced herself to reply positively, 'Good idea.' Joe reached for her hand and held it tenderly. 'It won't always be like this, Rose. It's the repercussion of war. It takes its toll.'

Rose put her other hand over Joe's, remembering his tragic loss and Peter's. She whispered, 'It takes time to come to terms with peace after war and it's not easy to pick up the threads of life.' She momentarily lapsed into silence, and then an idea came to her. 'Joe, I'll keep my eyes open for any houses or flats that become vacant to rent. I spend a lot of my time filling in forms for families to be rehoused; I'll bring you a form.' She glanced out of the window. 'The sun's come out. Shall we have a walk?'

'Can I see the boats?' Peter asked, his face lighting up with enthusiasm.

Hand in hand, Joe and Rose strolled down Earle's Road to the foreshore of the River Humber, with Peter running ahead, eager to see the boats and ships in Alexandra Dock. The wind blew Rose's hair across her face and eyes, and she giggled, trying to tame the unruly strands back into place, but without success.

'Here, let me,' Joe said, halting their steps. Gently, he brushed her hair back into place and secured it with a hairgrip. 'There.' He looked into her eyes.

Rose caught her breath, for she saw the longing in his eyes. He needed her as she needed him. She pulled him close, feeling the tremble of his body as he leaned into her.

'Rose,' he whispered. 'Oh, Rose.'

'Daddy, Daddy, look, boats,' Peter called, enthusiastically.

They broke apart and Joe went to his son's side. Rose watched father and son; she loved them both so dearly. More than anything, she wanted them to be a proper family, to be together. Love conquered everything or so they say, but the practicalities of life needed to be attended to. And we need somewhere for us to live together.

'Hello, Rose.' She turned to see Mr Elliott peddling his bike towards her. He pulled up sharply on his worn-out brakes, his tyres skidding. She stepped back so she didn't catch the dirty spray. 'Sorry,' he apologized, 'I'm just off to yonder.' He pointed to rough scrubland, just inland from the shore. Rose followed his gaze, but couldn't see anything. 'Land for allotments and I need to get my claim in fast.'

Joe came up, catching part of the conversation. 'Allotments, you say?'

'Aye, if you want one, best get there quick.' With that, he pedalled away.

Joe looked at Rose and they both laughed. 'What are we waiting for! Peter?' he called.

All three set off in the direction to where Mr Elliott was heading. When they reached the spot, surprisingly, quite a few people were there. Two official-looking men were marking out plots of land.

Rose stared at the rough, coarse ground.

'It looks as hard as iron,' she said to Joe.

He nodded in agreement and said, 'But it's earth.' He rubbed his head, thoughtfully. 'It's a challenge.' He bent down and touched the tired soil, scraping it with his pocket-knife; he picked up a handful, letting it trickle through his fingers. 'It needs plenty of back-breaking work to bring it up to scratch to grow a crop.'

So the next Sunday, instead of a sedate walk to East Park, Rose found herself walking alone down Earle's Road, but she wasn't unhappy. She strode on purposefully, swinging the basket on her arm, humming a catchy tune she'd heard on the radio. She waved to the distant figures, but they were too absorbed in their labours to notice her approach.

She walked up to them, her shadow falling across their vision. Joe looked up and smiled, and said, 'Hello, love. You are a welcome sight.' He laid down his spade, brushed the sweat from his brow with the sleeve of his shirt, and then kissed Rose on the cheek.

Peter, who had been playing with another boy of his age, came to Rose's side. She gave him an affectionate hug. 'You want to see what I've got in my basket?'

'Please, I'm hungry,' he said, hopefully.

All three sat on a makeshift seat, a plank of wood resting on three bricks at each end. Rose reached into her basket, saying, 'This is your very own picnic.' Her heart contracted with joy and love as Peter's face lit up in anticipation. 'Egg sandwiches,' she announced. One egg from Mr Reilly, which she had boiled and mashed with a drop of milk, adding salt and pepper. She was surprised how far it went. 'And for afters, Mam has made you her special fairy buns, with wings on.' She watched as both her men tucked in. For Joe, she poured tea from the flask and she produced a glass jar of milk for Peter.

Between mouthfuls, Joe said, 'My, this is a great treat.' Over Peter's head, who was sitting between them, he winked at Rose.

Peter, after eating and drinking his fill, went to play, and explore. Joe and Rose sat quietly, talking of plans for their future, of their hopes. Rose sighed heavily, and Joe took hold of her hand, saying, 'We have to be patient, Rose.'

'I know,' she said, and leaned her head on his shoulder.

'Dad, Dad!' shouted Peter as he squatted on the dirt earth. 'Come and look.'

Joe jumped to his feet and went to see the cause of Peter's excitement. He hunched down and looked at the long, moving earthworm.

'My, that's a beaut.'

Mr Elliott strode over and glanced down at the worm. 'Well, I am blowed. First worm, so there must be more. They irrigate the soil, make it fertile. I think we're onto a winner here, lad.' He bent down and ruffled Peter's hair. Then he reached for his baccy tin from the pocket of his old jacket. 'Fancy a roll, pal?' he asked Joe.

Later, Rose picked up her empty basket and they made their way home. She watched father and son chattering. Peter had lost his forlorn look brought on by all the disruption in his young life and was now a happy little boy. She caught up with the men in her life, and Peter slipped his hand into hers and looked up and smiled. Joe looked across his son's head to Rose, saying, 'Happy, love?'

A few days later, she had been out on a family call, when Rose spied Betty, pushing a pram, ahead of her in Wyke Street.

'Betty,' she called to the hurrying figure. But Betty didn't hear. It took Rose a couple of minutes to catch up with her. Betty, a headscarf covering most of her face, didn't look up as Rose walked by her side. 'Betty, what's wrong?' The only reply was a snivel-ling sound. Rose put a restraining hand on Betty's arm to slow her down, but she shook it off. They were passing wasteland, weeds sprouting in dusty earth, between bricks and broken framework of once family homes. No one was about, so Rose put her hand on the pram handle and pulled it to stop. The motion jerked Betty and her scarf fell to her shoulders to reveal a swollen black eye.

'Betty!' Rose gasped. 'Who did that to you?'

Betty began to sob uncontrollably, her body shaking.

'Come on, let's get you home.' Rose guided Betty and the pram to her house. Thankfully, the baby was asleep and didn't stir.

Once in the kitchen and Betty seated on the old chair, Rose filled the kettle and put it on the gas ring to boil. When the tea was made and poured, Betty's with a spoonful of sugar, Rose let her drink a few sips, then said, 'Now, Betty, tell me.'

Betty raised her head and said in a muffled tone, 'It's him. He lost it.' Her voice broke into sobs. 'He was never like this before, never. He just went wild. Mad. And then he cried.' She looked pleadingly at Rose. 'I don't know what to do. I'm frightened.'

From the passage came the wail of the baby in the pram. 'The children, did he?'

'No, he never touched the bairns. But they were frightened. What am I going to do, Rose?'

'What time is he home from work?'

Betty glanced at the clock on the mantelpiece. 'Ten past five.'

'I'm at the office until seven. If he wants to talk or if I can help in any way, I'll be there.'

Betty looked unsure and bit on her lip. Rose added, 'Let him have his tea first, and see that the children are out of the room. Ask him if he wants to come, but leave it to him to decide.'

Later that evening, Rose yawned and glanced at her wristwatch: 6.30 pm. She'd finished her paperwork and was thinking of home, and her tea. Her stomach rumbled. Perhaps Bob Duncan wouldn't come. Some men didn't want to discuss what was worrying them, especially with a woman. It was then she saw him, standing in the doorway, cap in hand.

She smiled and said, 'Come over, Mr Duncan, sit down.'

Slowly he came towards her, unsure of himself as he negotiated the piles of boxes. He seated himself on the chair she indicated. He put his hands in his pocket, then drew them out and began twiddling his thumbs. He shuffled on the chair, not meeting her eyes.

She opened the top drawer of her desk and brought out the emergency rations, as instructed by Mrs Butler. Rose opened the packet of Woodbines and proffered a cigarette to Bob Duncan and passed him the box of matches. His hand shook as he struck the match and lit the cigarette. She waited, watching him puff away until he began to unwind.

He spoke first. 'I'm a right bastard. I hate myself. I never meant to hurt Betty. I love her. It's just…' His voice trailed away.

Rose waited. She was used to hearing expletives from men so it didn't bother her. He drew deeply on the cigarette, then exhaled. Then he looked Rose full in the face.

'It's Civvy Street. It's not the same. They say it's peace time, but for me it's hell. I never expected it, not after fighting for king and country.' His body slumped in total dejection.

Rose needed to say something positive to him. She took a deep breath and said, 'You are working with the same firm as before the war?' She recalled Betty telling her.

'Oh yeah, I have a job. I'm the general dogsbody. At everyone's beck and call, sweeping the factory floor, fetching this and that. I ask you. Me, a corporal in the army. Men had to answer to me. And now I'm nothing. You wouldn't have thought I'd fought in the bleeding war. And for what?'

'Could you ask your boss for a better job?'

Bob stubbed out his cigarette in the tin lid, which served as an ashtray. 'It didn't do me any good. He said I'm lucky to have a job to come home to.'

Rose agreed, but she didn't say so. That wasn't the answer and there was no quick solution. She thought of Joe and the setbacks he faced. Life wasn't easy for a returning member of the armed forces or their families. The glory of winning the war fades fast and peace brings a whole new set of problems. They both sat in solemn silence.

Then an idea came to her. 'Bob, have you thought about an allotment?' He looked puzzled. She described as best she could. 'It's a plot of land where you can grow your own vegetables. There's an allotment site near the foreshore off Earle's Road. On Sunday, come along, bring your family. I believe there are still a few plots to be taken.' She crossed her fingers under the desk. 'Think of it as a new venture.' She offered him another cigarette and watched as he headed for the door, his stature more upright than when he came in.

EIGHTEEN

Rose had gone to bed early, but was unable to sleep because of the raised voices coming from downstairs. She couldn't hear what was being said though Freddie sounded angry and Elsa frustrated; so much so that she was speaking in her native tongue. Suddenly, the front room burst open and Freddie belted out. 'I do my bloody best!' He hurtled up the stairs, into his room, slamming the door. For a few seconds, the whole house shook.

Elsa's sobs floated up. Should she go down and comfort her? Though on reflection, Rose didn't want to interfere between man and wife, not knowing what caused the argument. Maybe in the morning, Elsa might confide in her.

In the next room, Freddie was moving about and Rose could smell the smoke of his cigarette. She huddled down in the bed and drew the counterpane over her ears to shut out Elsa's sobs. And, not for the first time, she wondered why Freddie and Elsa occupied separate bedrooms. It didn't seem natural for married couples to sleep apart, not in the same house. Ted had managed to secure a double bed in exchange for the old sofa, so there was ample room for Freddie and Elsa to share. But Freddie muttered something about Elsa needing her rest and he didn't want to disturb her as he rose early for work. Considerate of him, Rose thought, but if you were married, surely that didn't matter? When she and Joe married, she would always want to share a bed with him, no matter what the circumstances were.

Thinking of Joe, Rose drifted into sleep.

The next morning, Elsa kept to her bed. Rose came into the kitchen and glanced at her mother. Mary was sitting at the table enjoying her breakfast of tea and toast, and remarked, 'It happens between married couples, they have words and differences. Best let them sort it out.'

'I know, Mam, but I suppose it's with me

helping to sort out other people's problems.'

Mary eyed her thoughtfully and said, 'Do you think they are happy, Freddie and Elsa?'

Rose sat opposite her mother. 'I don't know. It must be difficult for them. They don't go out together. I know Elsa is frightened of upsetting the neighbours. The incident with Mrs Fisher really scared her. But they could go out for a walk, when it's dark.'

Mary sighed. 'Maybe when the baby is born, things will get better.'

That evening, walking home, Rose was startled when the screeching noise of bicycle brakes skidded alongside her. She turned to see the strained face of Freddie. He swung his leg over the crossbar, dismounted and walked alongside her.

'Hello,' she said, 'had a busy day?'

'Same as usual,' he said, in a deadpan voice.

As they walked down the street, his eyes downcast, Freddie mumbled, 'I'm sorry about last night, didn't mean to disturb you or Mam and Dad.'

'It can't be easy, not having a place of your own.' She thought of hers and Joe's predicament. 'It's difficult with the housing shortage. Some people with big houses are turning them into rooms or flats to let. But as soon as their advertisement appears in the newspaper, hundreds of people apply.' She looked at her brother, but he seemed lost in his own thoughts so she wasn't sure if he had heard her or not.

She heard the despair in his voice as he spoke. 'I suppose that's part of the problem. But there's more to it.'

'More to it,' she said, slightly baffled. 'What, Freddie?'

His voice sad, he said, 'I can't tell you, ever.' He mounted his bike and rode away.

Rose stared after him, her heart heavy. What did he mean? Whatever it was, it had left him scared. So lost in her thoughts, she didn't look where she was walking and caught her shoe heel on the uneven, broken pavement. Before she could save herself, her knees hit the cold, hard stone, jarring her whole body. She let out a cry of pain and irritation.

'Rose,' an anxious voice called. She felt gentle hands touch her shoulders. 'Take a deep breath. You're in shock.' Then after a few moments, she was carefully helped to her feet and Rose met the concerned face of the young woman. It was Sally, who hadn't spoken to her in weeks because of Freddie marrying a German girl.

'Thank you,' Rose gasped. She looked down at her legs to see her only pair of stockings sporting big holes in each knee and with ladders running in all directions. 'Oh, dear,' she exclaimed. She made to walk on, thinking that Sally wouldn't want to be seen with her, but she wobbled unsteady on her feet, her legs feeling weak.

'Come here, you daft bat,' Sally said, and linked her arm in Rose's.

Together in companionable silence they crossed over and round the corner into Hill Street. Had Freddie gone straight home? Rose felt uneasy about seeing him, not sure what to say to him after his strange statement.

They came to Sally's house, and Rose was just about to slip out her arm from Sally's when she said, 'Rose, come and have a cup of tea with me.'

Rose glanced towards the house. 'But your mother?'

'Mam's at her sister's. Anyway, she doesn't hold a grudge. She misses your mam.'

Gratefully, Rose went into the Wrays' house. It was quiet and calm. Sally poked the fire, stirring up the flames, then put the kettle on to boil. She left Rose sitting in front of the fire and went upstairs.

Coming down a few minutes later, Sally handed Rose a packet. 'Go on, undo it.'

With trembling fingers, Rose eased the packet open to reveal a new pair of fully fashioned silk stockings. 'But I can't accept them,' she said.

'Oh, give over and stop the dramatics. I've got another pair. It's one of the perks of working at Woollies. We get to buy the merchandise when it comes in. Now take off those torn ones and I'll bathe your knees and then you can put the new stockings on, and no one will be any the wiser.'

Ten minutes later, as they sipped their tea, they caught up on each other's life. Rose told about Joe and his allotment, and Sally told her about going out with Frank.

'I'll let you into a secret,' she said. 'We are going steady. We're not rushing into anything until Frank gets a proper job, so we can save up.'

'That's wonderful news. So you've given up loving and leaving them and having a good time?' Rose added, mischievously.

Sally blushed, and babbled, 'That was just talk. I quite fancied your Freddie at one time, but he wasn't interested.' Rose mused over this. How different it would have been to have Sally as her sister-in-law. But life, she was learning fast, was never quite so simple.

The following Saturday night, Peter came to sleep, so that Joe and Rose could go to the cinema. His landlady, Mrs Stepney, didn't like babysitting. When Joe and Peter arrived, Freddie and Elsa were in the front room listening to the wireless, which Freddie bought second-hand.

'Come in lads,' said Ted, eager for their company.

'And see what I've made,' said Mary. She opened the oven door and Peter peeped inside.

'What is it?' He sniffed. It smelt good. Mary produced her oven cloth and carefully lifted the dish from the oven. Peter's mouth watered and he licked his lips.

'There,' said Mary, as she placed the dish on table. 'It's bread pudding. It's a treat, though not like I used to make it before the war. Then I added grated lemon, orange rinds and crystallized peel. But I'm lucky because Mrs Wray's sister, she lives in the country, makes marmalade and Mrs Wray gave me a jar.'

Rose was pleased that her mother was once again friendly with Sally's mam, but Mrs Fisher still hadn't come round. She'd crossed over the street if she saw any of them.

In the cinema, they sat on the back row; Lovers' Row, as it was known. Joe slipped his arm around Rose's waist and she snuggled close to him. They didn't get many chances to be on their own and this was a wonderful opportunity. She loved the feel of Joe's strong arms around her. It made her feel safe, needed and loved.

'I love you, Joe Tennison,' she whispered in his ear. His arm tightened around her and she felt the beat of his heart.

He kissed her, passionately. Then he looked into her eyes. 'I love you, Rose. I never thought I'd love again. You mean the world to me.' His voice was thick with emotion.

'Shush!' a voice said in the darkness. They

both grinned and settled to watch the film: *The Jolson Story*, starring Evelyn Keyes and Larry Parks. It was an uplifting film though sad in parts; Rose loved it all: the music, the singing, dancing, costumes and the brilliant colour. On the way home, they sang songs from the film. Joe, entering into the spirit, went down on one knee and rendered a line from Al Jolson's signature tune, 'Mammy'.

The sound of clapping came from the shadows and Sally and Frank appeared. Rose and Joe stood perfectly still, clasping hands.

'That was nice,' Sally said.

'Aye,' echoed Frank. 'We saw the film yesterday.'

The two girls walked in front and the two men behind, all chatting about films they had seen. Then there was a lull and silence fell. On impulse, Rose turned round and said to Frank, 'We'll have to make up a foursome and go dancing.'

Frank looked taken aback and glanced at Sally. 'I don't know. I'm no good at dancing. I can shuffle a bit, that's all.'

Rose had another thought. 'What if I find someone willing to teach ballroom dancing?'

Sally slipped her arm through Frank's, saying, 'It could be fun. Shall we give it a try?'

'I'd rather play rugby,' Frank responded. Sally pinched his arm, and he added quickly, 'But if it makes you happy, I'll give it a try.'

Joe spoke up. 'How about watching a

match sometime?' The conversation turned to which team to watch; there was a choice of two rugby teams in the city.

Rose commented, 'Dad always says we should support the rugby team our side of the river.'

'Rovers it is, then,' said Joe.

Reaching home, the two couples parted. Nothing more was said about ballroom dancing lessons or watching a rugby match. But Rose decided not to let opportunities slip by. Quietly, they went into the house. The kitchen was warm and cosy. Ted was in bed, but Mary was waiting up, sitting by the fire, knitting a matinee coat for the expected baby of Freddie and Elsa. She wound her knitting up, saying, 'Kettle's on the boil and I've saved you some bread pudding. It's in the oven.' She looked at Joe, who was standing awkwardly by the table. 'Take your coat off, lad, and go up and see Peter.'

Noiselessly, Joe went up the stairs to Rose's room. He pushed open the door to see his son asleep in the little camp bed at the foot of Rose's bed. Peter was lying in the foetal position, with one arm outstretched. For a few moments Joe watched the gentle rise and fall of Peter's body, his heart overwhelmed with love for him. Then his eyes strayed round Rose's room and he moved forward to touch her pillow, breathing in her beautiful scent, and wishing...

He went downstairs. Mary said goodnight and Joe sat in her seat. Rose set a tray of mugs of cocoa and plates of pudding that Mary had saved for them on the wooden stool between them. They talked about the lack of housing.

'Oh, Joe, everything takes such a long time. Nothing has come up in housing or rooms to let.' She felt like weeping with frustration; instead she reached for her mug of cocoa.

Joe, sensing her downheartedness, said, 'Let me tell you some good news.' She sipped her drink, looking over the top of the mug at him. 'Betty's husband, Bob, has got an allotment. He's a good digger and he brings his son Billy along. We allotment holders are thinking of setting up a club, just something informal, to meet and swap ideas. What do you think?'

'Joe, it's a marvellous idea. Betty will be pleased to know that Bob is making an effort to settle back into Civvy Street.'

Rose got up and went to Joe and kissed him, tasting his bread pudding on her lips. He pulled her closer and she sat on his knees, pressing her body against his, feeling his heart beat against hers.

'Joe,' she whispered.

The kitchen door opened and a weary voice said, 'Water.' The heavily pregnant figure of Elsa, swathed in a nightgown, stood there, her face ashen. Quickly, Rose was on her feet and at Elsa's side, leading her to Ted's chair, and went to fetch a glass of water.

Meanwhile, Joe had risen to his feet and was putting on his coat. He signalled to Rose that he was going and blew her a kiss. Rose would have loved that kiss on her lips.

She turned her attention back to Elsa, who was sipping the water. Rose guessed that she wasn't sleeping very well and was uncomfortable. She couldn't understand Freddie's attitude, his lack of concern regarding his wife and their unborn child.

She left Elsa for a moment and went to her room to check on her bed and found it cold. Another reason for a husband, to keep you warm in bed. She thought about going to wake up Freddie, but if he was in one of his strange moods, it might make the situation worse.

Back in the kitchen, an idea came to her. 'Elsa, your bed is cold. I'll take the shelf out of the oven and put it into your bed to warm it up.' Elsa didn't seem to understand, but she watched. Cautiously, with a towel in her hand, Rose took out the hot oven shelf, wrapping the towel securely around it, and went to place it in Elsa's bed. Then after five minutes, she helped Elsa back into bed, first moving the covered shelf further down the bed so that Elsa could rest her feet on it. She relit the night candle and then sat on the edge of the bed, holding Elsa's hand.

'Forgive me,' Elsa murmured.

'You are no trouble.' Rose stayed by Elsa's side until she went to sleep.

Upstairs, in her own room, Rose was momentarily startled by seeing a sleeping Peter there. Her heart filled with love as she bent to kiss his forehead and he smiled in his sleep. She climbed into bed. She was so lucky to have Joe and Peter in her life.

NINETEEN

Rose went home bone weary. It had been a fraught day at work, one crisis after another. People losing their tempers, and who could blame them. She couldn't perform miracles, or scrape up money for the unemployed, who needed to feed their families.

Her mother was busy at the stove and on the table stood a batch of newly baked bread cakes. She looked up as Rose entered the kitchen.

'You look done in, love. Sit down and have a cuppa while the meal's ready. Ted, will you pour?'

Rose wriggled her toes to ease their ache and put on her comfy slippers. She sat down to drink the cup of tea Ted handed her. A delicious aroma of bacon frying filled the kitchen and usually the smell of food uplifted Rose, but not today. Not when the picture of the pinched faces of the little children who clung to their mothers' skirts was so imprinted in her mind. Tomorrow, she would have a word with Mrs Butler to see what could be done to help. Even if the children only had one decent meal a week, it was better than nothing.

'Well I never,' Ted exclaimed, rattling the newspaper he was engrossed in. 'I always knew he was a wrong 'un.'

Rose glanced at her father, not taking particular notice of his words. Her thoughts were buzzing in her head, like a bee caught in a web. 'I never liked him.'

'Who?' asked Mary, setting warm plates on the table.

'Why, Harry Carter of course.'

At the mention of that name, Rose shook herself. 'Harry?' she exclaimed. 'What's he done?' She hadn't seen him since they parted, and never gave him a thought.

'Involved in black market fiddling,' Ted retorted with venom. 'He's got what he deserves, a prison sentence.'

'A prison sentence!' gasped Rose. 'Isn't that a bit harsh?'

'No more than he deserves.' Ted returned to reading his newspaper. Then he looked over the top of the newspaper at Rose, and said, 'You've had a lucky escape, my girl.'

Strange, she felt sorry for Harry. Once she had loved him, or at least she thought she had. He was soon out of her mind. Between the frustrations at work, because of lack of funds and facilities, and juggling the atmosphere at home, her head reeled. The relationship between Freddie and Elsa was still strained, though there were no more rows. Perhaps when the baby was born, their lives would settle down. She knew Freddie was working hard at the metal factory, and he didn't go out much, only for the occasional pint with Ted. Sometime in the future, Freddie and Elsa and their baby would have a home of their own.

A week later, Rose had a short respite between clients. She leaned back in her office chair and stretched her arms, allowing herself to daydream of her future with Joe when they would be together in their own home, and she and Joe would have children so that Peter wouldn't be an only child.

'I am sorry to disturb you,' said a quiet male voice, breaking into her reverie.

Swiftly, Rose lowered her arms and sat up straight, putting on her professional face; she smiled and was surprised to see a clergyman standing before her. He wasn't known to her, although she often had contact with local church ministers.

'Can I help you? Please sit down.'

He put his bulk on the rickety chair and as

he did so, she studied him. He was of advanced years, with sparse hair and a neatly trimmed beard, and above his rotund red cheeks he had sharp eyes. It was these eyes which held hers now.

'May I introduce myself; I am Matthew Robertson, chaplain of His Majesty's Prison, Hedon Road.'

'I am Miss Ellerby, Rose.' She was puzzled as to why he was here. 'Perhaps you should see Mrs Butler; she's the senior officer here,' she offered.

'No, Miss Ellerby, it is you I have come to see on behalf of one disturbed young man.'

'I'll help you, if I can,' she said, not sure where this was leading.

He leaned forward. 'You can, Miss Ellerby. You are acquainted with Mr Henry Carter?'

Puzzled, she said, 'I don't know a Henry Carter.'

'He goes by the name of Harry.'

Her eyes widened. 'Harry Carter.' Then she remembered her father reading from the newspaper article. 'Harry's in prison, but I don't see how I can help you.'

'Henry – Harry came to me for help and guidance. He is much troubled.'

So he should be, Rose thought. Black marketing was not a fair system of distributing food and goods. She held back her words and waited.

'He is troubled because he did you an injustice. He needs to see you to make amends.'

Rose sank back in her chair, the sharp eyes of the chaplain watching her. 'I don't want to see him. I've nothing to say to him. What's done is done, and it's in the past.'

'Miss Ellerby, prison has a way of making some – I repeat – some inmates search their souls. They have a need to seek atonement for other misdeeds, not necessarily related to the crime they are currently serving.'

Rose couldn't believe this of Harry. He usually talked his way out of situations, not confronted them.

'I'm not sure what Harry has to be troubled about concerning me.'

'Miss Ellerby, you are a good person and you work tirelessly for people less fortunate than yourself. If I did not think Harry needed to see you, I would not intrude on your time.' He sat back, letting his words have their intended effect.

Rose ran his words though her mind again. She couldn't think what Harry would have to say to her that hadn't been already said. *I am a professional, she told herself, and must view Henry Carter in such light.* She drew a deep breath.

'Mr Robertson,' she wasn't sure how to address him, but his face remained bland, so she hadn't offended him, 'if you can arrange a meeting with Henry Carter,' his eyebrows arched slightly at her reference to Harry as Henry, 'I will see him.'

'You have a very compassionate nature, Miss Ellerby. Would the day after tomorrow be convenient to you?'

Rose thumbed through her home-made desk diary. 'The morning is best for me as I have clients in the afternoon.'

'Settled.' He rose from his chair and extended his hand. 'I'd be delighted to come and collect you. My Austin is quite reliable.'

'Thank you, Mr Robertson, but I can catch the number 47 bus, which passes the prison. Will you be there to meet me?'

And so it was arranged. Rose didn't tell anyone about her intended visit to see Harry, except Mrs Butler.

Mrs Butler cautioned, 'Rose, when I've made prisons visits, I always try to keep to the facts. These are best served by listening to the prisoner, but make no promises, other than to see if another organization can help.'

Now, as Rose alighted from the bus and walked up to the prison's huge, fortified doors, she felt every nerve in her body plummet. Once inside, she was relieved to see the chaplain striding towards her, hand outstretched in greeting. Niceties said, he led her along a corridor, through all the security checks, keys jangling, iron-railed doors clanging shut behind. She walked in a trance. Finally, they were in a small room, with a high, barred window, a wooden table and two chairs on either side. She coughed as the dank smell permeated her nose and shivered as the cold seeped into her body. She drew her coat closer and tucked her scarf more securely around her neck. The chaplain pulled out a chair for her and she sat down to wait, her hands folded on her lap. The chaplain remained quietly by her side.

Minutes passed, and then a narrow door opened in the far corner of the room, and Harry entered, flanked by a prison guard.

The first thing Rose noticed was the tension in Harry's body, his grey, pallid skin and sunken eyes, though his face lightened up a little when he saw her. She, in return, gave a weak smile. Harry sat down in the chair opposite her, his trembling hands resting on the table top. Rose was glad she had had the foresight to bring a packet of cigarettes with her.

She had them in her coat pocket; her handbag had been left at a security point. She placed the packet on the table and looked to the chaplain for guidance. He glanced at the guard, who stood by the door and nodded his assent. Rose pushed the packet across the table to Harry, who quickly extracted one and put it to his lips. Matthew Robertson produced a lighter and Rose watched the flame flicker and Harry puff and exhale then lean back in his chair.

The chaplain looked at his watch. 'You have twenty minutes and then I will be back.' He left the room. The guard remained on duty.

Twenty minutes, what a long time and what on earth would they find to talk about? She sat up straight and looked across at Harry.

'How are you?' she asked.

He leaned forward, saying, 'Thank you for coming, Rose. I wasn't sure you'd come.'

'It's my job.' Though she didn't mention this was the first time she had visited a prisoner.

'I always knew you were made of good stuff.' He drew on his cigarette, brooding. Then he blurted out, 'I did love you, Rose. I was such a damned fool to let you go.'

It was on the tip of her tongue to retort that he had been a fool, when she remembered Mrs Butler's words. She bit her lip and sat back in her chair to listen. She watched Harry pull a fresh cigarette from the packet and light it with the stub of the other.

'You're my first visitor.'

'Your mother?' she asked tentatively.

'Too ill,' he said, without much feeling. He drew on the cigarette, exhaled and added, 'When I get out of here, I'm moving on to pastures new.' He eyed her, as if trying to gauge her reaction, but Rose sat still, her professional smile in place. Harry shrugged and carried on. 'I wanted you to know that I'm sorry for the way I treated you. It's played on my conscience, gives me headaches.'

His hand was shaking as he put the cigarette to his mouth. Rose couldn't keep quiet any longer.

'Have you seen a doctor about your headaches?'

'No, it's nowt. I feel much better for seeing you. Do you forgive me, Rose?'

She felt her whole body give a deep sigh. She bore no malice towards Harry. Now, she felt only pity for him. She didn't want to discuss personal details with him; if they hadn't parted, she wouldn't be so happy with Joe. Instead she simply said, 'Harry, I do forgive you.'

His whole demeanour uplifted. 'That's a load off my mind.' He puffed away, and then he said, 'It was the damned war's fault. Turns a man upside down and inside out and when you fall, you're all cock-eyed.'

Rose looked at him in amazement. In one sentence, Harry had summed up the problems that many demobbed men and their families faced. The door behind her opened and the chaplain entered. The twenty minutes was up and it had passed so quickly.

The warden stepped forward and touched Harry's shoulder. He pushed back his chair and got to his feet.

'Rose.' He stretched out a hand to her.

She looked at him, a lump rising in her throat. 'Take care, Harry,' she whispered, their fingers touching across the table. As he was escorted back through the narrow door, he half-turned and glanced over his shoulder at her and smiled, and he was gone.

Rose stood still; it was quite an emotional moment, knowing that they would never meet again. Once, a lifetime ago, she had been a shy young girl who had captured Harry's heart and she had thought she was in love with him. She was twenty now, and her future was Joe.

On the bus home, Rose thought of Joe and her heart surged with love for him. She moved further up the seat for another passenger, who plonked her body next to Rose's. Rose turned to stare out of the window at the passing traffic and the clearance of bomb sites; they all slipped into oblivion, as her thoughts settled on Joe. She loved him with a fierce intensity and couldn't imagine her life without him. They were both saving hard for their marriage. Joe wanted to buy her an engagement ring, use his demob gratuity money, but Rose said to wait until they found somewhere to live because they might be required to pay a rent bond. When they fixed the date for their wedding, then he could buy her a ring. Sally had said Rose was too practical; if it was her, she would have had the engagement ring.

Every Monday evening, Joe went to night school to study for further qualifications for flour milling, which the war had interrupted. On Friday or Saturday nights they went to the cinema and Peter came to stay, sleeping in the little camp bed at the foot of Rose's. Other evenings during the long summer, all three of them went for walks, looking for empty houses or gazing in wonderment when they came across big houses with large gardens. Sundays were allotment and picnic days; Rose loved Sundays most of all. They would join other allotment holders, share food, talk about whose carrots were the best. Afterwards, they would all join in a game of rounders or just watch the shipping going up and down the Humber, guessing at the cargos being carried. They had such fun.

She sighed with contentment.

'My, that's a big sigh, love,' said the woman next to her on the bus.

Rose turned to look at her, saying, 'I'm happy.'

'I should bottle it, love. Happiness can fly out of the window and be gone.'

Rose laughed at the woman's bit of nonsense. But she would remember her words.

TWENTY

The house was quiet and still. Elsa roused herself. She moved awkwardly in bed, her nightgown clinging to her heavy body. The room felt stifling, hot and humid; she needed fresh air.

Slowly, she manoeuvred her legs to the edge of the bed; only a few steps to the window. She stretched up and with both hands, she pushed the wooden-framed sash upwards, but it refused to shift. She flopped back on the bed. Breathless, her lips dry, her throat rough and parched, she reached for the glass of water, which Mary had placed on the bedside table before going shopping. As her fingers clasped the glass, a sudden spasm of pain ripped through her swollen belly. She cried out.

The glass crashed down onto the linoleum floor.

Elsa hung on to the bedpost for support until the spasm subsided. Exhausted, she leaned back against the pillows, her legs dangling over the edge of the bed.

'*Mutti!*' she called out. She wanted her mother, her sweet-faced mother. Where was she? Both her hands cradled her stomach; it felt as if the baby was coming, but it was too early. She had another two weeks to go. '*Mutti*,' she called again. When her mother didn't come, she fell into a fitful doze, only to be woken again by the same gripping pain. Crying with agony, sweat running down her face, she gritted her teeth until the pain went.

Gasping, fighting to control her rapid breathing, Elsa knew that her baby was coming and that she needed help. Carefully, she put her feet on the floor, trying to avoid the broken glass. She managed to get the door open before the next spasm came. She clutched the door-jamb for support as the spasm swept through her. When it passed, she made it into the kitchen and sank into Mary's chair. Eventually, she reached the scullery sink and put her face under the tap to drink and to let the cool water refresh her.

Still leaning over the sink, Elsa listened; she could hear someone singing. It was coming from next door.

'*Hilfe!*' she cried, but no one responded to her cry for help. When the next spasm of pain passed, Elsa made it to the back door and opened it. '*Das Baby, hilfe!*' she screamed. The yard surface swam before her, the pain was unbearable. She felt dizzy, her body swayed and she tried to stop herself from falling forward. Reaching out she clutched at thin air, then the darkness engulfed her.

Mrs Fisher, who had been swilling her

back yard, and singing, stopped as she heard the piercing scream. She didn't stop to think, but rushed into next door's yard to see Elsa lying in a pool of blood.

'Oh, my Lord,' she gasped. She tried to pick Elsa up, but she was too heavy. She knew the signs; the baby was on its way.

She went to the yard gate and looked out, but she couldn't see a soul down the passage. 'Anyone there?' she yelled.

A gate further down opened and a man poked his head round: it was Mr Elliott.

'Come quick,' she yelled. The desperation in her voice carried to him. He came like a shot. Between them both, they managed to carry Elsa back to her bed.

On a quick examination, Mrs Fisher said, 'She needs a doctor.'

'I'll go on my bike.' Relieved to be away from the rigmarole of childbirth, he hurried off.

As he pedalled furiously down the street, he spied Mary talking to a neighbour. He shouted to her, 'Your Freddie's wife's bairn is coming.'

Mary hurried home as fast as her arthritis would allow. She dumped her shopping bag on the kitchen table, and still with her hat and coat on, she followed the trail of blood into the front room. Out of breath, not a thought for her own health, she rushed to Elsa's side.

'Oh my God,' she uttered, at the sight of all the blood.

'Get more towels,' said Vera, as she battled to stem the flow of blood. Mary lifted up the lid of a chest near the window, which she and Elsa had lovingly prepared for the birth, and grabbed towels. She was so relieved to see her old friend taking charge, for hadn't she delivered Freddie and Rose safely, and many other children in the street?

At last, the flow of blood stopped and Elsa began to come round, moaning. Mary wiped her face clean of sweat and Vera's as well. Elsa grasped Mary's hand, and whimpered, '*Mutti, Mutti.*' Her eyes were unfocused and she began thrashing about.

Mary touched Elsa's forehead. It was burning.

'She's got a fever.' She hurried back into the kitchen to bring a small bowl of cold water, but first putting the kettle on the fire to boil. Back in the room, with a flannel wrung out in the cold water, she bathed Elsa's forehead and gradually Elsa quietened.

Vera was examining Elsa and said, 'I can see baby's head.'

With that, Elsa gave a loud scream. 'Push, my girl, push,' Vera commanded.

Mary held Elsa's hand, not caring that her vice-like grip sent pains up her arm. Mary's only thought was for the well-being of her daughter-in-law. Elsa's screams became louder and then she stopped, her body sinking down onto the sodden bed. Then the faint whimper of a child, the most beautiful sound, resonated.

Vera, sweating and fatigued, didn't stop. She cut the cord and wrapped the tiny baby in a clean towel.

'Mother needs a doctor. He should be here by now.' She was worried; Elsa had lost a lot blood.

'Das Baby,' Elsa said weakly.

Vera gently placed the baby in Elsa's arms, and there were tears in her eyes when she said, 'You have a son, love.'

The doctor arrived, demanding a bowl of hot water and clean towel so he could scrub up. Both exhausted, Mary and Vera sat at the kitchen table having a cup of strong tea, while the doctor attended to Elsa. The clock ticked on.

'Another cup of tea, Vera?' asked Mary.

Draining her cup, Vera replied, 'I could drink the pot dry.'

Eyeing her old friend, whom she hadn't spoken to for many months, Mary said, 'Thank you, Vera. I know it can't have been easy for you, what with your lads being killed and Elsa a German. But I had to stand by our Freddie.' She watched Vera's shaking hand as she lifted her cup. 'It must have been difficult.'

'Stop your gabbing, woman. Have yer got

a cig?'

Mary smiled with relief and got to her feet. She picked up the packet from the mantelpiece and extracted two, passing one to Vera. Then she poked one of Ted's quills into the fire and lit the cigarettes.

After a few puffs, Vera spoke. 'If it had been one of my lads, I'd have done the same.'

Tears pricked Mary's eyes. Falling out with her dearest friend had been hard to bear. She smiled and nodded her thanks, not trusting herself to speak, for she would surely dissolve into tears.

They sat in companionable silence until the doctor entered the kitchen. Both with solemn expressions, they waited for him to speak.

'She's had a difficult time and lost a lot of blood. I have stitched her and administered medication. She is now stable, but she will need carefully nursing. I will call again in the morning. However, if there is any deterioration in her condition, send for me immediately and I will have her admitted to hospital.'

'Thank you, doctor,' said Mary, rising to her feet. 'And baby?'

He glanced at her in surprise. 'He birthed early and is small, but the baby is well, though mother will not be able to feed him for some time.' He raised his hat. 'Good day.'

Mary got to her feet, saying, 'I'd best get Elsa cleaned up and change the bed, and see to bairn.' She stood a few moments, straightening her aching back, feeling the tinge of arthritis.

Vera also got to her feet, saying, 'Come on, then, what're you waiting for?' And the two friends together went into the confinement room to attend to mother and son, the nationality of Elsa being of no consequence.

Rose arrived home from work to find her mother so exhausted that she had fallen asleep in her chair. When Mary told her daughter everything that had happened, Rose insisted that Mary went to bed.

'What about tea for Ted and Freddie? I can't think what to give them.'

Gently, Rose led her mother upstairs and helped her change into her nightgown. Her mother safely tucked up in bed, Rose kissed her on the forehead.

'Don't you worry about a thing, Mam. I'll see to everything.'

She went down to check on mother and baby, both fast asleep. The baby was nestling in the makeshift cot, one of the dressing table drawers. Ted hadn't quite finished making the crib, and Mary needed to line it.

Freddie went into the room to gaze upon his sleeping wife and bairn. He didn't know how he felt; relief that it was all over or was it just beginning? The child would always be a reminder. But he had made a promise. Tears filled his eyes and he roughly dashed them away. No time for regrets.

After having a quick mug of tea, Freddie cycled to the fish and chip shop at the corner of Hotham Street.

'Fish and two pennorth five times, please.' His hot newspaper parcel securely in his bike pannier, his next stop was the beer-off, on the corner of Ferries Street, and he bought two bottles of stout, one for him and one for Dad, to wet the baby's head.

After tea, he sat on the chair by Elsa's bedside, reading the evening newspaper, but he couldn't concentrate. He rose to peep at the sleeping baby boy, to gaze in wonderment at his face, the delicate features so well defined. So like... He bit back a choking sound.

From the bed, Elsa murmured, and he listened to catch her words, but she spoke in her native tongue. One word sounded familiar, but he couldn't be sure.

Freddie stayed by Elsa's side until Rose popped her head round the door.

'Gone ten, Freddie, you get off to bed. You've work tomorrow. I'll sit with her now.'

He looked so gloomy. She recalled the exuberant fathers' joy when their offspring had been born, when she'd been called upon to supervise the other children in the house. She glanced at the pale-faced sleeping Elsa. He must be worried about her.

Freddie got to his feet stiffly and motioned to the plate of congealed food on the tray.

'She didn't eat anything.'

'Don't worry, she'll get her appetite back. Mam's going to make a pan of broth tomorrow.'

It was Sally who had gone to the chemist shop for a tin of dried formula milk powder and feeding bottles and teats. Rose settled down to feed baby. He fitted snugly into the curve of her arm, his tiny body warm against her breast. She felt a surge of love and contentment as he sucked on the teat of the bottle.

'What's your name to be, little one?' she murmured.

From her bed, Elsa whispered, 'David.'

Rose turned so Elsa could see her son. 'David, that's a lovely name.' She was surprised, thinking Elsa would have chosen a Germanic-sounding name. Maybe it was Freddie's choice.

'David,' Elsa repeated, and then slipped back into sleep.

David settled back in his makeshift cot and Elsa was still sleeping, so Rose went to fetch her library book. It was an uplifting story of love and hope.

The hours ticked by; David had his next feed and she made him comfortable. Rose yawned and stretched and glanced at the clock on the sideboard: it was two in the morning. Saturday was here already. Quietly, she moved about, not wanting to wake anyone up. She didn't have to work today, but Ted and Freddie both had work until dinner-time. She went through into the kitchen to make a hot drink, then she heard Elsa scream.

She dashed back into the front room to see Elsa, bedclothes pushed back, clutching her stomach. Rose gasped, horrified to see blood seeping onto the clean sheet. Quickly, she picked up a towel to try and stem the flow of blood, but it was no use. She cast her eyes round the room for another towel. Elsa screamed again, clutching wildly at Rose's hand.

Just then, Freddie burst into the room, hastily buttoning up his trousers.

'Towel,' Rose commanded, nodding towards the clothes-horse.

Ashen-faced, Freddie looked on as Rose tried in vain to stop the bleeding.

'What should I do?' he asked, numbly.

'Fetch the doctor. Quickly!'

By the time the doctor arrived, topcoat over his pyjamas, Elsa had slipped into a coma.

'The ambulance is on its way,' he said. Mary held the whimpering baby close in her arms. Ted, not knowing what to do, put the kettle on to boil and stared out of the kitchen window.

Rose stayed with Elsa as the doctor examined her. Suddenly, Elsa gave a gasp, a rattling sound. The doctor put his stethoscope to her heart and listened. Then wearily he turned to Freddie, who stood motionless in the doorway.

'I'm sorry, Mr Ellerby, your wife has gone.'

Freddie, tears streaming down his face, stumbled to Elsa and flung himself over her still, lifeless body. He sobbed and sobbed. 'Forgive me, forgive me.'

Rose, stunned, unable to take in what had happened, froze to the spot. It was the doctor who gently guided her from the room and into the kitchen and seated her on a chair.

Ted, about to make a pot of tea, stopped and went to the cupboard by the side of the fireplace and reached for the small bottle of whisky, which he'd bought for the baby's christening. He poured a tot for the doctor and one for Rose. He looked at Mary, still cradling the baby in her arms, and she shook her head. He poured her a cup of strong tea.

They all drank in silence, as they listened to Freddie breaking his heart. Eventually, he quietened. Rose watched her grim-faced father pour a generous measure of whisky and take it to his grieving son.

TWENTY-ONE

Vera Fisher came later that terrible morning to lay out Elsa. 'It's the least I can do for the poor lass, for her to look grand for her maker. How's Freddie taken it?'

Grieving, Mary's eyes filled with tears. 'He keeps on blaming himself, saying he'd made a promise to take care of her and he can't forgive himself.'

'We all make that promise with our wedding vows, and when they go, it's hard to bear.'

'I know, but something else is troubling him and I can't quite put my finger on it.'

David cried. 'Feeding time,' said a harassed Mary. 'I was going to help you. But Rose was so worn out, so I've sent her off to bed.'

'I can manage,' Vera said. She looked at her old friend, and all the bitterness she'd harboured about Elsa being a German was gone. 'I'll do my very best for the baby's mother.'

'I know,' whispered Mary, biting her lip and close to tears. As she fed David, she could hear Vera singing a hymn: '*Dear Lord and father of mankind, forgive our foolish ways.*'

The next few days passed in turmoil, with all the funeral arrangements to be made and the stream of neighbours calling to pay their respects, and to bring food for the funeral tea.

'It's strange,' Rose commented to Mary. 'Because Elsa was German and felt unwelcomed by the neighbours, she scarcely left the house so she wouldn't know them nor they her, and yet they come to pay their respects now she's dead.'

Mary glanced up from re-trimming her black felt hat. 'It's tradition. And you know the old saying: do unto others as you would want them to do to you.'

'But they didn't like Elsa,' Rose argued.

'Given time, they would have accepted her. And, just think on, if any one of them did wrong, they would still expect the tradition to be carried out.'

Rose sighed heavily. 'Poor Elsa, all her family gone so I'm glad we were there for her.'

The June day was hot when Elsa was laid to rest. In the small church at Eastern Cemetery, the family gathered, and a few of the neighbours slipped into the back pews. Rose held a precious bundle, David. It was at Freddie's insistence: as he put it, 'Her son should be there.'

They sang the twenty-third psalm and Rose prayed that Elsa would find peace and be reunited with her loved ones. That was the only consolation, because she had left behind a grieving husband and an infant son. At the graveside, Rose put a single, fragrant, thornless rose into the tiny grasp of David's hand and together they let it fall onto Elsa's coffin. Rose turned to Freddie, to see if he wanted to hold his son, to draw comfort from the tiny body. But his face crumpled with sorrow. Rose, her eyes aching with unshed tears, watched as he turned to walk alone down the gravel path.

The days that followed passed mechanically. Rose, Freddie and Ted were all back at work. Mary was caring for David during the day and Rose took over in the evenings. She had him in her bedroom except for the nights when Peter came to stay.

Peter was thrilled with David. He stood over the cot, putting his little finger into David's tiny hand. The baby gurgled, enjoying the attention, and Peter, excited, exclaimed to Joe and Rose, 'Can I have a baby brother?'

Over the top of Peter's head, Rose and Joe looked at each other. For the first time, Rose noticed the rawness in Joe's eyes. He was working so hard studying and the lodgings where he and Peter lived were far from ideal. Rose reached out to take hold of Joe's hand and drew him close.

It was Saturday night, and Rose and Joe's night at the cinema, but it was such a lovely evening, that they decided to walk down to the pier. It was here that she'd met Joe. A lifetime ago. As if reading her thoughts, Joe said, 'It was a long time ago.'

They sat on a wooden bench on the upper deck of the pier, watching the sun setting in the West, its golden path of rays rippling down the River Humber. Colours of orange, gold and red streaked and swirled across the sky, making it look surreal.

Suddenly Joe said, 'I'm sorry, Rose.'

She looked at him in surprise. 'What for?'

He lit a cigarette and blew out smoke. 'A young girl like you should be off dancing and having fun, instead of being tied to a man like me who can't even offer you a home.' His face serious, he drew hard on his cigarette.

Taken aback for a moment, Rose said quietly, 'A man like you–'

He cut her off, about to say something, but she held her hand up. Her firm voice brooked no nonsense.

'Listen to me, Joe Tennison. A man like you is precisely why I love you. You are kind, honest, thoughtful and a passionate man. And, as for having fun, I enjoy being with you, it's sheer pleasure, and as for dancing, we will be doing just that, next month. I am organizing a summer ball. Come here.' She removed his cigarette from his mouth and stamped on it. Then she kissed him. 'Now, what have you to say to that?'

He crushed her to his body, murmuring

into her soft, sweet-smelling hair.

'Rose, oh Rose, you're the most wonderful girl in the world. I love you so much, it aches.'

'Hey up there, look at them two. Ain't you had no tea?' said a cheeky voice. Both Joe and Rose looked over their shoulders to see two youths walking by. One of the youths winked and said, 'She's a smasher, ain't you a lucky fella.'

Joe and Rose both laughed. He pulled her to her feet.

'Let's have a drink at the Minerva.'

Later, they arrived home to be met by an anxious Ted and Mary. 'Have you seen Freddie?'

'No, what's wrong?' Rose asked, knowing that Freddie was still grieving.

Ted answered, 'He was very quiet tonight, more than usual. I suggested we go for a pint, but he said he had things to think about and wanted to go out on his own. That was at nine and it's gone eleven.'

At once, Joe said, 'I'll go down to the pub to see if he's still there.' Through the deserted streets he hurried. The pub was closed, but a light was on. He banged on the door.

A voice within shouted, 'Bugger off, we're closed.'

Joe lifted up the flap of the letter box and called, 'I'm looking for Freddie Ellerby whose wife died.'

There was a shuffling of feet and the sound

of the door being unbolted, and the door swung open. The landlord, a big, wide man, sleeves rolled up, cigarette dangling from his moustached mouth, eyed Joe with caution.

'What's this about young Freddie?'

'He's not come home and his family are worried about him. Have you seen him tonight?'

'Aye, sat in corner on his own, only drunk one pint so he's not the worse for wear. He left on his own before I called time.'

Joe thanked him and headed off to search the streets for any signs of Freddie. When he reached the top of Ferries Street, he saw Freddie sitting on the low wall bordering the factory premises. He was just staring into space.

'Hello, mate,' Joe said quietly, 'mind if I join you?' Freddie didn't respond. Joe thought back to that dark time when his wife and un-born child had been killed in a bombing raid. He had sunk to the very depths of despair and had contemplated drowning himself in the Humber. 'It was Rose who saved me.'

Freddie looked at him, his face a mask of desolation. Joe shifted, not realizing that he'd spoken aloud. Speaking quietly, he told Freddie his sad story, finishing with: 'When I first met Rose, she had her own troubles and listening to her helped me to put my life back in focus. I have a young son, Peter; you've met him. He was evacuated and I hadn't seen him for some time. I was a stranger to him, but I am his daddy and I had to live for him.' He lit two cigarettes and gave one to Freddie, who took it without a word.

They sat on in silence, then Joe said, 'You have your son David to live for.'

Freddie let out an anguished cry and jumped to his feet.

'You don't know!' he shouted.

Joe put a steadying hand on Freddie's arm, saying, 'It's all right.'

In silence, they walked to Church Terrace where an anxious family waited. Joe put a finger over his lips to signal to them no questions, and just said, 'Freddie's tired.'

In hushed silence, they watched Freddie disappear up to his bedroom. Joe spoke to reassure them, explaining his own experience.

'Freddie's still grieving and it can be a slow process so it's best to be patient with him.' Though Joe didn't tell them that he suspected something else was on Freddie's tortured mind.

Freddie spent the whole of Sunday in bed. Rose glanced anxiously at Mary; there were dark circles beneath her eyes and the lines at the side of her mouth were more deeply etched.

'Don't worry, Mam, he'll pull through.' But Rose knew her mother was concerned about Freddie, as they all were.

David was a sleepy baby, only crying to be

fed and changed, but in time he would become more boisterous and demanding. Would Mary be able to cope?

'You have a rest, Mam. I'll take David for a walk in his pram down to the allotment.' One of the neighbours had loaned them the use of her pram.

At the allotment, Rose came in for some ribbing. 'By, that was quick, didn't know you were wed.' And, 'Does Joe know about this?' Rose laughed and was happy to do so because Elsa's death had hit them hard and a bit of gentle banter was a welcome relief.

Freddie continued to be quiet and distant. Everyone tiptoed around him, not wanting to upset him. One night, when Rose was looking after David and her parents were having a rare night out at the cinema, Rose needed to catch Sally at home. She was trying to arrange the summer dance and needed Sally's help. David was fast asleep in his cot, his new crib, made by Ted, and the inside lined in a pretty blue cotton, by Mary.

Freddie sat by the fire reading the evening paper and Rose said to him, 'I'm just popping to see Sally. Keep an eye on David.'

He looked at her over the top of his paper.

'Don't be long,' he said gruffly.

Sally was full of ideas for decorating the community hall. 'Balloons, I'll see what there is at work and then I'll cosy up to the supervisor. I can make bunting and Frank can hang it up. Oh, it's exciting.' They laughed and talked and the time passed too quickly.

'I must go,' said Rose.

'Stay for a cup of coffee.'

Enjoying their rare moments to chat together, Rose said, 'Just a quick one.' Mrs Wray came in and wanted to hear all about the dance arrangements so they chatted some more. Suddenly, Rose glanced at the polished wooden clock on the mantelpiece. She'd been here over an hour. She jumped up quickly.

'I'll have to go. I've left Freddie looking after the baby.'

'Well, he's the dad,' Sally griped, not wanting her friend to go.

She could hear David wailing when she opened the back door. Hurrying into the kitchen, she was surprised to see that Freddie wasn't there.

'Freddie,' she called, but no answer. David looked in distress and had kicked away his blanket and his tiny legs were drawn up in pain. She picked him up and put him on her shoulder and gently rubbed his back. He began to hiccup and then burp, bringing up the trapped wind. His lovely baby scent, mixed with talcum powder, filled her nostrils. This beautiful baby boy should have a mammy to love him; she closed her eyes and thought of Elsa. She would have made a wonderful mother. Life was cruel. She crooned to David to soothe him and he went to sleep. Gently, she laid him back in his crib and tucked the blanket up to his chin. Then automatically, he stretched his arms above his head. He looked so peaceful and contented.

She was still watching over David when Freddie came down the stairs. Rose rounded on him.

'Why did you leave your son in such distress?' she snapped at him.

He just stood there, his unshaven face a pallid grey. Then he spoke. 'He's not my son.'

Rose stared at her brother; his words shocked her. He was taking his grief too far.

TWENTY-TWO

'Not your son!' Rose blurted. 'How can you say that?

'Sit down, Rose,' Freddie said, but he remained standing.

She glared at him, but there was something in his manner, his stance, which made her do his bidding. Still angry, she waited for him to speak.

Freddie closed his eyes, as if seeking composure. When he opened them, he looked away from her, and in a strained voice, said, 'I can't live a lie any longer.'

Now confused and not understanding what he meant, Rose asked, 'Freddie, what is it?' But he didn't reply. And a growing unease filled her, as he sank heavily into a chair and covered his face with his hands. The clock ticked, marching away the seconds. David murmured in his sleep. This sound seemed to rouse Freddie. He lifted up his head and looked at his sister, his face twisted in agony and he groaned, 'If only Elsa hadn't died I would have tried to make a go of it. I made a promise to take care of her and broke it. Now, I just can't go on.' Again he covered his face with his hands, he wept.

Stunned, numb, Rose was unable to take in her brother's incoherent words. It seemed to her that his grief, the death of Elsa, had affected him so deeply that it might have upset his mental balance. Without a second's thought of her earlier anger, she was on her feet and by his side. Sorrow filled her very being to see this dear, big brother of hers so heartbroken.

Gently, she put her arms round his shoulders and drew him close to her. As she did so, images of their childhood flashed through her mind; of Freddie, the strong boy, protecting her from the dangers of slipping into a stream and catching her as she fell from the branches of a tree.

It was to this poignant scene that Mary and Ted entered. Rose saw the alarm on both their faces and she put a finger on her lip for them to be silent. Quietly, Mary put the kettle on the stove to boil, and Ted hurried from the house.

Eventually, Freddie's sobs subsided and he pulled away from Rose. Blindly, he stumbled through into the scullery to swill his red-blotched face in cold water.

'What's happened?' whispered an anxious Mary.

'I'm not too sure,' Rose replied. 'From what I can make out, it's to do with Elsa's death and for some reason he's rejecting David as his son.'

'Oh, my God,' Mary gasped, her hand going up to her mouth in despair.

Rose could see her mother about to crumple. 'Make the tea, Mam,' she said firmly, wanting to give her something positive to do.

Ted, out of breath, came hurrying back into the kitchen. He plonked a small bottle of brandy on the table and dropped onto a chair. Mary brought the teapot and cups and saucers to the table.

'He'll want a mugful,' Ted snapped at his wife.

Mary's lip quivered, but she didn't say a word. She poured out half a mugful, and Ted filled the other half with the brandy.

They waited in silence until Freddie came back. Beneath the red blotches on his face, his skin was tinged a dirty grey.

'Sit down, lad, and drink this,' Ted said in a soft, soothing voice.

In a trance, Freddie obeyed his father. All three sat and watched him drain the mug. Then he pushed back his chair, saying, 'I'm off to bed.'

From his cot, David started whimpering, but Freddie didn't acknowledge him.

'Poor little mite, he's hungry,' said Mary, lifting him from his cot. She cradled him in her arms, while Rose made his feed.

The next morning, Monday, Rose was up early. She'd given David his feed and went to tell her mother, who was still in bed, that she was going to work.

'I'm going to ask Mrs Butler for a week's leave. Freddie needs our support.' Mary nodded her agreement.

Mrs Butler was sympathetic to Rose's request. She recognized Rose's deep resolve to support her family, to bring them comfort, and to put them before her own needs. This was her great attribute, a powerful trait in one so young, and one of the reasons why she had employed Rose. She hadn't been wrong in her assessment; Rose had proved to have exceptional qualities in dealing with people at all levels, a talent that came naturally to her.

As Mrs Butler watched Rose walk out of the building, she sighed. It was one thing to deal with outsiders and their problems, but family problems? She hoped it would not overwhelm her at this stage of her life, thinking of Rose's intended marriage to Joe.

On her way home, Rose called at Bennett's shop on the corner of Empringham Street, where they were rationed for groceries. There was always a queue and people, mainly women, liked a bit of gossip as they waited; for some it was a form of social recreation. As Rose entered the shop they naturally stopped talking for a moment, to see who it was, acknowledged the person and usually carried on with the conversation. But not today: all eyes were focused on Rose.

'Oh, Rose, lass, sorry to hear your Freddie's right cut up about his loss.' A large woman with metal pin curlers wound tightly in her hair spoke. 'And yer poor mam, having to cope with a bairn at her age.'

Rose pasted a smile on her face. 'Thank you. It's hard for Freddie to lose his wife in childbirth, but he'll pull through with the family's help. And you'll be pleased to know, I have taken a whole week off work, so Mam can take it easy.'

'You're a good daughter. Come to the front of the queue,' a little, thin woman said.

Rose opened her mouth to say no, she couldn't possibly, when she found herself gently being eased forward. Tears of gratitude at this wonderful camaraderie filled her eyes. These were women who had kept families fed and clothed through the hardships of the war, on next to nothing, and still they were giving.

'Thank you,' she said, her voice on the verge of breaking.

Back home, she entered the still kitchen and listened. She could hear her mother out front in the terrace, talking. She left the bag of groceries on the kitchen table and went to open the front door. Mary was hanging washing on the rope line strung across the terrace and Mrs Fisher was pushing David backwards and forwards in his pram. Both women were chatting. Rose watched for a moment, so pleased that their friendship was resumed. She felt a little flush of happiness. Her voice light, she said, 'I'm back, Mam. Shall I put the kettle on?'

Mary glanced at her daughter and with an apologetic look at Vera said, 'Freddie's still in bed and I don't want to disturb him.'

'I'll put my kettle on,' said Vera.

Back in the house, Rose put the shopping away. Then she made a strong mug of tea and went up the stairs to Freddie's bedroom. She tapped on the door, and said softly, 'Freddie, are you awake?' She heard a movement. 'Can I come in?'

'If you must.' His voice was croaky and he coughed.

She went into the dark, small room, standing for a moment to accustom her eyes to the gloom. The room smelt stale and sour, of cigarette smoke and body odour. Rose wrinkled her nose, ignoring the unpleasantness. Treading carefully, for clothes were haphazardly strewn about the linoleum floor, she placed the mug of tea on the chair by his bedside. 'How are you feeling?' she asked, sitting on the edge of the bed.

Freddie looked terrible; dark hollow eyes and another day's growth of beard made him look grim. He heaved himself up in bed, reached for the mug and drank. He licked his lips and sighed. 'I was parched.' He flopped back on the pillow and looked at Rose. 'I'm a right mess,' he said bitterly.

'You are not,' she replied, gently touching his arm. 'Losing Elsa was a great shock to you. And you had so little time together. Let yourself grieve, Freddie. Mam and I will take care of David for you.' She saw him wince. Oh my God, was the reason he was denying David as his son because he blamed him for Elsa's death? Feeling she was intruding on her brother's grief she moved to the door and then turned, to say, 'There's plenty of hot water for a wash, and I've ironed you a clean shirt.' Not expecting him to answer, she was surprised.

'Thanks, Rosie,' he said. He hadn't called her Rosie since childhood.

Back in the kitchen, Rose set about preparing dinner: herb omelettes, made with reconstituted dried egg powder, beans, and thinly sliced potatoes, dipped in a batter and fried.

She heard Freddie come downstairs and go into the scullery to wash. And, ten minutes later, he came into the kitchen looking marginally better for a wash, shave and clean shirt. But his eyes still held the haunted look.

At 12.10 pm sharp, Ted came home from work on his dinner break and Mary came in, leaving David outside the front window, sleeping contentedly in his pram.

Dinner was a quiet affair, no one speaking. Ted went back to work, Mary went to check on David and bring in the washing ready for ironing. Rose was clearing the table when Freddie said, rising from his chair, 'I'm off for a walk.'

Rose gave him an encouraging smile, saying, 'The fresh air will do you good.' She would like to have added, *Take David for a walk in his pram*. But she didn't.

The week passed and each day, to take the burden off her mother, Rose did the household chores, and fed David. And each day, Freddie would go out. He became secretive about his movements and the family, not wishing to upset him, didn't press him.

She began to worry how her mother would cope when she went back to work.

Rose voiced her thoughts to Sally, who had dropped by to keep her up to date with the Summer Ball plans.

'Don't worry. My mam will help with shopping. You only have to ask.'

Snatching precious moments with Joe was her lifeline. He called on his way home from night school and they were outside in the backyard, talking about how well Peter was doing at school, when Joe gently touched her arm and asked, 'Rose, what's bothering you?'

She looked into his warm, brown eyes. He knew her so well.

'It's Mam; I'm worried about her coping when I go back to work. The neighbours are good, but they have their own families to see to.' She sighed heavily. It wasn't her intention to waste these precious moments with Joe to dwell on her family problems.

'Surely Freddie can take care of his son to give you and your mother a break?'

'Oh, Joe, if only, but I don't want to trouble you with family matters.'

He placed an arm protectively round her shoulders and looked steadily into her eyes. 'Have I ever told you what beautiful eyes you have?'

She laughed, saying, 'Do you think so?'

He pulled her closer. 'And what a pert nose you've got,' he said, kissing the tip of her nose. She giggled. 'That's my Rose,' he whispered. And so they talked pure delightful nonsense. When they finally kissed good-night, Rose went into the house with a lighter heart and a lovely warm feeling of being loved and cared for.

Joe walked slowly to his lodgings, his mood serious. He loved Rose with a fierce passion, but he was beginning to doubt if he was the right man for her. He was six years older than her, had a son and no home of his own, so what had he to offer Rose? She should be with someone of her own age, having fun, going dancing before settling down and thinking of marriage. She was obviously up-set by her brother's behaviour, so she had enough family problems without him add-ing to them. He had intended to ask Rose if Peter could come to their house after school until he came home from work. Peter loved it when he stayed over when Joe was at night school, like tonight, but how long could that go on for? His landlady, Mrs Stepney, said she was too ill to care for Peter after school and that he must make other arrangements, but with whom? Joe stopped to light a cigar-ette; drawing deeply, he pondered.

Monday, and Rose was back at work. She was kept so busy that she didn't have time to think how her mother was coping on her own.

'Goodnight, Stan,' she called to the warehouse man and hurried off to catch her bus home.

Rounding the corner of Hill Street, she came face to face with Mrs Fisher wheeling David in his pram. She looked upset.

'He should be ashamed of himself,' she flared.

Baffled by this outcry, Rose asked, 'Who?'

'Your Freddie. He's upset Mary and made her cry.'

Without another word, Rose dashed home to find her mother, red-eyed, sitting at the kitchen table. 'Mam, what on earth has happened?'

'I don't know. I only asked him when he was going to register David's birth. He said he wasn't. So I said I'd do it for him.' Tears threatened again.

'Take your time,' Rose said soothingly, sitting on a chair next to Mary.

Mary dabbed her eyes and then continued, 'He shouted at me. Said he wasn't David's father, never was and never would be.' Mary's voice broke and her lips quivered, but she forced out the words. 'Said we were to stop interfering in his life and mind our own business. He was so angry, but I only wanted to help,' she stammered. 'I don't understand.'

'Me neither. Something has tipped Freddie over the edge, but what? He seems to have lost his mental reasoning altogether,' Rose said, feeling concerned and helpless. 'But what can we do about it?'

TWENTY-THREE

Freddie did not come home that night. Mary fretted; Ted was angry.

'He's no right to put you through it,' he fumed. They were in the kitchen having breakfast; at least, Ted was. Mary just couldn't eat. No matter how old her son was, she was still his mother. She worried about him. He'd never been the same lad since coming back from the war, and married to a German girl. Elsa had been a nice girl, but she and Freddie never seemed right together. Then aloud she said, 'What did you think, Ted?'

He looked at his wife, not sure what she was on about. He pushed back his chair and got to his feet.

'Time I was off to work,' he said briskly, making for the door. Then he saw Mary's face, and for the first time he noticed the lines of worry around her pinched mouth. His voice softened and he said, 'Don't worry, love. He'll walk in as large as life.'

But Freddie had been seen at Paragon

Station, boarding the London train. It was a long, anxious week, before Freddie walked through the door of number nine, Church Terrace.

It was early evening. Rose had gone to see Joe, and Mary was upstairs, putting David in his cot. It had been a hot day and heat hung around in the kitchen. The back door and window were both wide open and Ted was sitting in his chair, reading the newspaper, when a voice said, 'Hello, Dad.'

Ted lowered the newspaper and glared at his son. 'I hope you have a good explanation for tearing off like that. Your mam's been worried sick.'

Exhausted, Freddie dropped into a chair. 'I'm sorry.' With the sweep of his hand, he pushed back a lock of his unruly hair from his forehead. 'I've been trying to sort things out.'

'Have you?' Ted demanded. 'I'll tell you this: I'm not having your mother upset again.'

Freddie sat up straight. 'Can I tell you what happened, Dad?'

Calmer, Ted said, 'Aye.' He offered his son a cigarette and they both lit up.

Freddie hesitated, and then said, 'It all started at the end of the war. My pal and I had been through thick and thin together. When war ended, we were sent to the German town of Bielefeld, where the army had taken over a three-storey house for headquarters. General dogsbodies we were, fetching and carrying, moving office equipment and furniture. On weekends we had a bit of spare time, so we went exploring bierkellers, and my pal got friendly with a girl. She used to collect the empty glasses. Sometimes all three of us would go for a walk. Then my pal started to slip out on a night to meet her and I would cover for him. I warned him not to get too friendly with a German girl because they spell trouble.'

Freddie drew on his cigarette, regrouping his thoughts, his head aching. He needed to tell all, get it off his chest before it choked him. 'Then a few months later, we were out with a party from our unit. We were merry, singing as we walked to good old British songs. When suddenly, this car comes hurtling towards us, out of control. We all jumped, but my pal caught it...' His words drained away.

Ted broke the silence. 'What happened to your pal?'

Freddie looked into space, beyond his father. 'He died in my arms.'

'Oh, son, I'm sorry.' Ted had seen many atrocities in the Great War. He glanced at his son's grave face, and asked quietly, 'What was your pal's name?'

Freddie, not looking his father in the eye, said, 'David. David Merchant.'

'David,' Ted repeated. 'You called your son David, after your pal.'

Freddie sank back in his chair, weary and drained of everything, his voice barely a whisper. 'No, Dad, Elsa named him David after his father.'

Ted stared at Freddie, not fully understanding, and then: 'You, you are not David's father?'

'No.' Freddie stared down at the worn fireside rug, reliving that fatal night and the sheer horror of those bizarre events which followed. He didn't want to go on, but he knew he must tell the whole story or go mad. He lifted his head up and felt tears wet his lashes.

His voice quiet, he continued, 'David died in my arms and his last words to me were to ask me to promise to take care of Elsa, who was pregnant with his child. I promised to marry her and take care of her.' His voice broke, 'I failed, Dad. She died. And the child, I can't care for him because I've nothing left to give. Nothing!'

Suddenly, Mary appeared in the room, not glancing at either man, and said, 'I'll put the kettle on.' She moved stiffly; it had been uncomfortable sitting on the stairs, but she didn't want to interrupt Freddie's heart-wrenching story.

After a mug of hot tea and a cheese sandwich, and his boots, with holes in them from the miles he'd walked, discarded, Freddie felt a bit more human.

'But why did you go to London?' asked Mary.

'That's where David came from. I went to try and find his parents. I wanted them to know that they have a grandson.' He saw Mary's face quiver. 'I'm sorry, Mam. But they had moved and no one seemed to know where they'd gone. I tramped and tramped the streets and asked at the shops and pubs.' He shrugged his shoulders, dejected. He laid his head on the back of the chair and closed his eyes and within a few moments, he emitted gentle snores.

'The lad's fair worn out,' said Mary.

Ted scratched his sparse hair and said, 'It's a right pickle. What's to be done about yon bairn?' He glanced upwards to the bedrooms.

'I really don't know,' answered Mary, 'but I'll tell you this: that bairn will be loved and looked after by me until...' Here her voice faltered, she gulped back tears and swallowed hard. 'Until we find his true grandparents.' She let out a heavy sigh. 'Though how we'll do that, heaven only knows.'

Rose walked slowly home from Joe's lodgings. She had hoped that they could have gone for a stroll, it being such a lovely summer's evening. But Peter was in bed and the landlady wasn't well enough to keep an eye on him. Coming home from school, Peter had fallen, hitting the stone pavement hard, and hurt his knee; nothing serious, but he'd cried for his mother. Mrs Mitchell, Joe's old landlady, had taken him home and bathed his wound and bandaged it. He had stayed for tea, and it was her daughter, Maureen, who brought Peter home. And when she heard of Joe's predicament, she suggested that Peter, after school, could come home with her children and that Joe could collect him on the way home.

Rose felt pleased that Peter was being taken care of, but she wanted to be the one to do so. More than anything, she wanted to be married to Joe, to be his wife and to be Peter's mother.

She didn't want to go home, not yet. She stood at the top of the street not knowing where to go or what to do.

'Just the girl I want to see,' said a cheerful voice behind her.

'Sally.' Rose hugged her friend. 'I'm glad to see you.'

Sally glanced at Rose's unhappy face. 'Want to talk about it?' Rose nodded in response. Sally thought for a moment, then said, 'There's a houseful at home. Shall we take a pew over there?' She pointed to the bombed area, where earlier, a few children had been playing and had built a haphazard wall of bricks. They crossed over the road and sat on the wall, facing away from the street, looking westwards to where the sky was a brazen kaleidoscope of red, orange and yellow, streaked with an artist's brush.

Rose contemplated this beauty of nature, wanting it to make her feel better, but it didn't. From the pocket of her skirt, Sally produced a packet of Woodbines and a box of matches, and Rose gladly accepted one.

They puffed in silence for seconds before Rose said, 'Do you really want to listen to my tale of woe? I shouldn't be moaning, I have a job, good health, a roof over my head, but...' Here, her voice failed her. Sally glanced at her, but didn't speak. After a few more puffs of her cigarette, she continued, 'It's Joe. I feel as though we've come to a full stop.'

'He hasn't packed you in,' Sally declared, hotly.

'No, it's nothing like that. It's just that we don't seem to have time to spend together. There's always something in the way. There are a lot of ifs: if only Freddie hadn't come home with a pregnant wife. We could have lived at home. Mam and Dad get on well with Joe and they love Peter. If only we had got Mrs Mitchell's old house to rent, we'd have been married by now. And what with the housing shortage – I just don't know.'

Sally looked at her friend's weary, sad, miserable face and said, 'You need something to cheer you up, something to look forward to. The summer dance is next week and you and Joe can dance together to your hearts' content. Frank and I will take charge.' She put a finger on Rose's open lips. 'You'll enjoy yourself.'

Rose removed the finger. 'What about Peter? Mam will have her hands full with the baby.'

Sally tossed back her long, dark hair. 'I'll ask my mam. She won't mind this once.'

Rose felt a tiny frisson of excitement bubble inside her. She momentarily closed her eyes, seeing herself dancing in Joe's arms.

'Thanks, Sally, you're a good friend.'

'Come on,' said Sally, 'my bum's aching sitting on these bricks.' Both girls laughed and jumped up and, linking arms, they crossed over the road.

Feeling in a lovely, lighter mood, Rose lifted the back gate sneck and went indoors. The first person she saw was Freddie, sleeping in the armchair. Her mother and father were sitting quietly, Ted reading his paper and Mary unravelling an old jersey to re-knit a smaller garment. She was just about to exclaim her pleasure at his safe return when Mary put down her task and motioned Rose to follow her into the front room. Taken by surprise at her mother's odd behaviour she did her bidding.

The front room was still the same as when

Elsa occupied it. Mary hadn't the strength to sort it out and Rose hadn't the time. No one was using it, so what was the point.

Mary sat on the chair, and Rose sat on the edge of the bed. Rose noticed her mother looked wearier than usual.

'What's wrong, Mam?'

'Oh, Rose,' Mary sighed heavily. 'It's such a terrible muddle. I'll tell you everything.'

Rose listened in silence as her mother recounted Freddie's sad tale.

When she had finished, Rose stared at her mother, then she said, 'Poor David. No mother and no father. I knew something had been not quite right between Freddie and Elsa, but I never dreamed it was that. To take on another man's girl and his baby, that takes courage. I'm proud of our Freddie and I will do all I can to help him find David's grandparents.' With that statement, Mary burst into tears. Rose got up to comfort her, holding her close, feeling how thin she was. Rose's heart sank at the magnitude of the problem she'd taken on.

On his way home from work, Joe decided that before collecting Peter from Mrs Mitchell's daughter's house, he'd call on Rose to arrange a night out at the cinema or a drink at the pub. It seemed ages since they had last been out together. What with his circumstances and Rose's family problems, their lives were in limbo. He longed to hold Rose in his arms, to feel her young body close to his, to kiss her, talk to her, but there never seemed to be a right moment, so he was determined to resolve the situation.

Feeling more optimistic and with a lighter heart he entered the Ellerby household, to be met by the plaintive cry of the baby and a sickly stale smell. Rose was holding David, trying to pacify him. He noticed how exhausted she looked, so pale with her hair lank and untidy. He glanced at Mary and Ted; they too looked exhausted. Of Freddie, he saw no sign. Joe stood on the kitchen threshold, not sure what to do or say.

Rose gave Joe a weary smile. 'Sorry, he's cutting a tooth and it's painful for him and nothing I do seems to soothe him.' She continued rocking the wailing David.

Ted, suddenly aware of Joe's presence, said, 'Sit down, lad.'

Mary, who had been nodding in her chair, raised her head to look at him, but didn't speak. Joe looked at Rose; he desperately wanted to take her in his arms and kiss her, for her to reassure him of her love. Surveying the scene before him, he felt shut out. The baby howled louder.

'Thank you, I won't stay. I'm on my way to collect Peter,' Joe said. He looked at Rose, waiting for her to give David to her mother and come to see him out, but she didn't. She put the baby over her shoulder, patting his back. He turned to go and no one stopped him.

The atmosphere was very different as he entered the house in Hotham Street. He heard the sound of happy children's voices and the tantalizing aroma of food. His stomach rumbled hungrily. Mrs Mitchell and the children were pleased to see him and his heavy heart lifted.

'Dad, I'm winning,' exclaimed an animated Peter, waving his arms in glee. Joe bent on his haunches to glance at the Ludo board and watch as Peter rolled the dice.

'Double six,' he yelled, and rolled the dice again.

Joe straightened up, saying, 'Time to go, son.'

'Dad, I can't, I'm winning.'

Mrs Mitchell spoke. 'Stay for tea, Joe. It's only stew and I can make extra dumplings.'

Joe felt guilty about imposing on her good nature.

'It's kind of you, but we have to go.'

'Please stay, Joe.'

He glanced at Maureen, who had just entered the kitchen. She was looking quite attractive in her coral-flowered dress with her light-brown hair hanging in curls to her shoulders. She smiled provocatively at him, coming up to him and placing a hand on his arm. Through the material of his work jacket, he could feel the warmth of her touch, which sent shivers through his hungry body. He knew he should resist the invitation, but the kindliness showed by mother and daughter was hard to refuse.

'Just this once,' he said. He looked down at his grubby hands. 'Can I have a bit of a scrub?'

'Come through to the scullery,' said Maureen. Joe followed, watching as she poured water into an enamel bowl. Then she stretched up to the wall cupboard to reach a clean towel, her dress riding up, showing her bare, shapely legs. He was aware she knew he was taking in her movements. She bent over, to look under the sink for a bar of soap, letting her dress ride up even further, showing a pretty lace petticoat.

She heard him step forward and when she straightened up, he was there, right next to her. It was the most natural thing for her to stand on tiptoes and kiss him.

At first, Joe didn't respond, and then with such a force, he wrapped his arms around her, pressing his body close to hers. Feeling her softness, the swell of her breasts and the tantalizing smell of her scent, he groaned inwardly. More than anything, he wanted Rose, the girl he loved. If he closed his eyes, he could pretend. And so he did.

Later, as he tossed in bed unable to sleep, he thought of Rose, his sweet Rose, and his conscience troubled him. He liked Maureen: she had come to his rescue by collecting Peter from school and letting him stay in her home, and Joe was grateful. But he didn't love her, nor want to be with her; it was just that he was feeling so helpless, which was no excuse for his actions. He wanted to blame the aftermath of the war. From what he heard and observed, things were even harder. Men coming home from the war to peace, to no jobs, less money, families to feed and clothe, and in many cases, like him, no proper home to offer. The future, if there was a future, resembled a dense fog. How long before it cleared?

That same night, Rose also lay awake in bed. Finally, she had settled David and he was sleeping; for how long, she wasn't sure. She closed her eyes, but couldn't sleep. She opened them and stared up at the darkened ceiling, her thoughts turning to Joe. Had he come for a reason early that evening? He didn't say and now she wondered what it might be. He didn't look happy and she was of no help. Tied to another man's baby, what must he think of her? But the child was defenceless, an orphaned infant who needed care and love. She couldn't abandon David. But Joe needed her, and Peter also needed her. It was a crazy situation to be in and one for which she couldn't see any instant solution. With mixed-up thoughts simmering in her head, she fell into an uneasy sleep.

In the early hours of the morning David began to wail. She changed him and gave him a feed, but still he cried. She walked up and down her small bedroom space, rocking the crying infant in her arms. His tiny fists struggled to punch the air, then he rammed them in his mouth. 'You poor little boy,' Rose crooned, nuzzling her lips against the soft down of his hair, feeling an overpowering sense of love and protection.

Suddenly, the bedroom door opened and Mary entered.

'I forgot about this.' She held up a dummy, a baby's comforter. 'Vera bought it for David.' She reached over and carefully eased it into his open mouth. Both women watched as he sucked on the dummy. They saw the gentle motion of sucking visibly relax his tiny facial muscles, until he closed his eyes.

At first, Rose was reluctant to put him back in his cot in case he woke up.

'Come on, love, I'll put him down,' said Mary, taking the sleeping baby from her daughter's arms. 'It's time you were getting ready for work.'

Rose glanced at her alarm clock, not that she needed the alarm since David had shared her bedroom. She yawned and stretched her arms.

Later at work, Rose couldn't stop

yawning. She apologized to Mrs Butler.

'What is the problem?' the older woman asked.

'Is it that obvious?' She tried to keep family matters separate from work, but she needed to confide or she would explode. So out came the story of the baby not being Freddie's and how he had tramped London looking for the grandparents and having no luck, and Freddie unable to acknowledge David, the son of his best pal who was killed and his only reason for marrying Elsa. Finishing the tale, her voice full of desperation, she said, 'I don't know what to do next.' Then, with a pleading look at Mrs Butler, she cried, 'I don't want to involve the welfare.' She felt the colour drain from her face. 'It wouldn't be right,' she said.

Mrs Butler was gentle, but firm. 'My dear, please do not be upset. You obviously need some help. I can arrange for one of our volunteer ladies to give your mother some free time, say two or three times a week, to help care for David. Your mother will then be less tired and able to cope and therefore you will be less stressed in the evenings.' Amusement played round her soft brown eyes. 'Perhaps you can spend time with your young man.' Before Rose could utter a word, she continued. 'Now for David's grandparents. If you can let me have their names and any details you may have, I will write to our London office and they will know who to contact for information. Then we will take it from there.'

'I don't know how to thank you,' said Rose, not sure if she wanted to laugh or cry.

Mrs Butler stood up, saying, 'You can thank me by putting the finishing touches to the Summer Ball. Go down to the hall and see how arrangements are progressing.'

Outside, in the warm August air, the colour returned to her cheeks. Rose strolled down the street, savouring the freedom, if only for a short time. Mrs Butler knew that the arrangements for the ball were well in hand, and Rose knew she was blessed with an understanding boss.

The war had been over for a year and the city centre, which had suffered great devastation, was gradually being tidied up. Her mother's favourite store, Hammond's, was badly damaged to a flat bleakness. There was talk of a new department store to be built. Rose wondered if it would have a dance hall, like before. She'd often listened to her parents talking about their courting days, dancing in the grand hall.

Crossing over North Bridge she glanced up the River Hull, its waters busy with activity, of boats, loading and unloading. She thought of Joe, working at the flour mill near to Drypool Bridge; would she see him tonight? Absorbed in her thoughts, she never gave the other side of the bridge a glance. If she had done so, she would have seen the man, loitering. He was watching her intently from the corner of Lime Street. A man dressed in rough clothing, with a flat cap pulled down, which partly hid his face. As she crossed over to walk down Holderness Road, he shrank his body into the shadow of the buildings. She passed him by without a glance. He lit a cigarette and moved off slowly in the wake of her footsteps.

The hall was further down the road, near to Craven Street. This location was handy for those who lived off Hedon Road. It was an easy walk down the alley to climb the steps leading up to the flyover of the railway lines and onto Craven Street. Though Rose had to admit, it could be a lonely walk in the dark on your own.

On the way, she met Betty Duncan, pushing the pram with baby fast asleep.

'Come and have a look at the hall and see what's happening,' Rose offered.

Betty accepted, saying, 'I don't know if we'll make it to the dance.' Her voice was wistful.

Rose gave her a quick look. 'Nothing worrying you?' she asked anxiously, knowing of Bob's past fit of temper and lashing out at Betty.

'No, it's just that money is tight and the bairns need new clothes. They're shooting up so fast, especially our Shirley.' Then in a confidential tone she said, 'She's started her periods.'

Rose smiled. 'She is growing up fast.' They walked on in silence for a few steps, then Rose said, 'Now don't be offended.' She knew how proud Betty was. 'Why not come along to our clothing store and check out if we have anything suitable?'

'I don't want charity,' Betty stated.

'Of course not, but you can always bring along what your children no longer need.'

Betty pondered. 'I suppose I can.'

They reached the hall and Rose unlocked the door and they went inside.

The man, who had followed them swore under his breath. He stood for a time, watching the door until he saw a police constable walking his way.

'Another time,' he muttered. He hunched his shoulders, pulled his cap further over his face and stalked away in the other direction.

TWENTY-FOUR

'Joe,' Rose called, as he was about to mount his cycle to leave work. She ran across Drypool Bridge towards him.

'Rose,' he said, looking concerned. 'Is there anything wrong?'

She came up to him, suddenly feeling very shy as she looked into his big brown eyes.

'No, I just wanted to see you.' She reached out to touch his arm.

'Aye, aye, some people have all the luck,' said an older man walking by. 'Hold on to her, Joe, boy, or I might be in with a chance.'

'No chance,' Joe called in reply, humour in his voice. He laughed, his face crinkling, then turned to look at Rose.

'I'm sorry, Rose. We haven't had much time together. What with no one to look after Peter when he's in bed, it's difficult for me to get out. Mrs Mitchell and her daughter,' he was cautious not to mention Maureen by name, 'take care of him after school, and when I'm at night class.'

Rose felt her facial muscles tense; she tried to smile, to be cheerful, as she promised herself she would.

'I understand, Joe. It's hard for both of us. And with my family circumstances, it makes it even more difficult.' She shrugged. She wished with all her heart it wasn't so.

A horde of workers, bent on getting home, were hurrying across the bridge and Rose and Joe had no option but to walk on down Clarence Street. Lost in the crowd, they didn't notice the roughly dressed man with a flat cap pulled over his eyes, walking just behind them.

'I'll walk you to your bus stop,' said Joe.

'I was hoping you could walk home with me,' Rose began, but glancing at him, she saw his face drop.

'I'm sorry, love. I'm expected to pick up Peter straight after work and if I'm late they'll worry.' He looked at her disappointed face, willing her to understand his predicament. 'It's difficult,' he sighed, then he tried to inject cheerfulness into his voice as he said, 'Mrs Mitchell will look after Peter while we are at the Summer Ball. That's good, isn't it?'

By now they had arrived at the bus stop and the man who was walking behind them also stopped, dodging into a nearby shop doorway. He lit a cigarette, blowing out the smoke.

Joe caught the whiff of tobacco, longing for a cigarette, which he didn't have. He needed the money for Peter's birthday present. He focused his attention back to Rose.

She smiled at him, her voice too bright. 'Of course. Sorry, I'm being selfish.'

'No you're not. It won't always be like this, Rose.' He had thought that once the war was over and there was peace, life would return back to some kind of normality, but it came with a whole set of new problems. 'Come to the allotment on Sunday; we'll walk down together and talk. It's Peter's birthday picnic.'

'I'm sorry, Joe. I feel guilty now because I've forgotten Peter's birthday, but I'll make it up to him on Sunday.' After that, they ran out of conversation and she was glad to see her bus coming. She went upstairs and sat at the back of the bus because she felt utterly miserable, and didn't want anyone to see the tears which stung her eyes.

Joe cycled off, lost in thoughts. He would have loved to have carefree time and walk home with Rose. But Peter's welfare, for now, must be his main priority. His son had suffered the loss of his mother, been evacuated and adjusted to strangers, whom he had grown to love and feel secure with. Then his father, this unknown person, had wrenched him from the only home he could remember. Peter needed him more than ever. It seemed to work, the bonding of father and son, when he lodged with Mrs Mitchell. At one time he thought that he and Rose would marry and live with her parents until they could set up their own home, but now that was only a pipe dream. He pedalled furiously, not noticing the bus pass him and Rose's face peering down at him from the upper window.

On Sunday, Rose stood at the kitchen sink, watching the torrent of rain gushing from the guttering, her spirits low.

'No walking to the allotment today,' Mary said, looking at the sparse assortment of vegetables – half an onion, carrot and two potatoes – on the kitchen table. 'I was banking on having fresh veg. Never mind, I'll make a casserole with the ham shank.'

'I'm going upstairs to see what I can wear for the dance. I'll feed David when he wakes up,' Rose offered.

'I was going to make you a new dress,' said Mary. Abstractedly, she ran her hands through her greying hair, which was in need of a perm.

Meanwhile, at his lodgings Joe was also staring out of the kitchen window, feeling hemmed in, restricted in more ways than one. Peter was sitting at the kitchen table, fixing together a small model aeroplane made of balsa wood, his birthday present from Joe. He was planning a picnic at the allotment to celebrate his son's birthday, a happy occasion. He glared out at the pouring rain, seeing no signs of a break in the sky. So it would be just him and Peter for the birthday tea; his landlord and lady still liked their afternoon rest on a Sunday.

Saturday, 27th July, the evening of the Summer Ball, was a lovely, sunny day. A shaft of light stole through a chink in Rose's bedroom curtains. Quietly, so as not to wake David, who had cut his first tooth and was still fast asleep, she dressed, and tiptoed downstairs to make a pot of tea. The tea caddy was almost empty.

'Drat,' Rose groused, using just a few

leaves; rationing seemed to be going on for ever. Cradling her hands round the mug of weak tea, she looked out of the kitchen window, embracing the soft blue sky and tiny, delicate, fleeting clouds. She loved these few moments of bliss before the household woke up. But most of all, she was looking forward to seeing Joe tonight and dancing with him.

Later on, Rose was on her way to the community hall. She hummed as she strode out.

'My, you've got a spring in your step,' remarked Mrs Fisher, on her way to the corner shop.

Rose couldn't keep the happiness from her voice. 'It's the dance tonight.'

'Aye, I know it is. Me and Alf are coming.'

'And Joe's coming.'

'I should hope he is. Mind you don't let any other girl dance with him,' Vera chuckled. 'If I was younger...'

Rose laughed and went on her way, down Raven Street, through the alley, up the steps and down Craven Street to Holderness Road, still humming to herself. She didn't see the man, the same rough-looking man who had followed her before.

She arrived at the hall and her fingers traced the smooth wood of the freshly painted door; a lush shade of green, the colour of early summer grass. Rose unlocked the door, letting out the trapped stuffy heat, and left the door open to let in the bright, clean air of the day. She went through into the small kitchen to check on the boiler for hot water, though she did not think that many would want a cup of tea tonight, except maybe some of the older generation. As she turned to check the list for cool drinks, she saw a shadow flit across the doorway.

Unperturbed, she called, 'Have you come to help?' No one answered. She went through into the hall and gasped, her hands going to her mouth.

'Hello, Rose. Pleased to see me?'

'Harry! What are you doing here? I thought you were still in prison.' She stared at him, shocked by his dishevelled appearance. He'd lost weight, his clothes were threadbare and dirty, his boots worn and down at heel. His face, unshaven, was gaunt beneath the growth of beard, and his eyes were dark and sunk, his hair unkempt.

His voice gruff, he replied, 'I've served my time. I just wanted to see you, to talk to you.' He fished in his jacket pocket for his cigarettes, his fingers trembling as he struck a match. Then some of the old spark returned as he said, 'How about a cup of tea and a biscuit?'

'Come through to the kitchen.' As he came closer to him, she caught the odour of his unwashed body and she held her breath.

She made him a big mug of tea and found a few biscuits at the bottom of a tin. She watched as he gobbled down the biscuits and swilled the tea down his throat. When finished, he said, wiping his mouth with the back of his grubby hand, 'That was good. A lifesaver.' Then he sat down on a chair and looked at her.

She moved to lean against the draining board. Adopting her professional voice, she asked, 'Where are you living, Harry?'

He shrugged. 'Here and there.'

She'd heard that quote so often since the war had ended.

'Are you homeless?' she asked.

Anger flared in his eyes. 'No bugger wants me now. Not even my own mother.' As quickly as his anger erupted it died. 'I'm beaten, Rose. You were the only good thing in my life and I messed that up.' His dull eyes became wet with unshed tears.

Feeling cold shivers run down her spine, Rose felt appalled that a man who had served his country at war was now reduced to this way of living; if it could be called living. She moved to where her handbag was resting on a chair and took out her purse. She had five shillings and tuppence. She emptied it out and pressed the coins into Harry's hand. Then she looked him full in the face.

'You didn't treat me very well, but that doesn't matter now. Go and buy fish and chips and use the rest of the money to pay for two nights' lodgings. Then on Monday morning, come to my office and I will see what can be done to help you.'

He looked at the money and balled it in his fist, mumbling, 'Thanks, Rose.'

She watched him go, a forlorn figure, his shoulders hunched. She didn't think of Harry as once being her sweetheart, but as a soldier returned from war, wanting peace but only to find his life in pieces, scattered to the uncaring winds. His life seemed meaningless and Rose didn't know the answer. She only knew that while the war raged, everyone, whether armed forces or civilians, pulled together and morale was high, because the aim for all was to win. Now the war was won and greeted with victorious glory. After the war peace was declared, but then the shadows crept in, and for many, an unseen future loomed.

She picked up a cloth, damped it and began vigorously to wipe dust from bottles of cordial, venting her pent-up emotions, her inability to make things right.

'Hey, lass, you'll wear that bottle away.'

Rose, her face still wreathed in fury, looked up. She blinked for a second, and then recognized the man. She took a deep breath and felt calmer.

'Hello, Denis, how are you?' He was one of the band members playing tonight.

'Better than you,' he commented. 'What's upset you?'

She threw the cloth into the sink. 'Injust-ice.'

'Ah, there was a lot of that after the Great War.' There was a loud shout from the hall. 'That's my mate. He's helped me push the handcart. Best bring the drums in now.'

After that, helpers came to set up the tables and chairs around the dance floor. Sally called in after work with colourful bunting.

'Me and Frank are coming early to fix it up. Is Joe coming early?'

'He'll try, but he's to take Peter to Mrs Mitchell's daughter's house first.'

'She's a flighty piece is that Maureen. She's works part-time in our works canteen. Likes the fellows, she does. I should watch her with your Joe,' Sally added.

Rose replied, stiffly, 'She's a great help to Joe, taking Peter home after school.'

'If you say so. Cheerio, see you later.' Sally mimicked a waltz step as she left the hall.

Rose, suddenly feeling tired, sat down heavily on a chair, oblivious to the noise going on around her. She had tried not to think of Joe spending time at Maureen's house and seeing Maureen more than he saw her. But she couldn't change the situation, not while David was still in her family's care.

TWENTY-FIVE

After making sure that everything was in readiness for the Summer Ball, Rose hurried home. She felt hot and dusty and in need of a good strip wash, and to wash her hair. How she wished, like in the American films, she could have a good long soak in a bathtub, with scented bubbling water. Instead, she would make do with the ewer and boil a kettle to take upstairs into the privacy of her room, and a jug of rainwater to rinse her hair.

The house was quiet when she arrived. Propped on the mantelpiece was a note from her mother, saying she had taken David for a walk in his pram.

'Bless her,' Rose murmured.

Upstairs in her room, she laid her underclothes on the bed, the ones she had made for her bottom drawer. Lovingly she'd sewn them using material of artificial silk, bought before the war, of a delicate shade of pink and embroidered with tiny rosebuds. The silk stockings Sally had given her, and her blue dress was the one her mother made her last year.

At last she was ready; hair shining and still damp, she coaxed it into waves to hang onto her shoulders. With her precious stub of lipstick, she carefully painted her lips bold red. Slipping her feet into white, wedge-heeled sandals, she checked her appearance in the mirror and smiled. She was looking forward to seeing Joe.

Mary and David were home. Rose glanced at her mother's worn-out face, feeling guilty.

Then Mary said, 'Rose, you look lovely. By the way, Mrs Butler has arranged for a helper to come on Monday so I'll have time to myself. Now you go and enjoy yourself.'

Rose kissed Mary on the cheek, and said softly, 'Thanks, Mam.'

The early evening was still warm and Rose strode out to the community hall, with a surprising spring in her step. Tonight she would be dancing in Joe's arms.

The musicians were first to arrive: they liked to tune up and have a practice together. The piano, donated by an old man who had no further use for it, had been tuned. The pianist, a young demobbed sailor, was eager to get into a band and perfect his playing. He had brought along his mate who served with him and who played the guitar. There was Denis on the drums and Eric the saxophonist, who could also play the clarinet. Rose listened as they practised, her feet tapping to the music as she began to set the buffet table.

'Go on, give us a dance, Rose,' called Denis, good-naturedly.

Rose obliged, performed a quick-step, holding the arms of her imaginary partner. 'I'm in the mood for dancing,' she sang out.

'The party's started early!' Sally and Frank came into the hall and everyone laughed. After that, people began arriving, and Rose became caught up in the spontaneous activity of the offerings of cheese sandwiches, savoury rolls, packets of Smith's crisps complete with their tiny blue twists of salt. One man brought bottles of pale ale, and another a bottle of port wine. She was overwhelmed with the kindness and the generosity of folk.

'Rose!' She turned to see Joe and immediately she went into his arms, so pleased to see him. He held her close; his lips on hers were warm and tender. He smelt divine, of male freshness and Brylcreem.

'Love you,' she whispered in his ear.

'Let me look at you.' He held her at arm's length. 'Rose, you are beautiful.' They gazed into each other's eyes. 'I've missed you so much.' He pulled her close again.

Rose felt as though they were the only people in the room and that they could dance in each other's arms for ever and ever. Then the spell was broken, someone called her name: they couldn't find the bottle opener.

'Come and get a drink, Joe,' she said, taking his hand.

'Bring me one, Joe.'

Rose turned to see Maureen.

'We came together,' she said.

Rose looked at Joe, and he whispered, 'When I took Peter for Mrs Mitchell to babysit, she asked if she could walk down with me. I couldn't very well say no.'

The evening passed in a swirl of dancing, swinging music, and 'Good grub,' a man said. It was Bob, Betty's husband.

'Hello,' Rose said in surprise. 'I didn't realize you were here. How's the allotment doing?'

'Great onions, though Betty's fed up of them. Women are a damned mystery to me,' he added, with a twinkle in his eye. 'But I'm working on it.'

Betty came up to join in the conversation. 'Sorry we were late. My old aunt forgot she was babysitting and we can't stay too late. So come on, Bob, let's get dancing.'

Rose, collecting empty glasses on a tray, looked round for Joe. He was waltzing with Maureen, who was clinging to him in an intimate manner, and they were laughing together. An uncontrollable pang of jealousy stirred in Rose and she wanted to rush onto the dance floor and knock Maureen out of Joe's arms.

'You're shaking, let me take them, love.' Mrs Fisher took the tray from Rose, and following Rose's gaze, remarked, 'I should watch that hussy.'

Rose waited until the dance finished, and

then she went to claim Joe. She took hold of his arm and, smiling sweetly at Maureen, she steered him away.

The evening whirled by and now the band was playing the last waltz. Rose was tidying up in the kitchen and jumped when Joe came up behind her and slid his arms around her waist and nuzzled her neck.

'May I have this dance, Miss Ellerby?'

She twisted to face him and with a hint of mischief in her voice, said, 'Yes, Mr Tennison.'

Joe led Rose onto the dance floor. They waltzed to a lover's melody; her feet were gliding on air. He held her close and ripples of heady sensations filled her very being. Her fingers caressed the nape of his neck. She heard his soft intake of breath, his voice low, barely audible, 'Miss Ellerby, I wish you were Mrs Tennison and we were going home together.'

'Oh, Joe, so do I,' she whispered, her lips seeking his.

All too soon, the music ended. Everyone clapped in appreciation. Rose's attention was torn from Joe, as dancers came to congratulate her on arranging such a grand evening and when was the next one to be.

Rose laughed and said, 'If it was only up to me, we could have a dance every week, but funds and work commitment wouldn't allow.'

People started drifting home and Rose set about making sure everything was safe and in order, for the hall was used by other groups. Sally and Frank were helping and Joe too, when Maureen appeared with her coat on and said to Joe, 'It's late, and Mother will be wondering where we are, and you have Peter to think about.'

Joe looked apologetically at Rose. 'I'm sorry, love, but I have to collect Peter and it's late.' He gave her a hasty kiss and went with Maureen in tow.

Outside, a balmy breeze stirred in the night air. Joe was thinking of Rose, paying no attention to Maureen. Neither of them noticed the man lurking in the shadows who started to follow them as they set off.

They walked in silence, Maureen sniffing and coughing every now and then to draw attention, but Joe seeming unaware of her. They walked over the flyover and down the steps leading to the dark alley, when Maureen tripped and caught hold of Joe's arm.

He stared at her; he'd forgotten she was there. Remembering his manners, he asked, 'Are you all right?'

She rubbed her ankle. 'I've twisted it.' She leaned against him, clutching his arm.

Joe looked down, but he couldn't see anything for it was too dark.

'Can you walk on it?'

'I'm not sure.' Her voice wobbled. She made an attempt to stand up on her own, and wincing with pain, overbalancing, she fell heavily against Joe, her arms flailing, her hands gripping round his neck. Endeavouring to steady her, he put his arms around her waist.

'What a fetching sight.' The sarcastic male voice was menacing. 'You two-timing bastard.'

Joe, still holding Maureen, turned his head to see who it was and didn't see the fist. The blow to his chin knocked him sideways and he lost his footing, and his hold on Maureen slipped. She screamed, hitting the hard surface of the alley. Staggering, blood oozing from his mouth, Joe looked for his attacker. Just at that moment, a crying Maureen pulled at the leg of his trousers, sending Joe tumbling over her. All the time the attacker hurled a torrent of abusive words. As Joe was about to scramble up, he felt the attacker's boot hit his solar plexus, winding him, taking his breath away. He bent double and as he clutched his abdomen, a wave of nausea swept through him. Before he could pull himself up, he felt the boot again, this time aimed at his head. A seething hot pain burst within him and a flashback struck him; in vivid colours of reds and oranges with streaks of blue interspersed. He was back at war, trying to rescue a comrade from a burning plane. The noise and cries around him were heart-wrenching and warm blood spattered his face; was it his or his comrade's?

The shouting came nearer and footsteps, running on hard ground. It was strange, he remembered thinking, because the field was thick with slimy mud, which made a slithering sound and he was slipping on it. Suddenly, he saw a white flash of light; gasping for air he felt a queer sensation of being weightless, floating, before he entered a tunnel of blackness.

It was Frank who first reached the crumpled, silent figure of Joe on the hard ground of the alley. At the top of the steps, Rose saw the figure of a man running away towards Hedon Road. She knew him.

'Harry,' she uttered in disbelief. Then she hurried down the steps, Sally following her. On reaching Joe, she fell to her knees. 'Oh, my God!' she cried. 'What has he done?' She made to cradle his still form in her arms.

Quickly, Frank said, 'Don't move him. Not until we know the extent of his injuries. I'll go for help. Will you be all right?' They both nodded.

'What about me?' Maureen whined. She was sitting with her back against the alley fence.

They hadn't noticed her there. Rose, concerned about Joe, just glanced at her. Sally went to her side.

'Did he attack you?'

'No, but I've hurt my ankle,' she sobbed.

Sally kneeled to look at the swollen ankle, and then she straightened up, saying, 'You've only sprained it. You'll live.' Accustomed now to the darkness of the alley, she could see Rose's face, pale and strained. She went to put a comforting arm around her shoulders.

'His pulse is weak and he's cold,' Rose said. She pulled off her cardigan and laid it gently across Joe's body. 'I wish someone would come and help,' she cried, plaintively. It was then they heard the clanging bell of an approaching ambulance.

By now, a small crowd had gathered, wondering and speculating what had gone on.

The attendants were quick and efficient and they soon had Joe on a stretcher and into the ambulance. Rose, in a state of shock, went with Joe, not wanting to be parted from him.

At the infirmary, a doctor took charge of Joe and he was whisked away to be examined. Rose was left to give the receptionist Joe's details. Then she went to sit on a hard chair, in the small, sterile waiting room, her mind now completely numb. The only other occupant was a woman who stared at Rose in her blue dance dress. Rose hugged her arms around her trembling body and let her chin sink to her chest.

After a while, her body stopped its trembling and she prayed that Joe's injuries were not life-threatening. But why had it happened? What was Harry thinking of? His mind must be deranged. She would have to tell the police that she saw him running away from the scene. Her thoughts circled her numb brain, nothing making any sense. She sat for hours, waiting.

She was startled when the door opened and the doctor came in. 'Mrs Tennison?' he asked.

She struggled to her feet. 'I'm Joe's fiancée, Rose Ellerby,' she said, her voice sounding hollow in her head. She stared into the tired face of the young doctor, wanting good news.

He seemed to sense her anxiety and his voice was calm. 'Mr Tennison has two broken ribs, a broken nose and missing teeth.' He paused a moment. 'He has a fracture to his skull and is suffering concussion. We will need to keep him in hospital to monitor his condition.'

Shock again reverberated through Rose's body. She whispered, 'Can I see him, please?'

'A nurse will come and take you to him, but you can only see him for a few minutes.'

The time dragged. At last the nurse came. Rose followed her along a silent corridor.

Joe was in a small ward in a bed near to the nurses' desk where a nightlight shone. She approached the bed and gasped on seeing Joe's brutally beaten face and his head covered in bandages. She wanted to smother his injuries with kisses, but she just sat down on the chair and took hold of his hand. It felt light and limp in hers. Tears filled her eyes, and she whispered, 'Joe, my sweetheart.' She couldn't say any more because words choked her. She sat quietly, holding his hand, watching for any sign of movement.

The nurse reappeared. Rose looked fearfully at Joe.

'Is he going to be all right?'

'He's stable. Come back tomorrow, then the doctor will speak to you.' Rose bit on her lips to stop the tears from overflowing.

Outside the infirmary, the early morning was warm, but Rose shivered. She made her way to the porters' lodge to ask if they could call her a taxi to take her home.

'Rose.'

Out of the shadows stepped a figure.

'Harry,' she gasped. Anger spiralled within her and without thinking, she flew at him, her nails scratching his face and drawing blood.

He caught her arms and held them in a vice grip. 'Rose, I did it for you. He's not worth it. Two-timing you with that bitch, I caught them at it. It's me you should be marrying.' His voice was hysterical and she could smell the beer on his breath.

She struggled to free herself from his

strong hold, yelling, 'I don't love you, Harry Carter, and never will.'

'What's going on?' Two porters, reporting for duty, came into view. On seeing them, Harry immediately released Rose, turned and fled.

TWENTY-SIX

Joe was in the infirmary for two weeks. There was no question of him going to his lodgings to recover from his injuries. Mrs Stepney, when asked, said she couldn't look after him.

Off the cuff, Ted made a decision. 'Joe and his son can come here,' he declared. They were in the kitchen and Ted was standing firm by the mantelpiece in reach of his pipe and baccy.

'Oh, Dad,' cried Rose, and flung her arms around his ample waistline. 'What a relief.'

Freddie, who had been listening, gave an angry reply. 'And just where are they going to sleep?' Freddie had moved downstairs to sleep in the front room so that David could have his small bedroom. Mary could attend to his needs, thus giving Rose more chance of a restful night. Not wanting to be thwarted, Ted snapped, 'Can't Joe share with you?'

'Like hell!' Freddie replied, jumping to his

feet. 'I live here and pay my way and I'm not going to be pushed from pillar to post.' He pulled on his jacket and stormed out of the house.

Rose stared after her brother and Ted lit his pipe, neither speaking. Mary came downstairs, after putting David to bed.

'What was that commotion about?'

Ted looked glum and Rose explained to her mother.

'I can see Freddie's point. He had a lot of upset, what with Elsa dying and the bairn not his. It's not easy for him.' Mary's voice was calm and sympathetic. 'And now you're worried about Joe and Peter?' Rose nodded. 'Let's have a good think what to do,' Mary suggested.

Rose and Mary sat at the kitchen table talking, thinking up ideas, but nothing seemed workable. Ted didn't add to the conversation, immersed in reading his newspaper, when suddenly he said, 'They could go next door.'

Both women stared at him, not sure what he meant. He gave a broad smile. 'Ask Mrs Fisher. She's got a front room.'

'Oh, Ted Ellerby, I could kiss you,' Mary said with joy. 'Why didn't I think of that?' She looked expectantly round the kitchen. 'I can't go empty-handed.' She got up and went to the pantry. 'I've got a rhubarb pie. It was for supper.' She glanced at Ted.

'Bread and dripping will do me,' he said,

pleased with his idea.

Mary went next door. Ted read his newspaper, and Rose began unpicking an old coat, hopeful that when she turned the material inside out, it would make a skirt. It was a laborious job, but it helped to keep her mind off Joe and his injuries, and recuperation.

Mrs Fisher was agreeable, and said that Alf would welcome a bit of male company. The question of board and lodgings would be sorted later.

Freddie came home, the worse for drink. Mary ushered him to bed, telling him everything was now fine and he mustn't worry.

Over the next few days, the Ellerby household was topsy-turvy, but gradually settled down. David continued to thrive, contented with his routine, and Irene, the help, was great with him, which gave Mary a chance to go and have her hair permed.

Joe came home to Church Terrace in a car, complete with a chauffeur, organized by his employers at the flour mill. The children, playing out in the street, came to gaze and admire the sleek saloon, all black and shiny. Rose went to meet him. Her heart sank when she saw the fatigue of his body and the grey pallor of his face, but she smiled at him, gently taking his arm. They slowly walked forward.

Mrs Fisher welcomed him by cooking one of her special meat and potato pies and Alf produced a bottle of stout, 'To build you up, lad,' he announced jovially.

While Joe was in hospital, a police constable had come to take a statement from him. Rose was by his side as he recounted the unprovoked attack.

'Maureen, Mrs Baker, was walking with me, her mother was looking after my son at her house, when she tripped and sprained her ankle. We were just seeing if she could walk on it, when he attacked. He came from nowhere, ranting and raving.' Joe closed his eyes for a moment. He didn't want to go over that terrible night, but he must. 'It happened so quickly and took me by surprise. One minute I was standing, the next on the ground. He laced into me with his boots, kicking me in the ribs and head, and...' He swallowed hard; this was difficult for him to say.

'Take your time, sir,' the constable said.

Joe's voice was low, almost a whisper. 'It was as if I was back on the airfield, trying to save the crew from the burning plane and I couldn't reach them...' His voice faded and he closed his eyes, not wanting to relive such terrible horrors.

Rose reached for his hand and held it. Joe opened his eyes, his jaw set in determination, his tone stronger. 'I recognized Harry

Carter's voice.'

Next, Rose told how she had seen Harry running away from the scene and the altercation outside of the infirmary. When the constable finished writing, Rose asked, 'Have you seen Harry Carter?

'No, miss. We checked the most likely places and believe he is hiding out somewhere, but we are on the lookout for him.' His voice took on a stern, warning note. 'If he should turn up anytime, please do not approach him. Contact the station and we will deal with him.'

The family rallied round and Joe was made comfortable in Mrs Fisher's front room. Peter was not sure what was expected of him, but he wanted to keep close to his dad. Ted brought the little camp bed and placed it next to Joe's makeshift sofa bed, so they were companions for each other. Peter would read to Joe from his treasured Rupert Annual, though Joe often fell asleep. Peter loved it when Rose came from next door and brought him a mug of cocoa and sometimes a biscuit and tucked him in bed. She would sit and hold his dad's hand and talk to him. Peter liked it here; he felt safe and happy. In his nightly prayers, he asked Jesus if he could stay here and not have to go back to Ferries Street.

Rose went round to Joe's lodgings to see Mrs Stepney, to explain that Joe and Peter were staying with her neighbour until Joe recovered. Mrs Stepney stood on the doorstep, her apron tight around her overweight body, her arms akimbo, her lips pursed. She did not ask Rose in.

'Um, well, I'll tell you this, miss, I can't keep the room open. We need the money. I've already got a nice respectable couple wanting to come.'

Rose was taken aback by the woman's lack of compassion. Then she said, 'If we pay the board and lodgings, will you keep the room for Joe and Peter?'

'Well, I suppose I can.'

Rose saw the woman thinking of the money and nothing to do to earn it.

'I'll bring the money tomorrow.'

The woman smiled, which was more of a smirk.

By the end of the week, Joe was feeling so much better, in spirit and in health. 'I've never been so well looked after. Vera's cooking and your mam's baking has set me up a treat.' He patted his stomach. 'And your dad and Alf are so generous with bottles of stout.' He was resting on the top of his bed and stretched his arms luxuriously above his head.

Rose laughed, pleased that his recovery was going well. 'Don't get too used to it, Joe.

Another week or so and you'll be back at Mrs Stepney's.'

'Don't remind me,' he groaned. He glanced down at the sleeping figure of his son, tucked up in his camp bed. 'He'll miss being here. He's had a lot of unsettlement in his young life.'

Rose reached for Joe's hand. 'When we are married, he will have stability. If only there wasn't a shortage of housing.' The result of houses bombed during the war, in the daily newspaper it reported that plans were afoot to remedy this, but so far, nothing was happening, no new building was taking place. If rooms became vacant, they were soon snapped up. Mrs Fisher was kind enough to let Joe and Peter stay, but only for a short time. Alf was her paying lodger, with his own bedroom and use of the front room for his visitors. 'All above board so don't get any funny ideas,' she soon told any prying neighbours.

At work, Rose was busy and so was Mrs Butler. They were the only two paid members of staff for the WVS; the warehouse/driver man was paid by the council. The other workers, who were mainly part-time, were volunteers and very dedicated to the cause of helping people in difficult situations. There was no information from the London contact on the whereabouts of David's grandparents and Rose didn't like to pester Mrs Butler.

David was a lovely baby and in the short term, the family coped well with him, but long term? Rose put down her pen from filling in the endless obligatory forms. She cupped her chin in her hands. What if they didn't find David's grandparents and what would the future hold for him? One thing was for sure, David would not be abandoned by the family. Somehow they would manage. Freddie was still in shock at losing his comrade and Elsa. Rose gave a heavy sigh. In the meantime, she and Joe remained unwed.

The afternoon wore on; Rose didn't take a break at dinner-time so that she could, if possible, go home early to meet Peter from school. She was preparing to leave when a man entered her office space. It was the clergyman, Matthew Robertson, Chaplain to His Majesty's Prison, Hedon Road. Rose stared at him. Did he want her to visit another prisoner?

'Good afternoon, Miss Ellerby. I am sorry to intrude.'

She motioned him to be seated. 'How can I help?'

He sighed heavily. 'I have had sad news. I have just come from the mortuary.'

'The mortuary?' she repeated, feeling a chill run through her body.

'Yes, I was asked by the deceased's family to identify him.' He stopped speaking to let her digest his words. 'The body of Henry

Carter was found on the Humber foreshore.'

'Harry,' she whispered. She felt the colour drain from her face.

Matthew got to his feet and went to fetch a glass of water from the cloakroom.

She sipped the water and her colour and composure returned.

'How did it happen?'

'The police are not sure, but they think he must have slipped and fallen when walking along the riverbank near to the old town.'

Rose thought of Mrs Carter. 'His mother, how is she taking this?'

'According to Mrs Carter's sister, she has asked me to act on the family's behalf to make all the necessary arrangements. Because of Mrs Carter's illness, she will not be able to leave her and is therefore unable to attend the funeral. There are no other relatives. The police informed me of Harry's attack on your fiancé and I quite understand.' He paused, looking at her.

In a quiet voice Rose said, 'You are asking me to attend his funeral?'

'Yes, my dear. I believe you are a lady of Christian compassion.'

Rose found she was gripping her hands tightly in her lap.

'I must speak to Joe. He is my first loyalty.'

'Yes, of course.' He drew a single sheet of paper from his breast pocket. 'These are the details.' Slowly, he got to his feet. 'Good afternoon, Miss Ellerby. Thank you for your time.'

Rose watched him go and then she glanced down at the paper. Her Joe was alive and improving each day, and they would have a future together. Harry had been a tortured soul, a victim of the war. He had never known peace and for him there would never be a future.

TWENTY-SEVEN

Rose played over the scenario with the chaplain, until her head ached. She was on the bus going home, and stared unseeingly out of the rain-splattered window, unaware of someone coming to sit in the seat next to her.

'Penny for them,' said a cheerful voice.

Rose half-turned in her seat and exclaimed, 'Sally.'

'You look as though you are carrying the worries of the world,' Sally said, observing her friend's drawn face.

'Just heard sad news. Harry Carter is dead.'

'Dead, how?'

'Drowned.' Rose explained what the chaplain had told her.

'I never liked Harry, but I wouldn't wish him dead. Why did the chaplain tell you?'

Rose sighed heavily. 'He's given me a dilemma. He wants me to go to the funeral. Harry's mother's ill, and the aunt is looking after her.'

'But what will Joe say?' Sally asked.

'I don't know. I don't want to upset him, not now he's on the mend. He's suffered at the hands of Harry, an unprovoked attack of such fury. Harry must have been out of his mind. But now he can't hurt anyone, ever. The least I can do for him is to go to his funeral.'

'But are you sure you want to go?'

'If I'm honest, no, I don't. But who else will go?'

'Didn't he have any mates?'

'Not the sort you would call friends. I think they were responsible for him being in prison. He never told on them. When he came out, he had no job, no home, no one to turn to. He became a down and outer, living rough.'

Sally gave her a look of sympathy, not wishing for her friend's problem.

'It's our stop.'

Rose hurried off to meet Peter from school, glad of his small hand to hold. It comforted her. As a treat, he was having tea with them today. David was cooing in his pram in the passage and Peter went to talk to him and to play with his tiny fingers, which mesmerized David.

312

'You're quiet, Rose,' Mary said as she cut the cake for afters.

Rose finished laying the table and sat down and blurted, 'Harry Carter is dead.'

Mary put down the knife she was using and sat down opposite Rose. 'That's a shock.'

Rose told her mother the full story. When she had finished, Mary took hold of Rose's hand, saying, 'You must do what you think is best, but first, talk it over with Joe.' Then as an afterthought, she added, 'Peter can stay with us.'

After tea, Rose went up to her bedroom to freshen up. She changed into a clean blouse and sat at her dressing table. She stared at her reflection for a few moments. How would Joe take the news? Her troubled eyes looked back at her. She sighed deeply and ran her fingers through her hair. Taking out the grips, which were fastening it back, she let it hang loose.

Why did Harry, who once had loved life and sparked with energy, end up deranged and attack Joe? Now he was dead. What a waste of life. She banged down the hairbrush on the dressing table and jumped to her feet. The light, streaming in through the window, shone on her hair and it gleamed like the colour of burnished gold of autumn leaves.

In the kitchen, Mary was bathing David in a small tin bath in front of the fire, and Peter was helping. Rose watched this delightful family scene, her whole being filled with tenderness. Tears pricked her eyes, because more than anything, she wanted to marry Joe and be a mother to Peter and for them to be a family.

She turned away quickly, saying, 'Just going, Mam.' She stopped in the yard for a few moments to regain her composure and to let the cool air fan her face.

She knocked on Mrs Fisher's back door, calling out, 'It's only me, Rose.'

'Go through, he's waiting for you. I'll bring you both a cup of tea.' The older woman, on seeing the anxiety on Rose's face, looked questioningly, but for once she held her tongue.

Rose pushed open the front room door. Joe was sitting on a chair by the bedside. He still looked pale and his eyes were dull. She went to his side and kissed him warmly on the lips.

His eyes lit up. 'Hello, love.' He reached out to clasp her hands. 'They're cold.'

'Cold hands, warm heart,' she said, her voice too bright. She sat down on the edge of his bed, her knees touching his. How was she going to tell Joe about Harry? She couldn't do it, not just yet. Instead she asked, 'How have you been today?'

'I need to go back to work.' His voice was tense.

'You will, when you're fit enough. They're keeping your job open so don't worry.'

'Yes, but how long for? And another thing, I can't keep on paying for the lodgings in Ferries Street. It's taking all my savings.'

Rose guessed that Joe had been fretting all day. She had offered to pay towards the lodging fees, but his pride wouldn't hear of it. To cheer him up, she said, 'It's a nice evening, fancy a short walk?'

'Good idea, I need to get out.'

They wrapped up warm and strolled up the street towards where the air-raid shelters used to be. There was a path through to Lee Smith Street, where there were shops and a pub. The path was deserted and Joe, every now and then, stopped to catch his breath. They reached a pile of old timber and sat down. Joe was silent so Rose gazed at the wasteland where grass sprouted and intermingled with vivid pink wild flowers, emitting a bittersweet scent.

'I've made up my mind,' Joe said quietly. 'I'm going to walk each morning and night and next week, I'm determined to go back to work.'

Looking at his grey, strained face, Rose asked, anxiously, 'But will you be strong enough?'

'I'll have a glass of stout each night, that's a good tonic.'

So every morning, weather permitting, Joe walked with Alf, and in the evenings he walked with Rose. On one of the walks,

Rose told him of Harry's death, but not about her going to the funeral. She didn't want to spoil his progress. Joe was thoughtful for a moment, and then said, 'I wouldn't wish death on anyone so young, but he was a wrong 'un.'

Joe was unwavering in his fitness regime and in his determination to go back to work. On Friday evening, he asked Rose to walk with him to his lodgings in Ferries Street.

'I'm going to tell Mrs Stepney that Peter and I will be coming back on Sunday night and I'm going to work on the Monday.'

'Are you sure, Joe?' Rose glanced at his determined face. His answer was to take long strides. 'Slow down,' Rose puffed, trying to keep up with him.

Joe knocked on his lodgings door and looked at Rose in surprise because laughter could be heard from within. 'They must have company.' He knocked again.

The door was opened by Mrs Stepney, who glared at them.

'What do you want?'

Joe ignored her curt manner and said, 'I've come to tell you that my son and I will be coming back on Sunday, and–'

She interrupted him. 'You can't. I've got a respectable couple lodging now.' She made to shut the door, but Joe thrust his foot to stop this. 'I've been paying you to keep my lodgings.'

She sniffed. 'I used that money to paint the room. You left it in a disgraceful condition.'

Rose looked on in disbelief. 'You can't do that,' she cried in protest.

'Don't you tell me what I can and can't do in my own house.' Mrs Stepney hollered, placing her hands on her huge hips.

'I'll speak to the authorities,' Rose retaliated.

Joe put a steadying hand on Rose's arm. 'It's not worth arguing about. I'll find somewhere else.' He turned to Mrs Stepney. 'I'll have my belongings, please.'

'Bert,' she shouted. 'Bring that cardboard box.'

Bert came and shoved the box into Joe's arms and the door was shut in their faces.

For a few seconds, both Joe and Rose stood there.

'Come on,' Joe said gruffly. 'Let's go. I never did like it here.'

Mrs Fisher, when she heard the tale, said they could stay for the time being. Speaking to Mary later on, she said, 'I wouldn't throw them out on the street, but I miss not having my front room. It's my only bit of luxury and it's where I keep the photographs of my lads and Alf's lad. God bless 'em.' Mary smiled at her neighbour, understanding.

Joe came home after his first day at work, looking worn out. When Rose went round to

317

see him, he was fast asleep in his chair. Peter was sitting cross-legged on the clipped rug, reading his Rupert Bear book. As Rose entered the room, he put his finger on his lips to warn her. She was going to suggest to Peter that they have a game of tiddlywinks, but they would have been too noisy. Instead, she sat quietly.

She stayed for a good hour and still Joe didn't wake up. She made Peter a mug of cocoa and then helped him to get ready for bed; and, tucking him in, she kissed him goodnight.

For a few minutes, she stood watching Joe's rhythmic breathing. He looked so peaceful that she hadn't the heart to disturb him, and certainly not to tell him that she was going to Harry's funeral. She blew him a kiss and tiptoed from the room.

Harry Carter's funeral was a sombre occasion attended by just three. The brief service was conducted by a vicar Rose didn't know.

'Mrs Fisher's sister's clergyman,' the chaplain, Matthew Robertson, said. The vicar spoke about Harry's childhood and his service to king and country, but made no mention of his time in jail. The wind whipped through the graveyard and Rose held on to her beret, as Harry was laid to rest in the family grave. She felt sad. What a tragedy for one so young to die.

Their duty done, Matthew took hold of Rose's elbow and steered her along the grass path.

'Shall we go and have a cup of tea, my dear?'

They sat in the warmth of the Kardoma cafe, drinking tea and eating toasted crumpets. When finished, Rose sat back in her chair, thinking of Joe. Should she tell?

'You look deep in thought. Are you worried about something?' Matthew leaned forward, speaking quietly. 'Do you want to talk about it?'

Rose sighed deeply, and said, 'Yes, it would be a relief to. It's Joe, my fiancé. I haven't told him about me going to Harry's funeral. I know I should, but the time never seemed right. I don't want to upset him. He's suffered enough.'

Matthew made a steeple of his fingers and said, 'What if Joe hears it from another source and he is angry because you have not told him? Would not that upset him and you?'

Later that afternoon, Rose waited for Joe to leave work. When he saw her, his face broke into a broad smile. She kissed him on the cheek and workmates passing by gave a cheer. Rose blushed, but welcomed the good humour because it put her in a relaxed mood. They walked along together, Joe pushing his bike with one hand and holding Rose's hand with the other.

'This is a lovely surprise,' Joe said, glancing sideways at her.

Rose coughed and cleared her throat. 'I've something to tell you.' She looked at Joe, but he didn't say anything. 'I've been to a funeral today.' Still Joe didn't say anything. Her insides churned and she bit on her lip; it had to come out. 'It was Harry Carter's funeral.' She gave Joe a fleeting look. Had he heard her?

Then he spoke. 'I knew you were going.' They stopped walking to gaze at each other.

'But how?'

'Your mam let it slip. She thought I already knew. I promised her that I wouldn't mention it until you told me.'

'Oh, Joe, I'm sorry. I didn't want to hurt you. You've suffered enough. It's just that I was proxy for his mother and aunt, that's all. Otherwise I wouldn't have gone.' Tears were pricking her eyes and a lump came into her throat.

Joe leaned his bike against the gable end of a brick wall and took Rose into his arms. She put her head on his shoulder, letting her tears flow.

Joe whispered in her ear, 'That's why I love you, Rose Ellerby. You are a wonderful, caring woman and I wouldn't have you any other way.' He put his fingers under her chin and lifted up her face and kissed away her tears.

Some young men passing by gave wolf whistles. Rose blushed, feeling so much happier.

TWENTY-EIGHT

'Rose, come into my office,' Mrs Butler called.

Rose had just arrived at work and was hanging up her coat. Smoothing back her hair, for it was blowing a gale outside, she hurried into the office.

'Sit down,' said Mrs Butler, not in her usual brisk work manner, but kindly.

Rose sat, feeling a little apprehensive.

'Rose, I have good news for you. I have a letter from my London contact. They've found Mr and Mrs Merchant, David's grandparents. They're now living near relatives in Ely, Cambridgeshire.' Mrs Butler handed her the letter.

Tears sprang into Rose's eyes; tears of happiness and relief. These last few weeks had been stressful at home and to hear good news was a joyous welcome. Her hands shook as she read the letter; it was from a Mrs Welton, who was agreeing to act as an intermediary. Rose looked up.

'Freddie will be pleased and relieved.

Thank you, Mrs Butler, for all your help.'

Rose wasn't too sure what her mother's reaction would be. Mary had grown to love David, but Rose knew she could not carry on indefinitely caring for the child.

'Take the letter home for Freddie to read, and I suggest, if he is willing, he writes to Mrs Welton with all known details. She then can contact Mr and Mrs Merchant to acquaint them with the fact that they have a grandson, and the circumstances of his birth. One more thing, my dear: be prepared; Mr and Mrs Merchant might not accept David as their grandson or may not be willing to be his legal guardians or to care for him.'

Rose's face became sombre.

'Take one step at a time,' Mrs Butler advised.

For the rest of the day, Rose worked on autopilot.

Later, after work, she collected Peter from school and left him next door with Alf, who was going to show him how to play the game of draughts. Then she hurried home and into the kitchen, where Mary was cooking the tea.

'Smells good,' said Rose, hanging her coat on the door hook. She kicked off her shoes and put on her cosy slippers.

'Belly part of pork,' Mary said. Turning, she glanced at her daughter and remarked, 'You look pleased with yourself.'

Rose couldn't contain her joy. 'I've a letter to show to Freddie,' she burst out. 'It's from a Mrs Welton, who has found David's grandparents, and she has agreed to act as a go-between.'

Mary dropped into the nearest chair. 'Does this mean I'm going to lose him?'

Rose came to stand by her mother's side and laid her hand on her shoulder. 'Nothing is certain and this is only the first stage.' Then in a rush of optimism she ventured, 'When Joe and I marry, we will have lots of children and we already have Peter.'

Mary put a hand on Rose's, and said quietly, 'I sound like a selfish old woman, but you are right, David needs his family.' She was quiet for a moment, then added, 'He will be a blessing to his grandparents, their only son's child.'

Ted came home and was told the news, and said, 'Let's hear what Freddie has to say.'

Freddie arrived home, washed his hands and sat down at the kitchen table with his family.

'It smells good, Mam, and I'm famished.' Silently, all three stared at him. 'What?' he asked.

Rose, unable to contain her joy, said, 'A letter!' She thrust it under Freddie's nose. 'Read.'

As he read the letter, Freddie's face paled. With shaking hands, he rested the single sheet of paper on the table. 'So, they've found Davy's parents. I'd like to go and see them.' His colour now returned. He turned to look at Rose, seated next to him. 'Do you think it's possible?'

'If Mr and Mrs Merchant want to see David, then you could accompany him.'

'I couldn't manage him,' he cried, a surge of panic flooding his face and eyes.

Rose laid a soothing hand on his arm. 'I can arrange for an escort to care for David on the journey, but you will have to pay her expenses.'

Relief took over from panic and Freddie gave a low moan and uttered, 'Thanks.'

'Now that's decided,' Ted said, licking his lips, 'is that food I can smell, Mary?'

Later that night, Rose popped next door to see Joe and to tell him about the development. Peter was already fast asleep and, not wanting to wake him, they talked in low tones.

They sat on Joe's bed and he curved an arm around her slim waist and turned her to him. Rose looked into his warm brown eyes, seeing his adoration.

'Oh, Joe,' she whispered, 'I love you so much.' She flung her arms around his neck and cuddled in close to his body, feeling his heat against hers. His lips found hers. Their kiss was gentle at first, and then a fury of passion engulfed them both, so fierce, that they both fell back on the bed.

'When we are married we'll...' Joe whispered huskily. Voices came from the passage just outside the door. 'Vera and Alf,' he muttered. Not a minute too soon, he thought.

Hastily, Rose slid off the bed, smoothed down her skirt, and ran her fingers through her untidy hair.

'Time I was going, Joe,' she said loudly, 'I've told you all the good news.'

With that, there was a knock at the door, which opened and Vera popped her head round. 'Good news, did I hear you say?'

'Yes, but Joe will tell you. Goodnight.' A quick kiss on his cheek and she was gone.

Back home in bed, Rose relived those tender moments, the passion sizzling between them. She yearned to be Joe's wife and to share his bed. Aloud she said into the darkness, 'Before the year's out, I'm going to marry Joe, even if we've to live in one room.'

The next night, Rose sat at the kitchen table with Freddie, helping him to compose the letter to Mrs Welton. The hardest part for Freddie to write was how he came to marry Elsa. They were in the kitchen, David was in bed, and Ted and Mary had gone to see a variety show.

'You didn't love her?' Rose asked.

Freddie sat back in his chair, flung down his pen and lit a cigarette. He puffed on it a few times before answering, 'I did it for Davy. I promised him to look after her and his unborn child. To marry her and bring her home was the only way I could think of.' He looked down at the table and said angrily, 'And I made a bloody mess of that.' He scraped back his chair, got to his feet and went to stare out of the kitchen window.

Quietly, Rose went to put the kettle on the fire to boil, and mixed the cocoa. And from the pantry she brought a small apple pie Mary had baked for their supper.

When Freddie sat down again at the table, he was composed.

'Sorry, sis,' he mumbled. 'But since this war's ended, I feel a total waste. In the army, I knew where I stood, but now...' His arms went up in the air in frustration.

Rose remained calm, for this was a situation she had seen many times in her office and out on the streets. War was evil and yet men longed to be part of it again. Was it because they felt worthy then and now they didn't? She wasn't entirely sure. She sympathized with Freddie and all men in similar circumstances; their difficulties in trying to adjust to civvy life were fraught with uncertainties.

They ate and drank in silence. Then Freddie picked up his pen again and voiced his thoughts. 'What if Davy's mam and dad don't want to see me?'

Rose touched his arm, saying, 'I have the feeling that Davy's parents are good people and they will want to see you.' With her free hand, which was on her lap, she crossed her fingers.

On her way to work next morning, she posted the letter to Mrs Welton.

Sunday was a bright, sun-shining, late-October day. Rose and Joe walked hand in hand; every now and then they stole a quick kiss. Peter skipped ahead as they made their way to the allotment. As they approached, Joe gasped in amazement.

'Well, I'll be blowed! Bob said he would keep an eye on, but I never expected him to clear away all the waste stuff. Now I just need to turn it over and get it ready for winter.' He took off his cap and ran his hands through his dark-brown hair, face and eyes aglow with pleasure.

Just then one of the other allotment holders rode up on his cycle and stopped on the path. 'We've done a good job for you, Joe.'

Surprise mounted Joe's face. 'You helped as well, Eddie?'

'Aye and so did Jacko. We knew you'd do the same for us if we were taken bad.'

Joe gripped Eddie's hand, saying, 'You're the best mates I've got.'

Eddie's ruddy face went a deeper shade. 'Must get on,' and he cycled down the rutted path.

They watched him go. 'It restores my faith in mankind,' Joe said. 'Right, let's get to work.'

Rose shook loose soil from the late crop of potatoes. 'Mam and Vera will be pleased.'

'What are these, Dad?' Peter called.

Joe went over to his son. 'Onions, now that's a lucky find.'

A big grin appeared on Peter's healthy face, then it faded.

'Do I have to eat them?'

Joe ruffled Peter's hair. 'No, lad,' he laughed, and winked at Rose.

After an hour or so, they ate their picnic of apple sandwiches, the fruit scarcely seen since the war. The shiny red apples had come from Canada and, if sliced thinly, made tasty sandwiches and delicious pies.

Peter, enjoying his food but puzzled, asked, 'Aunty Rose, I know the apples came from Canada, teacher told us. Do they grow in the ground like potatoes?'

Rose, ignoring Joe's wide grin, replied, 'No, they grow on trees, apple trees.'

'Big trees?' Peter raised an arm up to the cloudless sky.

'Medium; they grow in a garden or on land which is called an orchard,' Rose said.

'Can we have an orchard, Dad?'

'Have you found any pips in your sandwich?'

Peter looked in the cloth his sandwich had been wrapped in. 'Three, Dad,' he cried excitedly, holding them up in his grubby hand.

'Put them in your pocket, carefully. We'll take home some soil and plant them in a jam jar. You can watch them grow and when they're big enough, we'll plant them in our allotment.'

Rose looked in her cloth. 'I've two.' She handed them to Peter. He thanked her and looked to Joe, who shook his head.

'I've got five,' Peter said with glee, his hand guarding the precious cargo in his pocket.

When they arrived back at Church Terrace, Mary and Vera were busy in the kitchen.

'We're having a joint effort for tea: savoury potato pasties, egg and bacon pie and apple turnovers and a special treat for Peter: chocolate buns.'

'I'll share 'em with David. He's got teeth now.' Off he went to the passage where David was cooing in his pram.

'He'll miss that bairn when he's gone,' Mary lamented.

Joe went next door to wash up. He found Alf and Ted having a smoke and drinking a beer. A lump stuck in his throat. He loved being part of this extended family, one of the best things that had happened to him. Bringing up Peter single-handed would have been hard. His love for Rose overflowed with passion and his dearest wish was to marry her. His number one priority now was to find rooms or a flat to rent. He'd make enquires at work and place an advertisement in the corner shop. He'd read in the local newspaper that the council were talking about building prefabricated housing, quick to erect, to ease the shortage of war-damaged houses. But he knew he couldn't wait that long. And nor could Rose.

TWENTY-NINE

'What is the matter, Joe?' Rose asked. This was two weeks later. He looked pinched-face and cold. 'I didn't realize you were working late or was it an extra night class?' Rose had David in his pram. He was restless and teething again and she was trying to get him to sleep. She was pushing him down the street, when she met Joe: a disappointed Joe.

'Another wasted journey: when I got there, the flat was taken. I went straight from work. I can't get away any earlier.'

'Let me try, Joe.'

'No, it's up to me.' The frustration rumbled in his voice.

Rose remained silent. She turned the pram

round and walked by his side. In her heart, she knew the situation was desperate. At work, when accommodation became available it went to large families, those who had been living with other families in crowded conditions. For single men, there was a hostel, but that had a waiting list.

The weekend was cold and wet. Rose suggested taking Peter to the cinema, but Joe said no; he was adamant.

'We need all our money for a home of our own or we'll never get married.'

Rose sighed inwardly. Joe was right, though it would be nice to go to the cinema or a dance.

'I must be thinking about making arrangements for the children's Christmas party.'

She glanced at Joe; he didn't seem to have heard a word she'd said.

Later that night, she stood at her bedroom window, gazing across the rainswept tiles of the houses of the next terrace. Suddenly into her head came a vision of apple blossom. She closed her eyes, seeing an apple orchard, the branches of its trees hanging low, heavy with crops of bright red apples. She could almost smell their sweet crispness and taste their juices. Her eyes opened and she saw only the lashing rain. She closed the curtains, but the memory of her vision stayed in her heart. One day, she would have an orchard, in the country, on the edge of the city, away from the dirt and dust of the streets.

The next morning at work, Rose was dealing with a Mrs Denton, and her four young children. Mrs Butler was very good at collecting used clothing, and families were often kitted out. Rose smiled at the woman to put her at her ease. The woman sat on the rickety chair and her children were squashed together on an upturned wooden crate. She had plenty to say. 'His seat of pants is out again and I can't keep up with the blighter.' She pointed to a boy of three. When his mother turned her back, he pulled out his tongue.

Rose suppressed a giggle. She opened the bottom drawer of her desk and brought out four small candy bars, courtesy of the American Air Force, and gave one to each child, 'You must be good children and sit quietly while I take your mother to the clothing store.'

Mrs Denton grumbled, 'You'd have thought this blooming government would know the war's over. We're worse off now than ever. I don't know what this country is coming to, I really don't.' Rose, listening in silence, had to agree with her.

Another week went by and then the long-awaited letter arrived from Mrs Welton, addressed to Rose but inside was a letter from Mrs Merchant to Freddie.

Rose hurried home. Vera and Alf were

meeting Peter from school and taking him out for a treat to the cinema. Freddie was home, sitting staring into space.

'A letter from Mrs Merchant.' Rose waved it under Freddie's nose.

Without a word, Freddie took it and slit it open with his forefinger and read its contents.

Quietly, Rose sat down in the chair opposite him and waited. When he had finished reading it, Rose saw that his eyes were filled with tears, which he hastily brushed away with the cuff of his shirt. He pulled a packet of cigarettes from his trouser pocket, his hand trembling as he struck the match, and the kitchen filled with the smell of tobacco smoke. At last, he spoke.

'They were heartbroken at the death of Davy. To take care of their only son's child is a dream come true. They thought they had nothing to live for and now...' Overcome with emotion, he puffed harder on his cigarette. Rose watched her brother, her heart aching for him.

Suddenly he said, 'They do want to see me.' He flung the cigarette in the fire and buried his face in his hands and sobbed, a heart-wrenching sound.

Rose went to put her arms about his shoulders and, holding him close, she cried with him.

After an eternity, Freddie's sobs ceased.

Rose went to look in the cupboard by the fire and found a tiny bottle of brandy, for 'medicinal purposes', Mary had said. Rose poured it into a glass and handed it to Freddie. He swallowed it in one go and then fumbled for his cigarettes. Rose sat down, staring into the fire, watching the flickering blue and red flames intertwining and then dancing apart.

At last, Freddie spoke. 'Thanks for your support, sis.'

Rose looked up and smiled at this dear brother of hers and said, 'I remember when I was young; you got me out of many a scrape.'

'Aye, I did,' he said, sounding more like his self again.

'Now to business,' she said, briskly. 'First thing in the morning, I will arrange for one of our volunteers to travel with you and David.'

'How soon?'

'Depends on who I can persuade at short notice.'

Freddie rubbed the stubble on his chin and said, 'I'll have to clear it with work.'

'Freddie...'

He looked at Rose; he knew that tone. 'First, you must register David's birth.' She held up her hand as he was about to speak. 'Baby's father, David Merchant, mother's name, Elsa Ellerby, both now deceased.'

Rose soon found a volunteer, Mrs Ashley, whose daughter and family lived in Ely so this would be a great opportunity to visit them and a bonus to have her train fare paid.

Within a week, all arrangements had been made. Mr and Mrs Merchant were expecting David and Freddie, and said they would love Freddie to stay with them for a while.

Mary was in tears. Despite the hard work of looking after a new baby, she would miss him terribly.

'I love the bairn like one of my own.' Lovingly, she packed his clothes, handmade by her. The ones David had grown out of, Mary packed separately with a note, which read: *Made with love by his dear mother, Elsa, Davy's sweetheart.*

Rose accompanied Freddie and David to Paragon Station, where Mrs Ashley was waiting. The weather had turned extremely cold, but they were all warmly clothed against the biting north wind. David gurgled happily, as if he sensed an adventure. Rose kissed and hugged him before handing him over to Mrs Ashley. She was a woman of ample figure, with a round, bonny face and a pleasant manner.

'He's a lovely bairn,' she said, cradling him in her arms.

Rose turned to Freddie and hugged him.

'Good luck and take care.' Then they were gone. Steam billowed from the engine, the guard blew the whistle and they were off. Rose waved until the train disappeared. Then she walked down the empty platform, feeling very sad. Would she ever see baby David again?

Heading for work, Rose decided first to call into Woolworth's to see Sally. She was in need of a friendly face.

'Rose, what a nice surprise,' Sally said. 'Have you come to buy or be a nuisance?'

Rose laughed. 'Neither. I just need cheering up.' And she explained what had happened.

'What are you doing tonight?'

Rose shrugged, 'Nothing planned. Joe's at his night class.'

'Mam and Dad are out tonight, come round and we'll have a good gossip. I've got something nice to drink,' she added mischievously.

'What about Frank, you're not seeing him?'

'No, it's cooled off a bit. I'll tell you about it tonight.'

'Are you serving, miss?' said an indignant voice.

Sally winked at Rose, and moved towards the customer. 'Can I help you, madam?'

That night, Mary was still upset about David's departure. Rose offered to stay with her, but Ted stepped in.

'Off you go to Sally's. We'll have a quiet night.'

'Thanks, Dad.' She felt guilty, but it was a relief to escape from the house.

The wind whipped through her coat as she

hurried down the passage to Sally's house. In the kitchen, a fire burned brightly and the wireless was playing a dance tune. Rose came in with a flurry, shivering, saying, 'There's snow in that wind.'

With a twinkle in her eye, Sally said, 'See what I've got for starters.' On the table were two spirit glasses full of mellow liquid.

'What is it?' Rose asked, taking off her coat.

'Best malt whisky, so I'm told.'

'Where did you get it from?'

'I met a Scottish man.' Sally put a finger on the side of her nose and tapped it. 'Come and sit down.' Both girls settled on chairs in front of the fire.

At first, Rose sipped her drink cautiously, but the smoothness of the malt whisky sliding down her throat warmed her whole body, relaxing her stressful mind. Soon she unburdened her worries to Sally. Not that she would do what Sally might suggest, but just to talk it over with a friend helped to release pressure.

Rose sat back in the chair, letting Sally top up her glass. Dreamily she said, 'I love Joe and he loves me and we want to marry, but,' she let out a long sigh, 'we have nowhere to live. Every time Joe goes hunting for rooms or flats, they're gone before he gets there.'

Sally, slouching in her chair, nodded then asked, 'Why are you in such a rush to get married?' Suddenly she sat bolt up, her words almost a gasp. 'You're not pregnant?'

Rose blushed, feeling the roots of her hair tingle. 'No, of course not, but it's tempting.'

'Ah,' said Sally, 'I wouldn't know.'

Rose, recovering her composure, quickly changed the subject. 'What about you and Frank?'

Sally glanced away and said, 'I love Frank like a brother, we're still friends, but we want different things. I want excitement and glamour, he wants to settle down.' She paused to drain her glass. Licking her lips, she added, 'I'm thinking of going to live in London.'

Wide-eyed, Rose stared at her friend, then said, 'What's brought this on?'

'My sister's coming back home with her four bairns, all because her husband has joined the merchant navy and she's frightened to be on her own. On her own, I ask you, with four bairns. Anyway,' she said, 'I've been thinking about it for some time.'

Rose sat forward on the edge of the chair. 'You never said.'

'You've had a lot on your mind.'

'I'll miss you, you're my best friend.'

'I ain't going yet. I've applied for a transfer at work; otherwise Mam wouldn't let me go.'

They chatted some more and drank all the whisky. They said goodnight and Rose put her coat on for home. Stepping out into the dark passage, the cold air sent her head spinning, and she wobbled unsteadily, colliding with someone, a solid figure, and she clutched at it.

'Rose, you've been drinking,' the male voice said, in astonishment.

She lifted her head just enough to squint up into his face. 'Joe,' she mumbled, 'take me home.' His strong arms held her upright and he walked her down the passage to her house.

There was no light on in the kitchen, Mary and Ted having gone early to bed. Joe was thankful that they didn't see their daughter in such an inebriated condition. He settled her on a chair and went to fetch a glass of water.

He held the glass to her lips and said in a low voice, 'Drink this.'

'No more whisky,' she cried.

'It's water, now drink it,' he said, sternly.

She drank and moaned, 'My head aches.'

He found aspirins in the cupboard by the fireplace and gave her two tablets. Watching as she closed her eyes, Joe sat with her, hoping that the water and tablets would ease her, at least so that she was able to take herself to bed. He would have done so, but he didn't want to disturb Ted and Mary; what would they think of him?

He eased back into the chair. He felt weary. What had caused Rose to get into this state? Was he to blame? Now, he was more than ever determined to get a place to live so that they could get married as soon as possible and he could take care of her. He had a few pounds saved, enough to give them a start. Tomorrow, he would ask the supervisor if he could leave work early so that he could get the first edition of the newspaper.

Rose stirred, and opening her eyes she said, 'Hello, Joe. I didn't know you were here.'

'You can't remember anything?'

Puzzled, she asked, 'What?'

'Doesn't matter, but it's time you were going to bed.'

She glanced at the mantelpiece clock and gasped, 'It's gone eleven! Sorry, Joe, have I kept you up?' Shakily, she got to her feet. 'I feel a bit fuzzy-headed.'

Joe made no comment, but gently steered her to the staircase. He kissed her cheek and watched her climb up to her bedroom. He listened for a few minutes, hearing the squeak of her bed springs. He turned off the kitchen light, bolted the door and quietly went out the front door; locking it, he slipped the key, which was fastened on a piece of string, back through the letter box.

He stood outside and lit a cigarette. There was too much on his mind for him to sleep.

THIRTY

The next day, Joe left work early and was on his bike, pedalling fast towards Lime Street. He wanted to be the first one to view the rooms to let. The house was the end in a row of eight, backing onto the River Hull; its foundations had been shaken when a bomb exploded nearby. He saw a man, dressed in a grey suit and smoking a cigar, standing on the doorstep. He parked his bike against the brick wall and addressed the man.

'I'm Joe Tennison and I've come to see the rooms to let.' The man's eyes narrowed as he looked him up and down. 'I've come straight from work,' Joe said, conscious of the white dust of flour on his overalls.

'I'm Murden. Give yourself a good shake before you come in,' he growled. And Joe did.

He stepped off the street straight into the living room. The smell of damp and mustiness hit his nostrils and he sneezed. Through the haze of dust motes, he was surprised to see an old woman, huddled in a chair. Murden said abruptly, 'My mother, she lives here, keeps an eye on things.'

She gave a toothless grin and reached in her apron pocket for her snuff tin.

Joe followed Murden, who spoke in mono-tones. 'Use of kitchen, scullery, copper, yard, coalhouse, lavatory,' he opened a door in the scullery, 'stairs and two bedrooms.'

'I'll need two bedrooms,' Joe said, as he followed the man upstairs, their footsteps heavy on the bare wooden treads. The bed-rooms were small; one overlooked the street and the other looked towards the river. As Joe peered through the dirty, cracked window panes, he saw a rat skulking along the bank and into the backyard of the house.

'Two bedrooms?' the man repeated.

'Yes, I've a son and a fiancée.' Joe turned from the window, about to mention the rat, but...

'No unmarrieds,' Murden barked.

'We're getting married.' Joe felt himself sweat in spite of the chill of the room.

'Can you pay up front?' By now they had come back downstairs.

'How much?' Joe asked, and watched the man calculating in his head.

'Four weeks at 11 shillings is £4.4s.'

Joe heart sank and he swallowed hard. That would make a big hole in his savings. He pulled his money out of his pocket, say-ing, 'I can pay 11 shillings now and bring the rest tomorrow.'

The man snatched the money and pocketed it quickly.

'Can I have a receipt, please?' Joe asked,

not sure if he trusted Murden.

'Don't give 'em. When you pay all the money you'll get a rent book.'

Joe looked towards the old woman, now dozing in her chair, and asked the question which was puzzling him. 'Where does she sleep?'

'Right there,' Murden said, 'she's never slept in her bed since the start of war.'

Back home in Mrs Fisher's house, Joe sat down with Peter and Alf to have tea. Mrs Fisher glanced at Joe as she served sausages and mash. 'You look like the cat that got the cream.'

'I have, but I can't tell you till I've seen Rose.'

After tea, Joe hurried next door to see Rose.

'I need to talk to you,' he whispered. He said hello to her parents; Mary sat by the fire darning socks and Ted sat reading the newspaper, neither listening to the two young people. They sat at the far end of the kitchen table.

Unable to hold back his news any longer, Joe burst out, 'I've got us a place to live.'

'Oh, Joe!' Rose said, her eyes shining with happiness. 'Does this mean we can be married?'

Joe took hold of her hands and pulled her closer to him and kissed her. 'Yes, as soon as it can be arranged.'

'That's the best news ever.' They both turned round to see Ted beaming at them.

'Oh, Dad.' Rose was on her feet to fling her arms around him.

'Whoa, steady on, girl, you'll have me over the chair.'

Rose hugged her mother, who asked, 'So where are you going to live?' Joe told them, and about paying the rent up front.

'Sounds to me you'll need all your savings to furnish the place, and make it fit to live in.' Ted lit his pipe and was thoughtful, then said, 'Joe, why don't you move in and let young Peter stay here.' He glanced at Mary, who nodded her approval. 'That way, you won't have to pay Vera board and lodgings.'

'It's short notice, do you think she'll mind?'

Mary answered. 'No, she'll be pleased to have her front room back.'

So it was decided. The next day, Joe went to see Mr Murden with the balance of the rent money, and to tell him that he was moving in at the weekend.

'Suit yerself,' was his sharp response as he pocketed the money.

Saturday, and it was raining when Joe and Rose set off to Lime Street armed with cleaning materials, but nothing could dampen their spirits. Rose, her mind full of ideas for their first home together, glanced at Joe, her heart brimming with love for him.

As they approached the house, in a part of

Hull she was unfamiliar with, she saw an unkempt street, of dirty windows and un-washed front steps. Rose felt her spirit sink a little, but she gave Joe a warm smile when he looked to her for approval.

Joe took the key from his pocket to unlock the door.

'It's not locked,' he said in surprise. The sound of voices was heard from within. Joe glanced at Rose. 'I've forgotten, Mrs Murden lives here as well.' He pushed open the door and Rose followed him inside.

She was taken aback by the four pairs of the staring eyes of puny-looking children and the toothless old woman. The house she was prepared for needing a good clean, but other people living here had not entered her thinking. She glanced at Joe.

'Are we in the right house?'

Feeling uneasy, Joe answered, 'Yes, but I didn't know about the children.'

Mrs Murden chortled. 'Me grandbairns, they always come on Saturdays. They like these.' From the pocket of her wrap-around faded-print apron, she produced a paper bag of boiled sweets shaped like fishes. Instantly the children grabbed the sweets from the bag.

'Show me round,' Rose said to Joe. In the scullery, he lit the copper for hot water. She sniffed the air, smelling damp and decay. Her heart sank, but she resolved to stay positive.

Upstairs, she inspected the bedrooms, trying to visualize how she could renovate them.

'Where does Mrs Murden sleep?'

Joe explained. Rose nodded and, turning to rub the grimy window, she glanced towards the river and then saw it, skulking along the bank and coming into their backyard. She uttered a cry and stepped back, nearly falling over Joe, who was bent over, examining the loose plaster on the wall.

'A rat,' she squealed. 'I don't like them.'

To keep upbeat, while Joe went to search out the rat, Rose set about cleaning. First tying up her long blonde hair in a scarf, turban style, she made a start on the bedroom windows. Next she attacked the cobwebs from the ceiling and walls, swept and scrubbed the wooden floorboards. She sat on the stairs for a breather and would have loved a cup of tea, but hadn't thought to bring the necessaries with her. Judging by the noise below, the children were misbehaving so she didn't hold out any hopes of Mrs Murden offering them one.

Joe came up. 'Sorted the rat and got rid of the nest and I've given the yard a good swill down.' He looked at Rose. 'You look tired. Shall we go and come back tomorrow?'

They stored the cleaning materials in a corner of the scullery and made ready for home. In the kitchen, Mrs Murden was fast asleep, and the children played on the dirty floor.

'Grannie, hungry.' One of the boys pulled at her arm.

Not pleased at being woken up, she retaliated with a swift clip to his ears. When she saw Joe and Rose looking at her, she gave an attempt of a smile and said, 'Always hungry, these little beggars.' From the recesses of her apron pocket, she brought out a purse and extracted eight pennies. 'Get some chips.' The lad, aged about five, snatched the coins and scarpered.

Rose and Joe edged forward. 'Goodnight, Mrs Murden.'

The old woman cackled a reply.

Outside, the air was raw, the wind blowing off the river smelling of snow. They quickened their pace to catch the bus home. On the bus, Joe said, 'I'm sorry, Rose. I should have told you about Mrs Murden. You still want to live there, don't you?'

Rose, who had thought of nothing else, sensed Joe's despair; she leaned close to him, feeling his strength.

'Joe, I made a promise to marry you as soon as you found us somewhere to live, and as long as we're together, we'll make the best of the house.'

Joe searched her face and he saw what he was looking for.

'You really do mean it?' He put a finger under her chin and kissed her tenderly, oblivious to others on the bus.

Mary and Ted were waiting eagerly, wanting to know more about the house. Rose glanced at Joe and said, 'It's fine after a good clean. Mrs Murden, the landlord's mother, lives there.'

'That's nice, love, someone to keep the fire going,' Mary said, brightly, thinking how much she was going to miss her daughter. She got up from her chair, saying to Joe, 'Stay for a bite to eat, beans on toast.' He nodded his thanks and hung his and Rose's coats up on the back door. Ted offered Joe a cigarette and they talked about rugby.

Rose cut the loaf and fixed a slice to the long-handled fork, and sat on a low stool in front of the fire, glad of a chance to thaw out. The coals were hot and she soon had a pile of toasted bread. The aroma of the toast was comforting and, accompanied by beans, the meal tasted delicious.

Joe, eating and drinking in this warm, welcoming kitchen, loved these folks and blessed the day he had met Rose. He sat back in his chair, basking in the love generated. Rose looked at him, giving a nod. He sat up straight and coughed, looked at Ted and Mary and said, 'We need your advice.'

'What's that, lad?' said Ted.

Rose slipped her hand into Joe's and squeezed it. 'I'm concerned about Peter having to change schools so soon after just settling in. What do you think?'

Mary pondered, but Ted was quick to say, 'Why not let him stay here to finish his school year, than he can move on more naturally.'

'Ted, you took the words right out of my mouth,' said Mary, with joy in her voice.

'Thanks, it's kind of you both,' Joe said. 'I'll talk to Peter in the morning. I don't want him to think I've abandoned him.'

Later Rose, tossing in bed, had mixed feelings about the Lime Street house. But one thing was sure; she would make the best home possible for her and Joe, and for Peter.

On Monday, plans were put in motion for the wedding. First Rose spoke to Mrs Butler, telling her about the rooms they were renting and that it was for financial reasons she and Joe were being married so hastily.

Mrs Butler smiled to herself at Rose's explanation. She stood up to shake her hand. 'Congratulations, Rose. I will help if I can. Use the office telephone.'

Rose spoke to the vicar of St Andrew's Church, the very church where her parents married thirty years ago. She replaced the telephone receiver, her mind in a trance.

'Have you set a date?' asked Mrs Butler.

Mentally, Rose shook herself and smiled, saying, 'He wants to see Joe and me and the only date free this year is Christmas Eve, Tuesday 24th December at 2 pm. It's really going to happen. I'm going to marry Joe.'

When Rose arrived home that evening and told her mother of the date, Mary went into a flap.

'It doesn't give me much time to find material and make you a dress,' she cried.

Rose, who up until then hadn't thought of what she was going to wear, gently hugged her mother. 'Mam, don't panic,' she soothed.

'I nearly forgot,' Mary said, 'There's a letter from Freddie. He's staying on a bit longer with the Merchants, but he'll be home for Christmas. He's got something to tell us.' She sighed. 'I just hope he hasn't done anything daft. Just wait until I write and tell him your good news.'

Joe and Peter came round and both were thrilled at the wedding date. Peter, his face all aglow, asked, 'Rose does this mean you'll be my mam?' The room hushed.

Rose felt her heart contract with such a powerful sensation of love. She bent down on her haunches, her face level with Peter's face, and looked into the beautiful brown eyes, of this wonderful boy. Her voice charged with emotion, she said, 'Is that what you want?'

Peter nodded his head, vigorously. 'Yes, please, so I can be like the other boys at school. They've all got mams.' And he added, shyly, 'I love you.'

'Peter, I will be honoured to be your mother and I love you dearly.' Tears wet her lashes and she hugged him close, feeling his young, sturdy body cling to her. Joe's hand touched the nape of her neck.

After that, Vera and Alf came to share the good news.

'I'll make your wedding cake, though only the bottom layer, top will have to be cardboard, but no one will know,' Vera offered. She nudged Alf's arm, saying, 'What about you?'

Alf chuckled and said, 'Before I retired, I was a sign maker, so I'm good at fancy lettering; I'll make your invitations. Now, let me put on my thinking cap where I can get card from.'

Ted and Joe came back in; they had been to the beer-off shop.

'Beer and lemonade, so it's shandies, and lemonade for Peter, to celebrate,' declared Ted.

Just then, Sally and her mother came in.

'The whole street knows,' said Sally. 'Am I going to be bridesmaid?' she asked enthusiastically. 'I can titivate my old dance dress up.'

Mrs Wray and Mrs Fisher, their heads together deep in conversation, came up for air.

'Settled,' said Mrs Fisher. 'Me and Mrs Wray will do the wedding tea and we'll get neighbours to give what they can.' She sat back in her chair, saying, 'I'm parched, where's that shandy?'

More neighbours came to share in the good news and soon the kitchen was a hub of friendly chatter.

'It's like the war, when we all pulled together,' someone remarked.

Much later, when everyone had gone home, Peter was tucked up in bed and Mary and Ted had gone to theirs, Rose and Joe sat quietly talking.

Joe said, 'Rose, first chance we get to have rooms or a house in Hill Street, we'll take it. Do you agree?' His strong hands cupped her face and his kiss was tender at first, until she melted into his arms.

After that, life moved fast for Rose. She was busy making the final arrangements for the children's Christmas party, answering questions about when rationing was going to stop.

'We're getting less now than we did in the ruddy war,' was the biggest complaint people made, especially women who found it difficult to concoct meals from the food restrictions still imposed. 'We can't even make a decent sandwich.'

Rose let all this wash over her head, knowing the grumbles released tension and she didn't have the power to change the system. She also closed her ears when she heard conversations where desperate women had sold their clothing coupons to enable them to buy food. But, despite their moans, they were always willing to help at the children's party. Best of all was the offer for a Punch and Judy show. Shirley came with her mother to make decorations. Another woman came with a bag of wooden pegs, scraps of material and wool, and made Father Christmases and angels. Mrs Butler's husband, Major Butler, secured a pine tree from the country estate where he worked.

The party was to be held on the Saturday afternoon before Christmas Day and on the Friday before, Mrs Butler came down to view the preparations.

'It looks wonderful, Rose, and the decorations are very festive. I think it should be utilized. Don't you agree?' she asked.

Rose, not sure what she meant, said, 'Yes.'

'Good, then I'll make it official for Tuesday 24th December.'

'But,' Rose faltered, 'I can't work then, it's my wedding day.'

Gently, Mrs Butler took hold of Rose's arm and said, 'My dear, you have worked commendably for the organization, the least we can do is to offer you this venue,' with her free hand she encompassed the hall and kitchen, 'for yours and Joe's wedding reception.'

Rose felt her eyes prick with tears and was so overwhelmed with happiness that she flung her arms round a startled Mrs Butler.

Later, at home, Rose was telling her parents of the generous offer.

'It's a relief,' Mary said. 'What with Freddie coming home and needing his room, it would have been a struggle to fit all the guests into our kitchen.'

After tea, Rose consulted her list, ticking off things done: 'Bouquet, buttonholes, shoes...'

'I'll need you to have a fitting,' said Mary. The dress was being made from two white damask tablecloths, salvaged from jumble, and over-laced with Nottingham lace, courtesy of Alf's curtains from the windows of his old home.

Later, Rose looked out of her bedroom window and, staring up at the twinkling stars in the clear, crisp night sky, she thought of Joe. Was he settling in at the house in Lime Street? They had furnished one bedroom from second-hand furniture, a bed, wardrobe and dressing table and there was her hope chest. They had enough possessions to start married life together. She sighed contentedly; what mattered most was their love for each other.

She turned away from the window, a feeling of joy wrapping round her. Everything was going to plan, wasn't it?

THIRTY-ONE

Joe was upstairs in his room in Lime Street, reading the newspaper or at least trying to. His mind kept wandering to Rose. What was she doing? And he missed Peter's cheeky grin. Startled, he heard the front door open and close with a bang and the sound of a woman's pitiful voice and the crying of children. He lowered the newspaper. The woman's voice rose in hysteria and Mrs Murden shouted. Joe stood up, hand on the doorknob, when the noise ceased. He didn't want to be involved in the Murden family matters. He turned off the light and climbed into bed, pulling the blankets over his head.

He must have been asleep for only an hour when he was jolted awake by hammering on the front door and a man bellowing, 'Open up, I know you're in there.' This was followed by a torrent of foul and abusive language. Shrieks from children and the screams of a woman reverberated round the house as the front door was rammed open.

Joe jumped from his bed, pulled on his trousers and raced down the stairs, his bare feet crunching on the cockroach beetles swarming the floor. In the kitchen, a thin, weedy man was swaying by the battered-down door, the cold night air racing in. The children and their mother huddled in a corner; the old woman hadn't moved.

'Who are you?' Joe demanded.

The man staggered forward, brandishing a long metal pipe. 'I'm her bloody husband. Who the hell are you?'

The man lunged at Joe, who leaped sideways, making a grab for the pipe. Both men fell to the floor grappling, and after a few minutes Joe snatched the pipe from him.

While all this was going on, one of the children ran out to fetch the police. A sergeant and constable came. The sergeant seized Joe by the scruff of his neck and yanked him to his feet and the constable held the man in an armlock.

In a voice of authority, the sergeant said, 'Now what's going on?'

The man, now subdued, said, 'I've lost me job and me home and now she's got a bloke.'

'Is this right?'

With the back of his hand, Joe wiped the dust from his mouth. 'No, I'm getting married soon and I and my wife-to-be are renting rooms here.'

The sergeant turned to look at the woman and the frightened children, still huddled in the corner. 'Why aren't the bairns in bed?'

The woman, pointing at her husband, said, 'It's his fault, gambled our money so

356

we couldn't pay rent and we got chucked out of our home.' She gave a big sob and howled and the children began crying again.

Joe felt his head spin. He went into the scullery to swill his face and then upstairs. Dressed, he came back down and addressed the sergeant.

'I'm going to work early. The bairns can sleep in my bed, for what is left of the night. Get hold of Mr Murden. Let him sort out the mess.' Outside, the air was frosty, but so fresh after the drama inside.

At work, Joe's mind was in turmoil. 'You're quiet, Joe,' said Billy, his workmate.

Joe glanced up, his tone bleak. 'I've got some business to sort out. I'll need your help later.'

After work, Joe went straight to Lime Street. Mr Murden was there, waiting for him on the doorstep, puffing on a cigar.

He greeted Joe. 'You'd think I was running a bleeding charity instead of a business.' He motioned him inside. In her usual place, Mrs Murden seemed unconcerned by all that had gone on. Her daughter, husband and their children, eyes cast down, were squashed together on a couch.

'Right,' said Murden. 'Sorry, Mr Tennison, I have no choice.' He gave his mother a quick look. 'My sister and children are homeless.' He didn't mention the husband. 'You'll have to vacate the rooms.'

Joe had no intention of staying, or to expose Rose and Peter to live in these conditions, but he didn't enlighten Murden.

'Go?' he stated. 'I've given you good money and cleaned up the place. Why should I go?'

Murden puffed up his flabby chest, preparing to do battle. But before he could, for the first time the old woman roused herself and rasped, 'Bleeding give him the money.'

'All of it,' Joe demanded.

Reluctantly, Murden handed over the full amount. 'I'll be back in half an hour to collect my furniture. I expect no trouble.'

He stored the furniture in one of the mill's outhouses. 'Only temporarily,' said the foreman.

Cold and hungry, Joe made his way to Church Terrace. With a cup of hot tea inside him, Joe explained. Rose, Mary and Ted listened in silence.

'Does this mean the wedding has to be cancelled?' Mary asked, tears in her eyes.

Before Joe could respond, Ted jumped in. Looking Joe full in the face he asked, 'Do you love our Rose?'

Rose was about to protest at her father's question, but Joe put a restraining hand on her arm and he met Ted's eyes.

'Yes, Mr Ellerby, I love Rose more than anything in the world and I cannot imagine my life without her.' Rose slipped her hand into his shaking one and squeezed gently.

Ted turned to his wife. 'What do you think, Mary, can we pack another into our house?'

Mary replied with confidence, 'Yes, we can.'

Rose, wide-eyed, stared at her parents and uttered a cry of delight. 'Do you mean Joe and I and Peter can live here when we are married?'

'That's what I'm saying, lass.'

'It might be a bit cramped with Freddie coming home, but we can manage,' Mary said. 'It will be lovely having us all together.'

Rose floated on a high. The wedding plans were all in place. Her parents had taken Peter to the cinema to see *Lassie Come Home*, so they had the house to themselves.

Joe was saying, 'There's a reason why I'm working overtime. I know we are both grateful to your mam and dad for offering to share their home, but I've plans for us to buy our own house.' He held her gaze, letting her absorb his words.

'A home of our own,' Rose whispered. 'Is it possible?' She stared at him, uncertain. Or just a dream?

He swept her up into his arms, saying, 'My darling Rose, of course it's possible.'

'Oh, Joe, you do mean it. I've often dreamed of a house of our very own, especially one with a garden.' She kissed him with a longing desire.

Tenderly, Joe sat her down, his optimism on a roll. 'I've read in the national newspapers that the government wants to get the country back on its feet. There has been quite a lot of discussion and I agree with the majority, that the best way forward is to build houses to replace the ones bombed and this will create new jobs. So the more we save, the better chance we have of buying our own home.'

Rose didn't understand politics, but she knew what Joe was saying made sense.

The weather turned bitterly cold and it was the day of the children's Christmas party and Rose was exhausted, but happy.

'Can I be your bridesmaid, Rose?' Rose, busy putting out the jellies, turned round to see Shirley, thinking what a pretty girl she was growing into.

'I would love you to be, but I haven't got a dress for you to wear,' Rose said, and there was nothing suitable in the clothing stock.

As if reading her thoughts, Shirley quickly replied, 'Mam said she can borrow a frock. Please, Rose, I've never been a bridesmaid.'

Her mother, who had just finished playing a game of ring-a-roses with the younger children, came across. 'I told her not to bother you, Rose.'

'Can you borrow a dress?'

'I think so. It belongs to my cousin's girl.

They're a bit posh. After I've put bairns to bed, I'll go round and ask.' Shirley did a little twirl and flung her arms around her mother.

When Freddie arrived home on Sunday, Rose greeted him with a hug, then held him at arm's length. 'You do look well and you've put on weight.'

'All that good country air and good food, but you make the best stew and dumplings, Mam,' he said swiftly as Mary looked at him.

Later, they sat down to a tea. Joe, now living next door again, was invited for tea. They talked, mainly about the forthcoming wedding and how the rooms Rose and Joe were renting had fallen through. Freddie looked thoughtful, but didn't say anything.

Mary spoke. 'Now tell us all your news, Freddie. I want to hear how David is.'

Freddie pulled out his cigarette packet from his trouser pocket and offered one to Ted. Inhaling and blowing out smoke, Freddie began.

'Little one is doing fine. His grandparents make a fuss of him and they love that he is called David.' He looked pensive for a moment, then added, 'They are older than I imagined, in their sixties. But they have a niece, Amy, who lives nearby and she's a great help. She's a nice, friendly girl. You'd like her, Mam, she reminds me of you. She's grown to love David too.'

'Oh, I am pleased,' Mary said. 'He needs all the love he can get.' Her eyes glazed as she thought of her precious boy; he would always have a special place in her heart.

They were all silent. The fire hissed and sparkled and the mantel clock ticked. Freddie lit another cigarette, and spoke. 'I've something to tell you.' He looked nervous. No one spoke; they just stared at him, waiting. He drew on his cigarette, gave a deep sigh and said, 'I've decided to stay down in Ely.'

'Do you mean a holiday or permanent?' asked Rose.

'Permanent. You see, I've become fond of the little chap and I want to watch him grow up. I've talked about it a lot with David's grandparents. They're happy about it.'

Mary's eyes brimmed with tears as she said, 'Oh, Freddie, will me and your dad be able to visit and see you and David?'

Freddie reached across the table and took hold of his mother's hand. 'Of course, Mam. I'd be upset if you and Dad didn't come.' He winked at Rose. 'You too, sis, with Joe and Peter.'

'Just one question,' asked Ted. 'What about your job here?'

'All taken care of,' Freddie replied, matter of fact. 'I called into work on my way here to tell the foreman I wasn't coming back. You see,' he shook another cigarette out of the packet and offered one to Ted, 'I've a chance of a job on a farm, labouring, but I intend to go to agricultural college to train for management.'

'Well, you've got it all worked out, son,' Ted said, hesitantly, then proudly. 'Fancy going down to the pub and celebrate?'

Mary and Rose declined but suggested, 'Ask Joe and Alf.'

Going out of the door, Freddie threw over his shoulder, 'The front room is all yours, sis.'

In the front room, Rose and Mary stood, surveying it.

'Why don't you and Joe use it as a bed-cum-sitting room,' Mary said.

'It's a good idea and Joe and I will get by until Freddie goes.' She blushed, tingling with pleasure as she thought of her narrow bed and how close she and Joe would be.

The wedding day dawned. It was a cold, frosty day. The men were ordered to stay in their beds while Rose had a bath and washed her hair in front of the kitchen fire. When she was enveloped in her mother's warm dressing gown, she towel-dried her hair and pinned it up with metal curlers.

'What would you like for breakfast, Rose?' asked her mother.

'Tea and toast, please, Mam.' Mary handed her the toasting fork and bread. Rose sat dreaming, looking into the flickering flames of the fire. She felt ecstatically happy. A lovely warm feeling ran through her veins; this was hers and Joe's wedding day. The yearning to be Joe's wife, and her complete loving of him, was soon to be fulfilled. She whispered to herself, 'Mrs Rose Tennison.' It was the most perfect name.

Later, Sally came to take out the pins and brush Rose's hair, letting it fall in waves, sweeping up the sides and front: a style suitable for the headdress of a garland of white silk flowers attached to a fine veil of Belgium lace; this was on loan from a workmate of Sally's. Rose dusted fine powder on her face and applied a dazzling pink lipstick.

Rose glanced in the dressing table mirror.

'Sally, do you think the colour is too flashy?'

'Not a bit. It matches your bridal bouquet of pink roses.' They were a gift from Mrs Butler and her husband, who had also loaned their Bentley for the bridal pair.

Finally, Rose was dressed in her wedding gown, which was made with love by Mary.

'You could never imagine that the raw material was two damask tablecloths and Nottingham lace curtains,' Sally enthused. The dress fitted perfectly over Rose's slender hips and tiny pearl buttons embellished the sleeves. The neckline of the dress was unadorned, with a Mandarin collar, and Rose's blonde wavy hair just touched the very top.

Mary fussed round her, adjusting a hem so that her satin shoes showed. Then, with tears of joy in her eyes, she stood back to gaze at her daughter.

'Oh, Rose, my darling daughter, you look so beautiful, a radiant bride. God bless you!'

Mary, in a pale blue costume and matching hat, went in the hire car with the bridesmaids, Sally and Shirley, and Peter, who was a pageboy. Suddenly, the house was very quiet after all the activity. It seemed unreal to Rose and her insides did somersaults; she wondered if it was just a dream and she would wake up. Then Ted appeared, looking smart in his best dark suit, white shirt and blue tie. He poured two measures of brandy.

'Drink this, love, it'll warm you up. It's chilly outside.' His voice was thick with emotion and pride.

Rose stepped outside to see the winter sun shining brightly in the clear blue sky. Neighbours lined the terrace to see the bride, and said ohs and ahs, and 'Isn't she lovely' and 'Good luck!' The chauffeur, resplendent in a dark grey suit and peaked cap, held open the door of the Bentley for Rose and Ted. Slowly, he drove down the street, and people stopped to wave. It had been a long time since a bride had graced Hill Street.

They arrived at St Andrew's Church with minutes to spare. The church was decorated for Christmas, with holly, greenery and gold painted cones. Candles were lit to illuminate the interior, matching the sunshine outside. Enthralled, she watched the light from a candle flickering against a magnificent stained-glass window, revealing its rich colours of blue, red and yellow. And as Rose stood on the threshold of the church, a wonderful sense of peace and love embraced her.

Music filled her ears as Mendelssohn's 'Wedding March' called her. She was ready to walk down the aisle to her destiny. Her heart quickened and her inside fluttered. She tightened her hand on her father's arm. Head held high, she glided towards the altar, seeing only a misty sea of faces turning to look at her.

Then she saw Joe, standing tall. She reached his side. He turned to look at her. His eyes mirrored hers, so full of love. They were soulmates on the brink of a new dawn of discovery.

She knew, whatever came their way, they would face it together. She slipped her hand into his and the wedding service began.

The publishers hope that this book has given you enjoyable reading. Large Print Books are especially designed to be as easy to see and hold as possible. If you wish a complete list of our books please ask at your local library or write directly to:

Magna Large Print Books
Magna House, Long Preston,
Skipton, North Yorkshire.
BD23 4ND

This Large Print Book, for people
who cannot read normal print,
is published under the auspices of

THE ULVERSCROFT FOUNDATION